If You Stay

BARBARA MEYERS

IF YOU STAY

This book is a work of fiction.

The names, characters, places, and incidents are products of the writer's imagination or have been used fictitiously and are not to be construed as real. Any resemblance to persons, living or dead, actual events, locale, or organizations is entirely coincidental.

Print ISBN: 978-1-951286-09-5

Digital ISBN: ISBN: 978-1-951286-08-8

1. Contemporary Romance – Fiction. 2. Ohio (U.S.) – Fiction.

3. Family Relationships – Fiction.

4. Small Town – Fiction. I. Title.

Chapter One

J oy parked across the street from her childhood home. The neighborhood hadn't changed much, but neighborhoods like this one never did. The houses stood like sentinels, successfully holding back time for the past hundred years or so.

Some of the homes had been updated, many restored to their original glory——peaked roofs and chimneys and clapboard, porches and gables and a turret or two. Mostly the way she remembered it.

She stared at the home she'd grown up in, the one where her parents still resided. A home and a family she hadn't seen in twenty-five years. She wasn't nervous, she realized, thanks in part to Devonny. Her daughter's journey gave her hope. Maybe it wasn't too late to bridge the span of time and space between her and her parents. And if it was? She still had Devonny and her new baby granddaughter, Lucy. She still had a family. And she could always comfort herself that she had tried. Tried to reconcile with those who'd abandoned her when she'd needed them most.

She got out of the rental car and stood for a moment in the damp air, the old cobblestones wet from morning rain. The trees were not quite ready to release their leaf buds, waiting perhaps for the exact right moment. Unlike her, they wouldn't wait too long. They'd know the right time to burst forward without fear of damage from yet another frost.

Joy stowed the car keys and hitched the strap of her purse higher on her shoulder before she strode across the street and marched up the steps. The porch looked cold and neglected. The wicker chairs had no cushions, and the swing sat sadly on the floor at one end. Flowerpots were full of dry dirt, dead stalks, and nothing else.

In another month, however, her mother would transform the space into one that welcomed and warmed. She'd plant her flowers and get Joy's dad to hang the swing. Her mother would wash everything down as part of her spring-cleaning routine and replace the cushions on the chairs. There'd be a discussion as to whether the floor needed a fresh coat of paint.

In the afternoons, her mother would sit in the rocker with her needlepoint or mending or perhaps the crossword puzzle from the morning paper. She'd visit with the neighbors before starting dinner.

Joy sighed as a thousand memories from her years spent here assailed her. Maybe, she thought, she'd make a thousand new ones.

Or maybe not.

She opened the storm door and knocked. The old house telegraphed movement from inside, the approach of footsteps. Behind the door's cloud of prismed glass, she saw her father. He seemed to debate for a moment before he opened the door.

"Whatever you're selling, asking for, or promoting, you're wasting your time."

He hasn't changed a bit, was Joy's first thought. Still as tall and stern and formidable as he'd always been. Joy bet Arthur Harmon could still put the fear of God into his parishioners even though his hair was a bit grayer, and he'd developed a slight paunch. But she wasn't afraid of him anymore. She didn't need his approval. Or his love. Or his forgiveness. She didn't need anything from him, except for him to see her as an independent adult with a mind of her own. And if he didn't want to accept her as she was, to be her father, that was his choice. She only wanted to give him one last chance.

"Hello, Dad."

He stared hard at her. She couldn't read all the emotions as he reacted to her greeting. Surprise certainly, from which he quickly recovered. No outpouring of love. No sigh of regret. He frowned. "Thought I told you never to come back here."

"You did. But it's a free country. And that was twenty-five years ago."

"What I said then still goes." He started to close the door, but Joy stepped into its path.

"Is Mom here?"

"You made your choice. You forced us to make ours. You'd best go back from wherever you were and leave us be."

"I want to see my mother first." Joy stared him down. She'd turned out just as stubborn as him. She'd nearly lost her own daughter by behaving as he had. But she caught her mistake in time and made amends. She'd learned to accept what she couldn't change, learned that children often made choices of which their parents didn't approve. But respecting a child's right to make those choices was the difference between having a relationship with the child or not having one.

"Who's at the door, Art? Who are you talking to?"

They both turned as Marcy Harmon approached. She stopped and stared. "Joy?"

"Hi, Mom."

Marcy covered the few steps between them, ignoring her husband's signal to stop. She enveloped Joy in a hug, crying over and over, "My baby. My baby."

Joy closed her eyes and let herself revel in the feel of her mother's arms around her, something she'd thought she'd never experience again. She breathed in the scents buried in her subconscious all this time: moisturizer and pressed powder, mint toothpaste, and a touch of jasmine perfume. While her father seemed not to have changed at all, her mother seemed smaller than she remembered, diminished, somehow, from the woman Joy had known.

"I can't believe you're here." Marcy pulled back and cupped Joy's face in her hands to look into her eyes.

"Come in. Come in. Art, why are you standing there with the door open?"

Marcy drew Joy forward.

"She's not welcome in my house," Art intoned. "She knows why. And so do you."

Marcy glared at her husband, her hand grasping Joy's. "You've kept us apart for too long, and I've had enough. Joy is my daughter, and this is my house, too."

Joy stared at her parents. She'd never known her mother to defy her father on anything. The Marcy she recalled had been a good, dutiful wife, deferring to her husband on all important matters. Marcy's domestic influence reigned supreme inside the house. Anything outside of that was Arthur's domain.

And Joy had been on the outside for a long time.

Arthur kept his hand on the door as if he could still slam it in Joy's face. "We agreed—"

"We *never* agreed. You dictated, and I swallowed my own objections. I've been choking on them ever since. Joy is here now, and she stays." Marcy tugged Joy's hand and Joy followed her to the kitchen, feeling her father shooting daggers of disapproval at her back.

Joy stopped at the threshold. "Wow. This isn't the same kitchen. It's beautiful." Not everything on the street or in this house remained exactly the same. Marcy's kitchen could have come straight out of a spread in *House & Garden*. It had been painstakingly updated without losing its original charm. Three curved windows enclosed a sunny, built-in breakfast nook with padded cushions in shades of yellow and blue.

"Hmmpf." Marcy busied herself behind the center island. "I learned a long time ago, when you can't have what you want, you take what you can get. Would you like some coffee? Tea? A soft drink?"

"Coffee would be great. But please don't go to any trouble just for me."

Marcy looked at her. "I have years of not going to trouble for you to make up for." When Joy didn't respond, Marcy indicated the nook. "Please. Sit. This will just take a minute."

Joy sat and looked out at the backyard. There were changes there, too. The trees she remembered climbing in childhood were taller than ever. A new shed sat at the back of the property, and a large plot of turned earth created space where a sizeable garden would go.

When her mother took a seat on the other side of the table, Joy said, "Mom, I don't want to make trouble between you and Dad."

Her mother's lips thinned, and her eyes sparked with barely suppressed emotion. "Your father made his own trouble with me when he hung up on you that night. When he refused to help me find you or let you come back home." Marcy looked away. She blinked. Her voice softened. "But I'm as much to blame as he is. I should have—overruled him. Fought harder for you."

"Is it even possible? To overrule Dad?"

Marcy gave her a bitter smile in reply. "Maybe not. But I should have tried harder than I did. I'm sorry that I didn't."

"Me too. I should have tried harder to get in touch with you."

"I know how difficult it must have been for you. But was it horrible? I prayed, Joy. I prayed for you every day. And every sleepless night, and there were a lot of those. You've always been in my prayers. You look wonderful, by the way." She cocked her head. "Successful."

"Thank you."

Marcy got up to pour coffee. "Cream? Sugar? That's one of those things I should know about you, but I don't."

"Black is fine."

They sipped their coffee while awkwardness descended. Neither of them, it seemed to Joy, knew where to begin.

"Why did you come back?" Marcy asked. "Don't get me wrong. I'm overjoyed you're here. Finally. After all this time. But I am curious. Why now?"

"Actually, it's because of my daughter."

"I always wondered if you had a boy or a girl."

"You're a grandmother. In fact, you're a great-grandmother. Devonny had Lucy in February."

"Devonny. That's a beautiful name."

"She lives in Iowa now."

"I want to meet her. And my great-grandchild."

"Of course. Dad won't approve of Devonny, though."

"It will be his loss, then." Marcy toyed with her coffee cup. "So, you came back because of Devonny?"

"Devonny made some choices I didn't agree with. She married a man I thought was as wrong for her as he could be. When he died, I said some horrible things to her. Things I couldn't take back."

"Just like your father did to you."

"I realized I'm more like Dad than I ever thought possible. Devonny left LA without a word to me. She wouldn't answer my calls. Texts. Emails."

"She was angry," Marcy said.

"Of course, she was, and she had every right to be. But I tracked her down and showed up on her doorstep."

Marcy smiled. "So, it's a habit with you. Just showing up."

Joy grinned. "Apparently."

Marcy snapped her fingers. "I have coffee cake. Baked it this morning. Would you like some?"

"I'm fine with just the coffee but thank you."

"So, you showed up. Go on."

"I'd never really told Devonny about you and Dad. About why I left or what happened to her father. But when I saw the pattern repeating, I knew I had to change it. That's what Devonny helped me see. I had to accept her right to make her own choices. I didn't have to like them, but I had to respect them if I wanted to be in her life."

"She sounds like a remarkable girl. Woman, now, I guess."

"She is. We talked about me coming back here. She made me see I had nothing to lose. I'd been without my family all this time. I'd proved I could make it on my own. If you still didn't want anything to do with me..."

Joy tried to read her mother's expression but couldn't.

"If your father still didn't want anything to do with you, you'd still have a family. Devonny and her baby."

"Yes."

Tears welled in Marcy's eyes. She reached for a paper napkin from the holder on the table and dabbed at them beneath her glasses. "Devonny must think we're horrible people."

"I'm sure she doesn't. But she is strong-willed. And she won't be disrespected."

A horn honked out front. Marcy jumped. "Oh, dear. That will be June Lethridge. On Fridays, the Ladies' Guild puts together lunches for the low-income children in the area. Let me give her the keys to the church basement and she can go on without me."

"Mom, no. I don't want to interrupt your routine."

"But you just got here. After all this time. I can't—"

Joy stood. "I'm going to be here for a few days. Maybe longer. We'll see each other some more."

"Promise me?"

"Mom. Of course. I'm here now. I won't leave without telling you. And I'm certainly not leaving today."

"Where are you staying, though?"

June honked again.

Joy started walking with her mother to the front door. "I'm at that new motel out near the interstate. Room 219." She drew a business card from her purse. "This has my cell number on it. Call me whenever you want."

Her mother hugged her fiercely. "I'm so glad you're here."

"Me too."

"I'll call you this afternoon."

Joy could feel June Lethridge studying her as she walked down the steps behind her mother. Probably, there'd be a lot of that if she stayed in town very long. She had no idea what her mother told people when her daughter left all those years ago. But Joy was pretty sure she knew exactly what her father would have said if anyone had the nerve to ask him.

Joy waved at her mother as June's car passed by. *I really don't care what they think. Or what they think they know. I'm free.*

Joy had to keep reminding herself of that. She had only herself to consider in her decisions and choices. Her grown daughter made it clear she valued her independence, and Joy had learned her lesson the hard way about attempting to interfere in Devonny's life. Joy did research for several clients, but with her laptop and internet access, she could work from anywhere.

She hadn't told Devonny, but she'd put the condo in LA on the market and all her things in storage. Joy didn't know her destination in much the same way Devonny hadn't when she left LA. Joy knew she needed a reset just as her daughter had. She didn't need to start over. She needed to start anew.

Chapter Two

J oy drove through the surrounding streets, reacquainting herself with the neighborhood. She drove past the park, the elementary and high schools, the community center.

The rental car seemed to know its way to downtown Liberty and steered itself into an angled parking space. She sat for a moment peering at the mix of old brick storefronts and new sidewalks of interlocking paving stones. The streetlights had that new vintage look. There was a coffee place on the corner and a bistro next to it. Not a café. Not a diner. A *bistro*. Joy grinned. Revitalization had come to Liberty, Ohio, while she'd been gone, like a hundred other small towns across the country. She'd bet they'd applied for and received grants to preserve historic buildings.

She squinted, almost certain she saw an art gallery combined with an interior design studio farther along the block. She wondered what had happened to Kahl's

General Store and the pharmacy with the ice cream counter and sweet shop.

She remembered twirling round and round on the red stools while waiting for her mother to conclude her business. If she behaved herself, sometimes she got a Coke or a single dip cone.

Joy got out of the car. The wind had picked up, and one glance at the overcast sky suggested more rain soon. It didn't bother her at all. After the dry, smog-laden air of LA, where water was a precious commodity, she relished the thought of a spring rain. She could always duck into the coffee shop for a hot chocolate or the bistro for lunch. *After* she checked out the art gallery, that is.

She purposely walked slowly, reading the menu posted outside the bistro and peeking into the coffee shop. There were small tables and a counter, and workers wearing tan aprons and matching hats. Only a few patrons were in line.

She crossed the street and checked out the art displayed in the windows of the art gallery. Curiosity piqued, she opened the door. A subtle bell sounded. A male head with lots of curly hair poked around a door at the back. "Be right out."

"Take your time. I'm just browsing," she called back. Joy loved art galleries and museums. She'd taken Devonny to them often because she'd wanted her home-schooled child to have a diverse education. Every learning experience Joy could afford, she'd given to Devonny. Concerts and music classes. Ballet performances and dance lessons. Plays and movies and books. Devonny had soaked it all up and then thrown her future away by marrying Jack Campbell.

No, Joy warned herself. Devonny simply made her own choices. Created her own life. Just as Joy had. *Just as I'm going to do again*, she reminded herself with a smile.

"Thanks for stopping in," said the man who approached from the back. "Anything I can help you with?"

"To tell you the truth, I'm still getting over my shock. An art gallery in Liberty? How did that happen?"

He tilted his head and studied her. "Do I know you?"

She returned the favor. "I'm not sure. I grew up here, but I've been away for a long time." She appraised the man a moment longer. The riot of sandy brown hair. The wire-frame glasses. The sweater vest. "Oh, my God. *Brian?* Brian Crowley, is that you?"

"Yes. But...Joy? It *is* you!" When Brian hugged her, a hundred memories of their friendship came rushing back. Brian pulled away first, but he held on to Joy's shoulders as he peered into her eyes. "I can't believe it. You're back? After all this time?"

"I'm back." She laughed, so delighted she could hardly stand it. She began to get a glimpse of what she'd missed by turning her back on everyone in Liberty, even the handful of close friends like Brian.

"Girl," he said, taking her hand drawing her to a stool near the counter. "You sit right here and tell me *everything*, and I do mean *everything* that's happened since you left town."

Joy laughed again. How she'd loved Brian. He'd been the closest thing she'd ever had to a brother. How foolish she'd been all these years, allowing her bitterness to take seed and grow. Leaving her home, her parents, her friends, everyone, and everything that made up her life to that point. Everything but Mike. And when he'd died, she'd stupidly taken her father's words into her heart and allowed them to fester like a wound that would not heal.

You've made your bed, now you can lie in it.

If that's how everyone felt, she'd decided, she'd damn well lie in that bed and forget them. Screw them. She'd ridden that wave of anger and resentment, and it had almost cost her her daughter. Her grandchild. Her father might never accept her, but he was only one of many people she'd left behind. She'd repair the relationships she could. First, she'd reconnected with her mother; now it seemed fate was handing her another opportunity. Another chance with an old and dear friend.

"I'm sorry, Brian."

Worry lines formed between his eyes. "Sorry?"

"For leaving the way I did. For not saying goodbye or staying in touch."

"Oh, that. Not going to say I wasn't hurt. Or that I didn't hate you." He grinned. "Mostly because you were the talk of the town after you left. 'Preacher's daughter runs off with notorious bad boy.' Oh, my, you had the gossips wagging their tongues for close to a year. I was *so* jealous."

Joy grinned. "You were not."

"Honey, if only I'd been lucky enough to be involved in such a delicious scandal, I could die happy."

"But instead, you...?"

"But instead, I went to college. Got an art degree. Came back here and started selling wallpaper and *objet d'art* to the discerning and sophisticated of Henry County. Dabbling on the side doing interior design."

"And you're good at it. And quite successful."

"Well...yes, I am."

"And what about your love life?"

Brian sighed. "Not quite as successful. Or good at it, for that matter. But you know what they say. You can't keep a good man down." He laughed. "I mean, we've made progress these past twenty years. There's a small contingency of us gays. We not only have secret meetings, but a secret handshake as well." He wrapped his fist around his middle finger and moved it back and forth a couple of times.

Joy laughed again. She reached out for another hug. "I didn't realize how much I missed you. How much I missed this."

"Well, you're back now, and we have to make up for lost time." The phone rang. Brian held up a finger and answered it. The bell over the door tinkled, and two women came in to browse. Joy didn't recognize either of them. Brian covered the phone with one hand and called, "Be right with you" to the customers."

Joy reached into her bag for a card. When she slid off the stool, Brian frowned at her, but she handed him the card and mimed a "call me" gesture. He nodded. She made her way out of the store.

The day had become even more dreary and drizzly as only spring days can be. Joy went back to her car and turned the heat on to dispense the chill. She began to drive around the town, past her old haunts. The schools again, and the parks. The bowling alley and the skating rink. The strip malls and the pizza joints, refamiliarizing herself with the area. Little had changed in all these years. A couple of restaurants had closed or changed hands. A big drugstore chain had gobbled up one of the pharmacies. There were some new gas stations and a dollar store.

The residential areas were less altered, except the trees were bigger, and the houses seemed smaller than she remembered. She stopped on a side street when she saw a sign that said *apartment for rent*. The traffic this time of day in a residential area was almost non-existent, and she stared out at the back of this house, a brick ranch style. Behind it stood an oversized, detached two-car garage and the apartment must be over the garage. A set of steps led up the side to a door on the second floor.

It couldn't be a very big apartment. A studio, she supposed. Probably one big room and a bathroom. She plucked her cell phone out of her purse and dialed the number on the sign, expecting to leave a voice mail. But a man answered. He said something that sounded like "Granger" in a clipped, what-do-you-want-I-haven't-got-time-for-this manner.

Joy hesitated a fraction of a second before she said, "Yes. I'm interested in the apartment you have for rent."

No response.

"Hello?" she said, thinking she had lost the connection.

"You want to see it?"

"Well, yes. If it wouldn't inconvenience you too much." He certainly didn't sound anxious to find a tenant.

"When?"

"Whenever it's convenient for you."

"Now?"

"I—I suppose." Put off by his demeanor, Joy wasn't at all certain she wanted to see the place.

"Where are you?"

"I'm on the street. Um…" She squinted at the sign on the corner. "Longfellow Lane."

"Be right there." The call disconnected.

Joy eased the car over to the narrow shoulder, which left half of it still on the street. But since not one car had gone by while she'd been idling there, she didn't think it would be a problem. The back door of the house opened, and a man came out. He gestured at her as he crossed the yard. The drizzle began to come down harder. Of course, it would.

Joy left her purse in the car and took only her phone and the keys, locking it with the fob. The man hesitated at the bottom of the stairs until he seemed certain she'd follow him before he started up.

Friendly, Joy thought sarcastically, *but built*. Broad shoulders covered by a faded navy blue tee shirt and a green-and-navy plaid flannel shirt he wore unbuttoned over it. Jeans that fit him well enough to give her a glimpse of a damn fine ass. The boots of a working man. A tradesman of some sort, she decided.

I don't have to be best friends with my landlord, she reminded herself. If indeed the place was habitable.

He unlocked the inner door and pushed it back, waiting for her to step inside ahead of him. She got a glimpse of his face. Hazel eyes. Dark waves of hair that hadn't seen a barber in a while. Ruggedly handsome. Tough. Guarded. And not terribly friendly. *Too bad-*. Because otherwise, she could be interested. And she hadn't been interested in a man in quite some time.

He stepped in behind her and eased the screen closed but left the inner door open. Good. In case she needed to make a quick get-away. He flipped a switch, and an overhead light came on, which did little to dispel the gloom. Then he leaned against the wall near the door and crossed his arms over his chest, watching her as she moved into the space. It was, as she'd thought, one big L-shaped room with a tiny galley kitchen featuring a counter on one side that overlooked the main space. It wasn't furnished, but she wouldn't need much furniture. She peeked into the bathroom. Small but adequate. The place didn't sparkle, but it was clean.

She turned back to him. He didn't look away. "How much?"

"Three hundred a month. First, last, and security deposit up front."

"Seems kind of steep for the area and for such a small space."

He shrugged. He didn't care if he rented it or not.

She'd already decided she'd stick around Liberty for a while. Even if she only stayed for a month, she'd still come out ahead financially. She wanted to spend more time with her mother and doing it at the home where she'd grown up wouldn't fly with her father. "Month to month?" she asked.

He appeared to debate that offer. "Not planning on sticking around?"

She tried a smile. "I don't know. Depends on how things go."

"I can do month to month. Doesn't change anything else. No pets."

"Haven't got any. Is there Wi-Fi?"

"Shouldn't be a problem."

"Is a check okay?"

"I'd rather have cash."

Joy laughed at his bluntness. He didn't look amused. She didn't care. "I'll have to go to the bank." She narrowed her eyes. "But I'll want a receipt."

His narrowed in return. "No problem."

"Will you be here the rest of the day?"

"Nope. If you come back after four, my daughter will be here. She'll give you the keys."

"All right."

She brushed past him, and he moved in behind her, making her all too aware of him. He reminded her a little bit of Mike. A bit dark. A bit dangerous. A bit of that taciturn bad boy thing going on even though he was a grown man, probably close to her age.

What was it about those kinds of guys that always attracted her? She'd never figured it out. She was a sucker for them, though. Maybe because of her conventional upbringing, following the rules, toeing the line, until she'd thrown herself over that line and left town, never realizing that once she did, she wouldn't be welcomed back.

She wasn't looking for a man anyway. Certainly not one who couldn't communicate. She needed an affordable place to live for however long she ended up staying, and Mr. Granger could provide it.

Joy didn't bother saying goodbye or thanking him. She went back to her car through the rain and didn't look his way again. He doesn't have to be my friend, she reminded herself again. He's just the landlord.

Chapter Three

G ranger Sullivan watched Joy's car pull away. He knew exactly who she was, even if she hadn't recognized him. And why would she? He no longer bore any resemblance to the boy he'd once been. He'd had a crush on her since forever, since the first day he'd seen her in church. Sitting with her mother in the front pew, her father up in the pulpit. He remembered the pink bow in her blond hair, the pink and green plaid dress she wore with another bow tied in the back, white Mary Janes, and white anklet socks with lace trim.

She'd seemed like an angel to him. The picture of delicate, sweet femininity. She was three years older, and he knew even then that he'd never catch up to her. She was out of junior high by the time he started and a senior when he entered Liberty High as a freshman. He'd lived on hope, because once they were both adults, he figured, all bets were off. The age difference wouldn't matter. He'd always be younger, but an acceptable younger.

Except he never got that chance. He'd watched from afar when she started seeing Mike Laurence. Everyone knew Mike's mom was a druggie, and they lived in a run-down trailer in a bad neighborhood. Mike had a lot of bad habits, and he rode a motorcycle. Granger about died the first time he'd seen Joy with her arms locked around Mike's waist as they roared off together on that bike.

Everyone knew her dad hated Mike. That she'd been forbidden to date him. But it hadn't stopped Joy. She snuck out of the house. She fought with her parents, especially her father. Mike was a bad influence, that's what Granger thought. That's what everyone in town thought. And he badly influenced the pastor's daughter.

And then, one day, they were gone. Just gone. Granger couldn't believe it. Neither could anyone else in town. Word filtered back that they were in California. There'd been an unconfirmed rumor that Mike died not too long after that. No one heard from Joy again.

He'd studied Joy while she looked at the apartment. She wasn't wearing a ring. He hadn't asked if there'd be other tenants. She seemed...alone. The same Joy he remembered, but different. That soft, sweet prettiness had developed some sharp and interesting angles. Her eyes were assessing. Her hair not as blond. And there were no bows anywhere on her person.

Wasn't that just the way the world worked? Maybe now he had a chance with the Joy Harmon of his dreams. Except he didn't have a damn thing to offer her. Hell, he hadn't even managed a smile.

Maybe it was the shock of seeing her after all these years, but he knew he'd come across as rude. She wouldn't know his reticence had nothing to do with her. He could have dusted off a few of his rusty social skills in honor of her return. Too late now.

He went back inside to finish his sandwich and send Cassie a text.

"How's it going?" Devonny asked when Joy called her that afternoon.

Joy gave a humorless laugh. "It's going."

"Did you see your parents?"

"I did."

"And?"

"Your grandfather tried to slam the door in my face."

"Oh, Mom." Joy welcomed Devonny's sympathy and found it comforting.

"But my mother wouldn't let him. When she saw me at the door, she stood up to him. Pulled me into the kitchen and sat me down for a cup of coffee." Joy cleared her throat as emotion welled into a lump and lodged there. "It was good to see her. Kind of weird, after all these years. But good."

"She must have been thrilled to see you, too."

"Yes. I never realized how my leaving would affect her. Never thought about it, really. Selfish of me. She was never the problem, except that she took Dad's side."

"Doesn't sound like she's doing that anymore," Devonny said.

"Oh, no. She's not afraid to stand up to him now, where I never thought so before. She's changed."

Devonny chuckled. "Haven't we all?"

Joy smiled. "True."

"So, do you think you'll stick around?"

"I told my mother I would. Oh, Dev, if you could have seen the look on her face when I gave her my phone number and told her where I was staying. You'd think I'd handed her a diamond tiara or something."

"I can't wait to meet her."

Joy could hear the wistfulness in her daughter's voice. "She's dying to meet you too—all of you. We'll have to figure out a way to get you together. Maybe this summer."

"I hope so."

"I rented an apartment."

"An apartment? Sounds like you're planning on staying for a while, then."

"It's a studio, and I can rent it month to month. Cheaper than staying in a motel. I ran into an old friend today, too. I guess I do want to give it some time, being back here. See what happens."

"I'm proud of you, Mom. For trying. Whatever happens."

The lump in Joy's throat rose again. "Thanks, Dev. If not for you, I'm not sure I would have done it. It's been a surreal experience in a way, like stepping back in time, but I'm glad I came."

They went on to talk of other things for a few minutes with Devonny providing an update on Lucy, before Joy said, "Well, I've got to go. I'm at the bank. My new landlord wanted cash up front."

Devonny snorted. "Sounds like a hard ass."

Joy grinned. "Maybe. Or maybe he just wants insurance against a tenant skipping town and screwing him over. I'll talk to you in a day or two, okay?"

"Sure, Mom. Good luck with everything. And everyone."

At 4:15, Joy knocked on the back door of the brick ranch since that's where Granger had appeared from. She'd driven by the front of the house to discover a long porch, curtains closed in all the windows, and unimaginative landscaping. No surprise there. This wasn't LA, where homeowners often spent thousands on such things.

There were curtains over the window of the back door and a storm door as well. She waited before knocking again, wondering if Granger's daughter was even here.

After she pounded on the door, she heard footsteps. The curtain twitched back not even long enough for Joy to see who was on the other side. Locks turned, and a teenage girl with hazel eyes even more penetrating than her father's greeted her.

She had the most gorgeous black hair Joy had ever seen. It looked entirely natural, but maybe extensions were the thing with the high school set in Liberty. The girl's long-sleeved, peasant-style top and leggings emphasized her willowy shape. Her feet were bare.

"Hello," Joy said. "I need to pay for the rent on the apartment."

"Yeah, I heard." The girl stepped back and held the door open wider.

Joy experienced a wave of nostalgia looking around, the kitchen so reminiscent of the kitchens from her childhood. Most of the appliances were black, except for a newer dishwasher finished in stainless steel. The creamy color of the wallpaper had darkened with age and featured teapots and teacups in its pattern. Four chairs sat around an old oak table. The battered porcelain sink held a few dishes. Joy took all this in before addressing the girl who stood staring at her.

"I'm Joy, by the way. Joy Laurence."

"Okay. Whatever."

Perplexed by her attitude and lack of manners, Joy said, "And what's your name?"

The girl gave a sigh, probably meant to convey her opinion of all adults and their insistence at knowing such things. "Cassie."

Joy tried a smile. "It's nice to meet you, Cassie."

Cassie rolled her eyes. "You want to pay for the apartment, or what?"

"Yes. Thank you." Joy decided to be even more polite and upbeat just to get under the girl's skin. If Devonny ever displayed such borderline rudeness to an adult in a similar setting, Joy wouldn't have thought twice about calling her out. But this wasn't her daughter. It wasn't her problem. And, she reminded herself, she knew absolutely nothing about this child. There might be a very good reason for her sullen demeanor.

Cassie turned to the counter and picked up an invoice. "It's seven hundred and fifty dollars," she said.

"Could I see that?" Joy asked.

Cassie sighed and handed it over. Granger had apparently already filled it out and signed it. She saw no designation for a business or personal name and address. Just an invoice number, the date, and what it was for.

"You have to put your name in the box at the top," Cassie informed her. She held out a ballpoint pen. Joy moved to the table and set her purse down. She filled in her name and took the bank envelope from her purse. She counted out the cash and handed it to Cassie, who counted it again, even though she'd watched Joy's every move.

Satisfied, Cassie ripped the triplicate invoice apart and handed Joy the pink copy. She held out one of those cheap key rings with the round cardboard attached to it, which held a single key. Someone had written "Apt." on the cardboard.

"Thanks!" Joy purposely brightened her tone and gave Cassie a huge smile. "Lovely meeting you."

Cassie rewarded her with a glower which made Joy wonder what the girl looked like when she smiled. If she smiled.

The door closed behind her and the lock snapped into place. Joy's momentary sense of triumph faded. Cassie reminded her of someone. The sullen attitude.

The barely disguised mistrust of adults. The disgust of having to deal with them. Cassie reminded Joy of herself as a teenager, although she didn't think she'd ever had an attitude to the same degree.

But she could hardly be an impartial judge of her own behavior. She did recall feeling suffocated by her parents, their rules, and the small town where, "What will people think?" took number one spot on everyone's priority list. She hadn't cared what people thought, and once she got together with Mike, he fed every wild impulse she'd ever had.

She wondered if Cassie had a boyfriend. A girl who looked like that? Joy would be shocked if she didn't. She seemed the kind of girl who could be easily led astray. Or maybe already had been.

Not my problem, Joy reminded herself as she crossed the yard and mounted the steps to the apartment. She wanted to take another look around. Her mother had called earlier, and they'd agreed to meet for dinner at the diner near the highway. Tomorrow, Joy would shop for a few basic furnishings. She wasn't going to invest much because she didn't know how long she'd be here.

Chapter Four

C assie parted the kitchen curtains an inch and watched the new tenant cross the yard and mount the steps to the apartment. Something didn't add up. That woman had too much class, and probably too much money, to want to live in a place like Liberty. Especially in a shitty apartment like the one over her dad's garage.

Cassie hadn't missed the Coach purse and matching wallet or the Polo logo on her blazer. No way was she from around here. Her hair looked like she'd stepped out of a salon, the subtle caramel highlights and the layered bob that fell below her chin but not to her shoulders.

Cassie knew what the new tenant was doing, too, when she'd adopted that spunky tone and exaggerated her upbeat responses to Cassie's lack of effort with the conversation.

After the woman disappeared inside the apartment Cassie looked at the name on the receipt. Joy Laurence.

She fingered the cash in crisp hundred-dollar bills and one fifty. Her dad would notice if it wasn't all there, of course. Adults could assume many things about her, but Cassie wasn't a thief. She clipped the cash to the invoice and brought it into her dad's home office, which used to be the guest room. But they never had guests. When her mom left, Dad got rid of the bed and moved in a desk and filing cabinets.

The bed had gone into the apartment when Cameron lived there for a short time after he graduated college and before he moved to Cincinnati.

Cassie wished she were Cameron. An adult with his own life. *Freedom.* That's what she wanted more than anything. Not to be under her dad's thumb, following his dumb rules, cleaning his stupid house, and making him dinner.

Sure, in return for her chores, he gave her a more generous allowance than any of her friends got. And she was learning life skills. At least, that's what her dad told her. She grudgingly had to admit he was right. She knew more about being self-sufficient than most of her friends who'd never done laundry or cooked a meal. Cassie didn't mind cooking. She'd got pretty good at it, as a matter of fact. She loved Pinterest and TikTok because there were always interesting recipes, even though she usually stuck to the basics. Otherwise, her dad's eyebrows would go up and he'd sniff suspiciously at what she put on his plate and say, "What's this?" He liked to be able to identify his food.

Maybe, she mused as she flopped back on her bed and reached for her phone, she'd go to culinary school. Maybe she'd become a famous chef and have her own cookware and TV show, like the Pioneer Woman. Yeah, maybe.

She saw she'd missed a text from Kye.

Practice 2nite @7. Wanna come?

Cassie sighed. Everything was so complicated. His cousin Patrick's band needed a drummer and recruited Kye to join them.

No way would her dad let her go out on a school night. No way would he let her hang around with guys who were nineteen or twenty, even if there were other girls there. Not without *adult supervision.*

Her dad was very big on adult supervision. If she wanted to spend the night somewhere, he called the parents and made sure they were going to be home. He often dropped her off and picked her up. If he didn't know them, sometimes he said no. Her dad had trust issues. She guessed being super overprotective was how dads showed love to their daughters. Mostly though, she just felt like her dad didn't trust her.

A couple of weeks ago, instead of asking permission she'd sneaked out to listen to Kye's band on a school night. She didn't even know how her dad found out. She thought he was asleep. She'd barely made a sound raising her window. But he had super-sensitive hearing or something. She'd run to Kye's car parked down the street. She hadn't realized her dad went out the back and followed them in his truck. She'd been drunk on the excitement of sneaking out, of having Kye, a junior, come pick her up, thrilled that he'd even invited her.

He'd introduced her to the other guys in the band. A couple of them sort of gave her the creeps with their stringy hair and tats and appraising eyes. Their groupie girlfriends weren't much better. Cassie had cringed a little bit when the term *white trash* crossed her mind. She tried not to judge. But it was hard when a girl had blond hair with black roots and too much eye makeup and wore a too-tight tank top with black bra straps showing.

Cassie sat in one of the beat-up lawn chairs as the band started up. It wasn't even her kind of music, and she couldn't understand the lyrics. The lead singer, Zak, didn't enunciate. She got the impression the song was about contemplating suicide. Driving off a cliff and letting go. She wasn't exactly having a good time, but at least she was doing *something* besides sitting at home.

She concentrated on watching Kye, who didn't look like he fit in with the rest of the band. His clothes were too clean, his hair too short. His parents let him be in the band and go practice at night as long as he didn't miss school and kept his grades up. Plus, practice was at his cousin's house, and his aunt and uncle were supposed to be keeping an eye on things.

When the band started a second song Cassie tried to get into it. One of the other girls lit a cigarette and offered the pack to Cassie. That's when her dad walked in. He didn't say anything. He didn't have to. He gave her *the look* and waited for her to get up and follow him out. Her dad excelled at waiting.

She'd rolled her eyes. Waved to Kye because they hadn't even stopped their song. Her dad held the door and followed her out. He didn't say anything on the way home. Neither did she. Her dad didn't have to say anything. She knew which of the rules she'd broken to guarantee herself even less freedom than she'd had before.

So, no, she wouldn't be going to band practice with Kye tonight or any night.

God, she was stupid.

That evening Joy arrived at the diner before her mother and was looking over the menu when she arrived. Marcy bent and pressed her cheek against Joy's. "I still can't believe you're here," she whispered. "Finally."

She drew back, but not before Joy saw the glimmer of tears in her mother's eyes. Marcy settled on the other side of the booth and smiled. "I'm so happy you're here. You're going to get tired of hearing me say that."

"No, I won't. Not if you don't get tired of hearing me apologize for the way I left. The way I stayed away. I'm sorry, Mom. I don't think I can make it up to you, and I know I can't change it, but I'm truly sorry for the pain I caused you."

Marcy sat back and cocked her head. "But it was painful for you, too. We weren't there for you when you needed us."

"*You* would have been," Joy said quietly.

"I did try to find you, but I didn't get very far with it." Marcy looked down at her menu. Joy knew she'd put her mother in the unenviable position of once again siding with her husband or her daughter. Marcy couldn't defend her husband, but she didn't want to admit disloyalty to him either. They both knew, if not for him, the rift in the family wouldn't have existed or lasted this long.

"Let's make a pact," Joy said, reaching to cover her mother's hand with her own. "Let's start fresh. Let's forgive each other and begin right now on being mother and daughter again. How does that sound?"

Marcy's lips trembled, but she tried to smile. "I'd like that."

Joy squeezed her hand. "Great. Now, I'm buying dinner. No arguments. What's good here?"

The waitress arrived with water glasses, and they both ordered chef's salads. "Tell me what happened," Marcy said once the waitress left. "From the beginning. Tell me everything I missed."

"The first thing you should know is that Mike and I stopped in Vegas and got married."

"Then you went to California?"

"Mike was sure he could get work in LA, and he did. It was tough at first. We didn't have much money. And I got pregnant almost as soon as we got there."

"How did he feel about that?"

"Not especially happy, if I'm being honest. But he wasn't angry about it or anything either. I think at that point we realized, whatever was going to happen, we were in it together. Where were we going to go? Not back here. So, we had to stick it out with each other."

"Did you love him?"

Joy looked away from her mother's eyes that seemed to pierce right through her. "I don't know, Mom. I thought I did. I know you and Dad thought he wasn't good enough for me. He was definitely rough around the edges. Rebellious. He didn't abide by other people's rules, probably because he'd been raised without them. That's what I liked about him. He was so different from me. But he wasn't unkind."

Was that the best thing she could say about the boy she'd run away with? That he wasn't unkind? But it was the truth. Her memories of Mike weren't all that vivid. Was it possible he hadn't, in the end, made much of an impression on her? Or had she simply been too young and inexperienced to understand what she felt?

"A drunk driver clipped his bike and threw him into the canyon. That's how he died before I had Devonny."

"I'm sorry," Marcy said. Her eyes were glazed with tears. She reached for Joy's hand. "So sorry, honey."

Joy smiled grimly. "I was terrified. I didn't have much money, no insurance, and a baby on the way. No friends. That's when I called home."

Marcy's mouth hardened into a thin line. "And your father answered."

That Joy did remember. Quite clearly. She knew she'd never forget it.

"I was devastated, as you can imagine. I didn't know there'd be an insurance settlement or Social Security benefits for Devonny. I grew up fast after that, especially after she was born. My landlady's son had recently passed the bar exam. I became one of his first clients. He went after the driver's insurance company before he pursued a civil suit against the driver for wrongful death. A young mother with a high school education and no prospects drew a lot of sympathy from the jury."

The waitress returned with their salads and, once she ascertained they needed nothing else, disappeared again. Joy picked up her fork. "I used some of the money as a down payment on a condominium in a decent neighborhood and invested the rest. When Devonny turned a year old, I started working from home, mostly doing research for writers, professors, doctors. Seemed like everyone wanted to write a book or an article. And research assistants were in demand."

Joy paused to dribble dressing on her salad. "Since I worked from home, I home-schooled Devonny. I'd researched that as well and realized I could probably give her a better education than the public school system."

"Go on." Marcy sprinkled the small packages of bacon bits and croutons on top of her salad.

"Devonny turned out to be a math geek. She had a full ride to Stanford on a math scholarship, but she never went to Stanford."

"Because she got married? To the man you didn't approve of?"

"Yes." Joy wasn't proud of her behavior toward her daughter. It made it a little too easy to understand her parents.

"Why didn't you like him?"

That was a good question. Why hadn't she liked Jack? Because he was an actor? He was older than Devonny? Because he'd interfered in her vision for her daughter's future?

"I don't exactly know. But Devonny loved him. And frankly, I think he adored her. It's funny how she ended up in similar circumstances. Pregnant and widowed."

"But she's doing all right?"

"Yes. She moved to Iowa, of all places, and she seems to be thriving. So is the baby. And she's got a new man in her life."

"Do you have pictures?" Marcy asked. "I'd love to see them."

"Of course." Joy pulled out her phone and accessed her photos. "I have quite a few. I visited them before I came here."

Marcy pored over the photos.

"That's Luke," she said when she saw Marcy studying a shot of the three of them.

"I can't wait to meet them." She handed the phone back to Joy. "When do you think we can arrange that?"

"I don't know. I'll talk to Devonny about it." Should she tell her mother about Devonny's adult films? The ones she'd made with Jack. And the others she'd made with Cherry. Did her mother need to know this before she even met her granddaughter? Joy decided it wasn't her place to enlighten her mother. If Devonny wanted her to know, she could tell her when they met. Maybe Marcy would never have to know.

They ate in silence for a while before Joy said, "Your turn. Tell me what I've missed."

Marcy gave a small shrug.

"The gossip about me leaving must have hurt."

Marcy's eyes flashed with indignation. "Sticks and stones," she said.

"I talked to Brian Crowley. Remember him? He said I was the talk of the town for about a year."

"Water under the bridge," Marcy insisted.

"What about your friend June? Didn't she have something to say when she saw me this morning?"

"Of course, she did. I told her the truth. That my daughter is here for a visit."

Joy laughed. "So, by now, everyone who goes to First Congregational knows I'm back in town."

The corners of Marcy's mouth turned up. "Probably."

"Daddy won't like it."

Marcy's expression hardened. "We all have to deal with things we don't like in this life."

Joy leaned across the table. "Mom, I love you. I love Daddy, too. I didn't think about how hard this would be for both of you. I only thought...about myself, I guess, and I wanted to see my family again. It was selfish of me now, that I think of it. As selfish as when I left."

"Sweetheart. I wanted to find you. I tried but," she paused. "It didn't happen. Still, not a day went by that I didn't want you here. There never will be. Whatever happens is going to happen. I can't control what others think or say. Neither can you. So, like you said let's start fresh. The two of us. Even if no one else can."

They lingered over decaf coffees while Marcy relayed some of the highlights that had occurred in the town during Joy's absence. The ice storm a few years ago that sent tree limbs crashing into the roof of the church, causing extensive damage. Joy's cousin giving birth to triplets after fertility treatments. The high school principal suffering a brain tumor.

When they parted, they made plans to have lunch the next day.

As Joy drove back to the hotel, she realized she hadn't told her mother about her new apartment. She'd tell her tomorrow. Her mother might like to go shopping with her.

Chapter Five

T he next day Joy parked once again on the street across from her parents' home. Marcy had assured her the coast would be clear because her father planned to attend an all-day conference in Dayton. She noticed a truck parked in front of the house. The kind a tradesman would use with a ladder secured on top and a covered bed and compartments on the side for tools and such.

Her mother hadn't mentioned having home repairs scheduled. She bypassed the truck and went up the walk. The weather had dried up leaving behind a crisp coolness, the scent of rain lingering in the air, and the ground still damp. Soon her mother would plant flowers in front of the porch as she did every year. The storm windows would come off and the screens would go on. Joy had missed the rituals of the definitive seasons.

She rang the bell. After twenty-five years, it didn't feel appropriate to just walk into the house, especially since she hadn't been invited to do so.

Her mother pulled open the door, holding the phone to her ear. "Yes, Marjorie, I understand." She rolled her eyes at Joy and motioned her inside. She covered the mouthpiece with her hand and said, "I'll just be a minute," before she ducked into the office off the dining room.

Joy set her purse on the dining table and wandered back to the kitchen. She felt the most comfortable there, probably because it was almost exclusively her mother's domain—a part of the house where hardly any trace of her father existed.

She stopped short when she saw a man on all fours, his head hidden inside the cabinet under the sink, where he shone a flashlight around the space. "Oh! I didn't realize anyone else was here."

He backed out, turned around, and fixed her with those hazel eyes once again. At the same moment her mother came up behind her, edging past into the kitchen. "Have you two met? Granger, you probably don't remember our daughter, Joy. Joy, this is Granger Sullivan."

"I remember her," Granger said, his eyes still locked on Joy.

Her tongue stuck to the roof of her mouth while she searched for a proper reply. Finally, she came out with, "Nice to meet you."

"Any luck?" Marcy asked him.

For the first time, Joy noticed the number of towels banking the cabinets and base of the dishwasher.

Everything normally stored under the sink sat in a dishpan on the floor nearby.

"It might be a pipe behind the wall, which means I'm going to have to tear out the back of the cabinet. But first, I'll pull the dishwasher out and make sure it's not one of those connections."

"All right," Marcy said, not the least bit perturbed. "I left you a sandwich in the fridge for your lunch. And a slice of cake there on the table to go with it."

"Miss Marcy, you didn't have to do that."

"Nonsense. Now we're off to have lunch ourselves."

According to Marcy, the food and the prices were decent at the downtown bistro. Once they were settled, Joy said, "Tell me about Granger Sullivan."

Marcy looked up from the menu. "Don't you remember him?"

"Should I?"

"Maybe not. He's a year or two younger than you. But he and his father went to our church. Still do, as a matter of fact. Granger and his children are like family to us. I don't know what your father would do without them."

"Oh? In what way?"

"Maintenance, for one thing. Granger can fix just about anything. And you know, as old as that church is, there's always something going wrong."

"He does it for free?"

"Oh, my goodness, no. The church pays him. But he's reliable, and if it's an emergency, he'll be there in five minutes."

"I met his daughter," Joy said, glancing down at her menu even though she'd already decided on the chicken salad special written on a sidewalk chalkboard.

"Cassie? She's such a darling. We think of her as our granddaughter. Where in heavens did you meet her?"

Darling? Granddaughter? Had she and Devonny, in their absence, been replaced by Granger and his daughter?

"I rented an apartment from him. He told me she'd be there when I came back to pay the rent and the security deposit."

Marcy sat back. "You rented the apartment? You're staying? Oh, Joy."

Whatever Joy had taken from her mother when she'd left, when she'd stayed away, from the look on her mother's face and the happiness in her voice, she knew she'd just given it back. "He agreed to rent it to me month to month. I'm not sure I'm ready for a commitment any longer than that just yet."

Marcy's eyes brimmed with tears. "You don't know how happy that makes me."

"I have an idea."

They ordered and ate and chatted, and Joy invited her mother to go shopping with her. Marcy agreed with delight. "I don't need much," Joy said. "A bed. A table and chairs to start with. A coffeemaker."

Granger pulled into the driveway and parked the truck outside the garage workshop. He glanced up at the apartment. His new tenant hadn't taken up residence yet, of course, but just knowing she would be around in such close proximity gave him a feeling in his gut somewhere between anticipation and anxiety.

He'd given up trying to figure out why the only women he found attractive were guaranteed to leave. Maybe because he'd lost his own mother at such a young age. Had he figured that's what women do? They leave. Cause you pain and sadness and grief? If his mom hadn't died when he was eight, would he be guaranteed healthy romantic relationships? He guessed he'd never know.

He locked the truck and went inside. The kitchen smelled amazing. Cassie looked up from the stove, giving him a mirror image of his eyes. Their routine now meant they each took a moment to gauge the other's mood, determining whether it was safe to interact and at what level. He did his best, but he could sure use a guidebook on how to raise a daughter by himself.

Even though he was glad to see her, he smiled so rarely these days, it looked unnatural and forced. Instead, wary of pissing her off, he strived for a neutral tone. "Smells good."

Cassie raised one shoulder and returned her attention to stirring. Granger went into the bathroom, leaned against the sink, and stared at himself in the mirror. Why couldn't he bridge this gap between himself and Cassie? He loved her. He supposed, hoped anyway, that she loved him. Of course she did. But they couldn't get past whatever was between them. Anger? Resentment? Did Cassie hate him because he'd driven her mother away? Is that what she thought?

Maybe that's what happened, even though he'd never wanted Adele to leave. But what he wanted didn't factor into her plans. She'd had enough, she said. She wanted more, she said. Even that had confused him. She'd had enough but wanted more? He didn't understand where she was coming from. They'd been plugging along pretty good as far as he could tell. Cameron was almost done with high school. Cassie was heading into middle school. They were doing okay financially.

But Adele wanted more. Or less. Truth was, he didn't know what Adele wanted. Maybe she didn't either. He didn't know if she'd found it because he hadn't talked to her in about a year. If Cassie kept in touch with her mother, she rarely mentioned it. Granger would have welcomed Adele's help with Cassie.

She wasn't the easy little girl he remembered. The one who delighted in a trip to the park or the unexpected treat of an ice cream cone. Cassie had turned dark and mysterious, and she always seemed to be silently questioning him. He just wished she'd ask him. But then again, he didn't encourage it, afraid she'd ask something he couldn't or wouldn't want to answer.

He washed his hands and ran his fingers through his hair to dry them. He gave up staring at himself. What had he hoped to find? Clues? Answers? He went back to the kitchen.

Cassie lifted two plates from the cupboard and began filling them from the pots on the stove. Granger opened the refrigerator. "What are you drinking?"

"I have water," she said.

Granger poured himself the same from the filtration pitcher, then refilled it at the sink. By the time he took his seat at the table, she'd set a steaming plate at his place. He poked at a slab of something covered with gravy. "What is this?"

"Country-fried steak. Roasted red potatoes. Broccoli."

Granger raked his fork through the broccoli.

"It's good for you," Cassie informed him. "And I put cheese on yours."

Granger glanced up. "I didn't say anything."

Cassie gave him the one-shoulder shrug again.

He cut into the steak and took a bite. Girl could cook. He cut the broccoli into tiny pieces and gagged it down with the potatoes. The cheese helped. "The tenant show up?" he asked after a few minutes.

Cassie knew better than to talk with her mouth full. After she swallowed, she said, "Yes. The money and the invoice are on your desk."

"Good. Thanks." Granger ate some more before he said, "What'd you think of her?"

"I could tell she's not from around here," Cassie said.

Granger cocked his head. "What made you think that?"

"I don't know. Her clothes. Her hair. Her *je ne sais quoi*." Cassie almost smiled when she used the words. He wished she'd smile more. She had a beautiful smile.

"She actually is from around here," Granger informed her.

"No. Way."

"Way. She was born here. Lived in Liberty until she was eighteen."

Cassie waited.

"She's Pastor Art's daughter."

Cassie's brows knit. "I forgot they had any kids. They don't talk about her."

"She's been gone a long time."

"Why'd she come back?"

"You'd have to ask her."

"I don't care." Cassie returned her attention to her plate.

I do. Granger wondered how long Joy would stick around. Not long, probably, considering she'd requested a month-to-month rental agreement.

A couple of minutes of chewing and fork tines scraping plates went by before Cassie said, "Where's she been all this time?"

"I'm not sure. LA, I think."

"That's dumb."

"What's dumb?"

Cassie shot him a look. "If I got out of this town and made it to LA, I sure wouldn't come back."

Granger looked down at his plate, that old sadness surging through him. Yep. His life seemed to be filled with females who were destined to leave him.

Chapter Six

Reverend Arthur Harmon sat at the desk in his small home office and stared unseeingly at the draft of Sunday's sermon. His mind was a million miles away, unsettled, and chaotic. Joy's arrival had shattered the fragile peace he'd managed to create during her absence.

Marcy had left him a sandwich for his lunch after informing him that she planned to meet Joy. Again. She'd used that clipped, no-nonsense tone she'd developed which meant, "Don't even bother objecting."

They'd simply looked at each other before Arthur had said, "Fine." He couldn't hold Marcy's gaze when she glared at him anyway. That look made him feel small and *wrong* somehow. Even though he knew he hadn't been wrong. Wasn't wrong.

His daughter had come between him and Marcy in big ways and little ways since the moment of her conception, it seemed. He'd wanted to feel joy when his first child arrived, his only child, as it turned out. But after a difficult pregnancy, Joy's birth had nearly killed Marcy, and faced with the possibility of being without his wife, Arthur had resented his daughter ever since.

He'd had many moments when he thought it would have been better to be childless. He loathed himself in those moments of weakness. Children were a gift from God. They were often mentioned in Scripture, used to demonstrate innocence and God's love.

"God loves all his children. Isn't that what you preach?" He could still hear the echo of Joy's defiant teenage voice as she threw the words at him when he'd forbade her to associate with that good-for-nothing Michael Laurence. He'd seen their relationship developing as one would see an oncoming train if one were trapped on the tracks. He couldn't stop it, but God knew Arthur had tried. He'd seen nothing but heartbreak for Joy if she continued down the path she'd stepped onto. He wanted to spare her that, to turn her around before it was too late.

Where had Marcy been then? Why hadn't she backed him up? Why hadn't she been stronger? Because, as she'd spat at him more than once over the days and weeks that followed Joy's exit, she'd been a good and *submissive* wife, just as she'd been trained to be. She'd been following *The Word* as handed down by the *Reverend Arthur Harmon*. And it had cost her her daughter.

Lord knew Marcy had never forgiven him. He'd tried to compensate for Joy's absence. Finally agreed to join the bowling league with her. Created outings he thought she'd enjoy. Touring Broadway shows. Nature hikes.

A river cruise. Enlarging the garden. Remodeling the kitchen. On the surface, Marcy put on an agreeable demeanor, but the loss of her daughter had changed his wife in ways Arthur shied away from contemplating. It was almost as if she'd begun channeling Joy, challenging him in big ways and small. Defying him. Subtly undermining his authority. But she hadn't done what Joy had done. She hadn't run away. There were days when Arthur didn't know if that was a good thing or a bad thing. Marcy was no longer the girl he'd married. She'd become a stranger who second-guessed his decisions at every turn. He'd lost her trust and didn't know how to get it back.

Not true. He knew how. But reconciling with Joy, condoning what she'd done, *apologizing* to her? Those were things Arthur simply couldn't do.

He stared at the papers on his desk, the words blurring before him. He took off his glasses and dug his knuckles into his eyelids. He thought about laying his head down on his desk, giving in to the doubt and confusion and sadness that stuck in his chest like a heart attack waiting to happen. He wouldn't, though. Those negative emotions were the work of the enemy. Arthur Harmon followed the Lord. And no one could cause him to stray from that path. Not his wife. Not his daughter.

Marcy hummed to herself as she prepared dinner, marveling at the return of her appetite. She and Joy had spent a lovely afternoon together, and nothing could have brought Marcy more joy than knowing her daughter planned to stay in town indefinitely. Finally, she reminded herself with a smile, her prayers for her daughter's return had been answered. Marcy wanted nothing more than to make up for lost time. She could call Joy whenever she wanted. Hear her voice. Hug her. Spend time with her. Marcy did a little dance as she opened the drawer for silverware and spun around in delight as she closed it.

She stopped humming and dancing, however, when she spied her husband in the doorway. She stared at him across the center island, daring him to trample on her happiness the way he'd done so many times. He didn't say anything, just gave her a searching look. Probably wondering about her dancing around the kitchen. Not that he'd ask. Not that she'd tell him. His lips parted but whatever he was going to say, she didn't want to hear it.

"Dinner in about twenty minutes," she informed him before she turned away to set the table. She listened to his footsteps retreat. Just like that, her happiness spillover from the afternoon dwindled away. Because being here, with him, was like having the life sucked out of her.

She loved Arthur almost as much as she hated him. She'd never stopped blaming him for driving Joy away. She'd never stopped blaming herself, either. The anger and the guilt and the recriminations had destroyed them both. They were two husks of a married couple occupying space under the same roof, going through the motions as their roles in life dictated, presenting a united front to the world. Living a lie. That's what it came down to.

But Marcy didn't know how to change it. She'd never known. A war had been going on inside of her for years. She'd married Arthur for better or worse. She'd made a commitment. She'd loved him and wanted to share his passion for ministry. But at the same time, after Joy left, when he wouldn't give in to her pleas to find her daughter, to let her come back home, the seeds of disappointment and heartache and resentment grew until they took over. They'd blotted out the love and admiration she'd once felt for Arthur.

Now that Joy was back, Arthur still took that hard line with her. His unforgiving heart embarrassed Marcy. Joy's desertion had hurt them both, and even though Joy had never asked for it until recently, Marcy had forgiven her long ago. Arthur never had. Perhaps he never would. They'd never be a family again.

It surprised Marcy to know she could live with that. She no longer felt a stronger loyalty to her husband than she did to her daughter. They'd both betrayed her in a way, but Joy had taken a huge step in rectifying the situation by returning, by her desire to make amends. Marcy didn't think Arthur wanted to make amends to either her or to Joy. Because Arthur didn't believe he'd done anything to amend for. To be forgiven for.

Marcy stepped to the stove and stirred the sauce surrounding the pork chops. She tested the mixed vegetables with a fork and drained them. The timer for the rice beeped.

"Dinner's ready," she called, not really caring if Arthur heard her or not. For once, facing him across the table, realizing she had nothing she wanted to say to him, didn't bother her. She'd said everything she needed to over the years. She was on her own now.

Chapter Seven

J oy parked her car next to Granger's truck. Lights were on in the garage and one of the overhead doors was up. She stepped carefully to the entrance to find Granger with his back to her, bent over and holding a blowtorch. Steven Tyler belted *Dream On* from a portable stereo. Sparks flew from the torch. A head covering and mask obliterated Granger's features. Not wanting to disturb him, Joy stood still and watched as he edged around his project inch by inch with the torch until he moved to the side of it, and she could see what he'd been working on.

Her eyes widened as she realized it was a sculpture. A work of art made of what looked like bits and pieces of scrap iron. Old faucets and spigots. The handle from a well. Knobs and brackets and other things she couldn't readily identify. He'd turned the collection of scraps into a clownish figure seated on a suitcase thumbing for a ride. The piece conveyed whimsy, but also a bit of sadness. Mesmerized, Joy studied the piece, searching for its essence, while also trying to figure out what exactly its parts were originally.

Eventually, her gaze roamed to the darkened half of the garage. It looked like there were more sculptures there, but in the dim light she couldn't tell how many or what they were. Distracted, it took her a moment to realize sparks were no longer flying from the blow torch. Granger removed his protective gear and stared at her.

She couldn't say his stance was forbidding exactly, or even unfriendly. More cautiously curious, she supposed. They'd be living next to each other for the foreseeable future. She hoped, at the very least, they could get along. But the way he looked at her unsettled her just as it had before, in a way she didn't fully understand, and wanted to think about even less.

"Hi...um, Granger? I'm, uh, sorry to disturb you." *Why*, she asked herself, *was she suddenly stammering?* "I wondered if you might have a tape measure I could borrow. I ordered a few pieces of furniture today, and I had to guesstimate. I just want to make sure they'll fit in the space before they're delivered. Because I can always cancel the order if they won't." She forced herself to stop babbling.

Granger turned to one of the many shelves lining the wall and pulled out one of several toolboxes. He set it on a workbench, opened it, and held a tape measure out to her. Joy had to walk farther into the garage to accept it, which put her level with the figure on the suitcase. She found herself drawn to it and bent to study the impressive detail, how he'd taken materials that were in no way human-like and turned them into a reasonable facsimile of a down-on-his-luck hitchhiker. He'd used nuts and bolts for eyes and buttons and bits of wire for hair. Fascinated, she circled the figure, barely realizing she'd forced Granger to take a step back or she'd have run into him.

"Wow. This is amazing." She arrived back at her starting point and looked at him. "How did you come up with this?"

He gave a half shrug. "Job like mine, you tend to collect a lot of scrap. Figured I'd see what I could do with it."

"And so, what? You just started making sculptures like this? Do you sell them?"

He snorted. "Who would want them?"

"Collectors. Art enthusiasts. Museums."

This earned her a hard bark of laughter. "Museums? Yeah, right."

Her eyes narrowed. "This is folk art. Better than a lot of what's out there. And yes, it is in museums. It's also in home décor stores, art shows, galleries."

Granger appeared unconvinced and loathe to take her assessment seriously. "If you say so."

"I do."

"Are you some kind of expert?"

"Hardly. But I've been to a lot of museums and probably even more galleries. I do a lot of research for work. I know what I'm talking about."

"If you say so," Granger repeated, but not quite as defiantly.

"Could I see the rest of it?"

"Sure. But not tonight. I'm beat, okay? Got a long day tomorrow."

"Another time then. Thanks for the tape measure. I'll bring it back."

"No problem."

"Good night."

"Night."

Joy turned to make her way up the steps at the side of the building. A weird hum of excitement rippled through her. Why? Because of him? Because he'd spoken more than two words to her for once? Because of his incredible art? Because an attractive, apparently unattached male lived close by, and she would inevitably run into him in the future? Joy didn't much care what the reason was. It had been a long time since she'd been excited about anything or anyone who wasn't still in diapers.

Granger walked around his hitchhiker slowly, trying to see it through Joy's eyes. Amazing? Saleable? Museum worthy? He doubted it, but the fact that she apparently thought so made him almost smile. He shut down the lights and closed the door, making sure to lock up.

He stepped into the quiet house. Cassie would be in her room, probably listening to music through her earbuds. Doing homework, he hoped. And not texting that kid, Kye, she seemed so hung up on. Granger started on the dishes that had been soaking in the sink while reminding himself that he couldn't keep her from texting a boy. Not unless he took her phone away. Being without a phone was like the kiss of death to a teenager these days. And he wasn't going to do that, mostly because he needed to be able to reach Cassie himself if he worked late, or if he needed her assistance, like he had with Joy dropping off rent money. And she needed to be able to reach him.

But he had installed one of those tracking devices on her phone and her laptop, and he made sure Cassie knew it. He could check up on her any time he chose. He could see who she interacted with, what she Googled, where her emails went, what she posted on Instagram or Snapchat. If she wanted a separate phone account, she could pay for it, and it would take most of her allowance money each month.

He wasn't sure exactly how they'd come to an agreement about the monitoring apps, but after he'd caught her sneaking out, she didn't fight him on it. He, on the other hand, had agreed not to check up on her or invade her privacy unless he caught her sneaking out again. Or did anything to make him suspicious.

"Define anything," she'd challenged him at the time.

Granger'd had to think for a minute. Because the truth was, he always suspected she might be lying to him and feared his own gullibility where she was concerned. "I can't say exactly, but it will include problems at school, your grades dropping, or time you can't account for when you're not at home or at school."

"I'm not Mom." She spoke so softly it took a moment for the words to sink in.

He knew in that moment his daughter understood him better than he'd ever given her credit for. "I know you're not." *And I hope to God you don't turn into her.*

He'd wanted to hug her then. Hold her and tell her he was sorry. Sorry he'd driven her mother away. Sorry he was doing such a lousy job as a father. Sorry for her unhappiness. But once again he waited too long, and the moment passed. Cassie said, "Okay, then," and went to her room.

Granger rinsed the plates and utensils and loaded them in the dishwasher before he scrubbed the pots and pans and set them on the drain board. He lifted the curtain over the sink and peeked out. Joy's car was gone, the apartment dark. But she'd be back.

A flutter of hope rose in his chest, and he found he didn't want to completely squelch it.

She'll be back.

Chapter Eight

Other than the occasional wedding or funeral, Joy hadn't been to a church service in all the years since she'd left Liberty. But today she'd decided to return to the church of her childhood. Her father's church. He could ban her from his home, but he couldn't lock the church doors against her. No matter how much he might want to.

She didn't know why she had this need to challenge his authority, to make him prove his points, to simply needle him. Theirs had never been an easy relationship. His rules never made sense to her. She'd decided he just liked rules. His way or the highway. If she asked for an explanation, something she didn't think was unreasonable at all, he exploded and sent her to her room.

"Well, you can't send me to my room anymore," she informed her reflection as she finished her makeup. She stepped back to get a glimpse of herself in the bathroom mirror. Would the weather ever warm up? She knew summer would be here soon, but this morning dawned cloudy and cool and still with that hint of rain in the air.

She'd chosen a royal blue cowl-neck sweater dress, matching it with a pair of ankle-high lace-up black boots. She carried an ivory pashmina as well in case she needed it.

"What you need is to find a gym," she told herself. She needed to get back to working out several times a week. Her visit with Devonny and the trip here had wreaked havoc with her schedule. But now, she could settle into her tiny apartment and get into a new routine. She exited the bathroom and glanced around the space. The bed and a single nightstand tucked in nicely behind the kitchen area, and the wall between gave it the illusion of being separated. The rectangular table would work well as a desk and an eating space for one, although she'd purchased the four chairs that came with it. Because one never knew when one might have company. Her mother certainly would visit. She envisioned morning chats with her over cups of tea, or the occasional dinner.

Joy hadn't brought very much with her. A variety of clothes, of course, though she'd left most in storage. She could have her things shipped and stored here, where she could access them if she needed them. It might make the most sense, but she wasn't ready to commit to a long-term stay.

She'd also purchased a comfortable rocker/recliner, laughing at herself when she'd chosen it. But it would be perfect for an evening of reading or to watch a movie. She just needed a small table or shelves to put nearby to hold a reading lamp and books or magazines or a drink.

She hadn't told her mother she'd planned to attend the service. She hadn't told anyone. She wondered if anyone else she knew would be there. Would they recognize her? Would they ask questions?

If they did, she'd already decided she'd tell them only what mere acquaintances deserved to know. They could fill in the blanks on their own. She didn't plan on questioning them about what they'd been doing since she'd been gone. Because it wasn't her business. She would assume they'd been living their lives, just as she'd been living hers. Yes, she'd left abruptly. And, she supposed, she'd returned just as abruptly. So what?

Done with her pep talk to herself, she went down to the car, looking up at the sky before she got in. Overcast. Again. But in LA, she'd probably be looking at a sky layered with smog. The sun might not be shining there either although the air would be drier. At least she knew what to expect in LA. From the sometimes smoky haze from wildfires to the June Glooms. She'd have to learn what to expect in Liberty all over again. And not just the weather.

She timed her arrival for just before the service began and slipped into a pew in the back as the choir and congregation stood for the opening hymn. She closed her eyes for a moment as the familiarity of it washed over her. How many times had she stood in this church and listened to these words? Every Sunday of her childhood.

Once everyone took their seats, her father offered the opening prayers, his hands spread and slightly raised as if beseeching heaven to rain down its grace upon him and his flock.

The first reading began, offered by a middle-aged man in a dark blue suit. Joy's mind wandered. She studied her father from a distance. Was he as hard on his parishioners as he had been on her? What did he do when they stepped off the path? Did he banish them? Tell them they could never come back? It seemed there had been many sermons on forgiveness, yet her father's heart held none. At least not for her.

And what about you, she asked herself. She'd come so very close to making that same mistake. She'd almost lost Devonny before she'd seen the error of her ways. She'd been angry with her daughter for making choices she had every right to make.

Joy had raised a smart, beautiful, talented daughter with a mind of her own. Wouldn't she have been disappointed if Devonny had been mealy-mouthed, timid, obsequious? No one had taken advantage of Devonny. She'd made her choices and stood by them and never felt she had to defend them.

Joy was beyond proud of her. *Now*. But she'd behaved toward her daughter almost exactly the way her father had behaved toward her. She refused to be like him, even if she saw more similarities between them than she cared to admit.

The Psalms soloist and choir completed their selection, and the same man gave the second reading. After that came a brief period of quiet reflection before her father took his place in the pulpit.

Joy lingered when the service ended, not wanting to be the first to leave, preferring to be part of the crowd. By the time she descended the steps outside, clusters of people were gathered, chatting with each other. She glanced around. If she knew any of these people, she didn't recognize them. No one greeted her. She felt isolated and alone in a way she never had before.

I don't belong here.

But she saw one face she did recognize. He looked up from his conversation, and she raised a hand in greeting. His daughter turned to look at her, and so did the couple next to him.

What the hell. She approached the group.

"Good morning, Granger." She somehow managed to tear her focus away from him. "Cassie."

Cassie looked more curious and less sulky than she had the other day right before she glanced back at her father and rolled her eyes.

"I don't believe we've met," said the older man.

"Sorry, Dad," Granger said. "This is Joy Laurence. Joy, this is my dad, Harold Sullivan, and my stepmother, Alison."

Joy nodded at them. "Lovely to meet you."

"Are you new to the church?" Harold asked. "Is that why we haven't seen you before?"

"Oh, no. I grew up here, actually. I'm just..." *Just what?* "Back for a visit."

"Joy rented the garage apartment," Granger said.

His father studied her for a moment. "An extended visit, then?"

"We'll see."

"Sweetheart!" Her mother slipped an arm around Joy's waist. "Hello, everyone." They all exchanged greetings, then to Joy she said, "I didn't know you'd be here this morning."

"It was a last-minute decision." Would God forgive her for a little white lie?

"Marcy, this is your daughter?" Harold asked.

Marcy gave Joy a squeeze and beamed. "That's right."

"Back for a visit, eh?" He seemed to appraise Joy in greater detail before he said, "We best be going. Nice to meet you, Joy." He ushered Alison away.

"I'll wait for you at the car, Dad," Cassie said.

"There's Diana Weller," Marcy said. "I need to speak to her about the women's luncheon. Darling, we'll talk later?"

"Sure, Mom."

She watched her mother join two other women. When she looked back at Granger, he'd shoved his hands in his jacket pockets and stood studying her. She wasn't quite sure what to make of him.

After another few seconds, she said, "That gaze of yours is quite intense."

He blinked. "Is it?"

"I can't believe no one's told you that before."

"Maybe."

Another few seconds went by. Joy fought the urge to squirm under his scrutiny.

He said, "I guess I tend to focus my attention on things that interest me."

"Things?"

"Or what fascinates me."

"What...?" Joy was at a loss.

"People, too. Sorry if I made you uncomfortable."

"No, it's..."

He glanced over her shoulder. "I should be going. Teenagers aren't long on patience." He lifted his hand. "Good morning, Arthur."

Joy turned to find her father coming up fast behind her. He waited until Granger moved beyond hearing range before he fixed her with a look and said, "Granger Sullivan's a good man. You stay away from him."

Resentment filled her, edging out everything else she'd just been feeling. "And if I recall correctly, Michael Laurence was a bad influence. You tried to tell me once before who I should stay away from, *Dad*. How'd that work out for us?"

She didn't wait for his reply but turned on her heel and strode fuming to her car. She got in and slammed the door, furious with him and with herself. Only he could do this, send her back to that place she'd been at eighteen, defiant, uncertain, dying to prove him wrong. Except now it seemed, her father saw *her* as the corrupting influence, and his surrogate son in need of protection from her advances.

A gray late model sedan drove past. She saw Cassie scrutinizing her with eyes just like Granger's.

Chapter Nine

What the apartment lacked, as did many of the homes in Liberty, was outdoor space. Even a small deck or balcony would have made a world of difference. Because of the conducive LA climate, most places, even the meanest apartments, generally had one or the other. If she stayed, she decided she'd look for a place with a porch, or a sunroom. Somewhere she could relax with a glass of wine in the evening and unwind.

Her mother had called earlier to say she wanted to plan a family reunion. Joy had cut off ties to everyone when she'd left, assuming the extended family would take her parents' side. She hadn't been especially close to any of them anyway, except for one of her girl cousins who was near her own age.

"What about Dad?" Joy asked.

She could sense her mother bristle through the phone connection. "What about him?" Joy detected Marcy's struggle to maintain a neutral tone.

"He won't want anything to do with it if I'm there."

Her mother must have been holding her breath because she let out a sigh before she said, "I can't control him, Joy. Neither can you. If he'd prefer not to attend, that's entirely up to him."

"But what will people think?" Joy gasped in faux horror.

After a moment, once Marcy realized Joy had asked the question in jest, she chuckled. "We can't control that either, I'm afraid. I know the family on both sides would love to see you. Maybe we can plan it around the time Devonny visits. Have you spoken to her about that?"

"No, but I will. I'll call her this week."

"Mondays, I go to Mother and Dad's. Why don't you come with me tomorrow?"

Joy hadn't thought through her return quite as carefully as she should have. She'd been focused only on reconnecting with her parents. Their extended family had hardly entered her mind. But she knew she'd have to see them all at some point. That's what being part of a family was all about. As grandparents went, her maternal ones were fairly innocuous. They'd be in their eighties by now. Perhaps not around that much longer.

"Joy?" her mother asked when she didn't answer immediately.

"Yes. Of course, I'll go."

"I'll pick you up around ten."

As evening approached, Joy gave in to her restlessness and admitted to herself she was the tiniest bit lonely. In her childhood, Sunday afternoons often meant a drive to one set of grandparents or the other for dinner. Usually included were various combinations of her parents' siblings and their children since most had settled in nearby towns within the area.

But now? Even a Sunday dinner with her parents was out of the question, much less an invitation to join them at a relative's home. How long, she wondered, and what would it take for her and her father to be on speaking terms again? Based on their interaction this morning? It would probably take hell freezing over. Maybe not even then.

She poured herself a glass of wine and stepped outside. The landing at the top of the stairs wasn't big enough for even a chair. She plunked down on the top step, leaned against the railing, and tilted her head to look up at the sky. It had warmed up since the morning, but the breeze remained cool, and clouds scudded across a pale blue sky.

A door opened and closed, and she saw Granger crossing the yard. She raised her glass in greeting as he came closer to the garage.

"Good afternoon."

He stopped at the foot of the stairs. "Is it cocktail hour already?"

She grinned. "It's five o'clock somewhere." She took a deliberate sip of the wine. "I'm willing to share."

"Thanks, but I'm not much of a wine drinker."

"That's all I have."

He climbed a few of the steps. "Sorry to make you drink alone."

"Maybe I do it all the time." She drank some more, aware once again of the intensity of his gaze.

"Do you?"

"Not really. Sometimes. More like nightly. Okay, you got me."

He laughed. Amusement suited him. Changed the lines in his face, lightened his eyes. She decided to see if she could make him laugh at least once, whenever she saw him from now on.

"I'm feeling a bit at loose ends, I guess. Still adjusting to being here. I was thinking of going for a walk later."

"A walk?"

"That's bad, isn't it?" she asked ruefully. "But I haven't been to a gym in ages. I figure a walk's a good alternative to another glass." She lifted her glass and drank. "Or to finishing the bottle."

"Want some company on your walk?"

"Really?"

"Family lore has it I've been doing it since I was a year old."

She chuckled. "Aren't you worried about your reputation?"

"What reputation?" Suspicion etched his tone.

"I have it on good authority that you're a good man, Granger Sullivan. And you shouldn't be dallying with the likes of me."

"Dallying?" He returned to being amused. "I can't imagine who used that word."

"No one did. I made it up. The dallying part. Not the part where I was warned to stay away from you."

"Let me guess. Your father?"

Joy raised her nearly empty glass. "Give the man a prize."

"Your father's not the boss of me."

"Oh, but haven't you heard? I'm the notorious Joy Laurence. Back in town to bring all the good men down to my level."

Granger rolled his eyes. "I'm not afraid of you."

Really? Didn't she unsettle him even a little bit? Because underneath the banter, there was a tingling anticipatory thing going on with her.

Stop it, she warned herself. *This doesn't have to be romantic.* It might be nice to have Granger Sullivan as a friend. And maybe that's all he was looking for as well. His behavior could hardly be termed flirtatious. They were both adults. Maybe they were simply in need of some companionship.

Joy drained her wine and set the glass aside. "I'm ready whenever you are."

"Let's go." He turned and gave Joy another view of his backside. The man looked good in those jeans. The whole world-weary, slightly rumpled look was growing on her after all the years of metrosexual types that seemed to breed like fruit flies in LA.

He waited for her at the bottom of the stairs, and they strode to the end of the driveway.

"Should we invite Cassie?"

"She's at her friend Abby's house, supposedly studying. Which way are you going?"

She pointed. "I thought I'd head toward the business district. See if I could find someplace to eat." She patted the pocket of her jacket. "I've got cash."

"Wing Lu's will be open," Granger said. "As far as I know, they're always open. That's if you like Chinese."

"I do."

He slanted a look her way. "Might not be like LA Chinese."

"I'm of the opinion they all went to the same school. Every Chinese takeout place I've ever been in has the same setup. Counter across the front, a few tables. Kitchen behind it where you can see them cooking. Same lighted panels above the counter depicting various dishes. Menus? Nearly identical."

"I notice the smudges on the windows."

"Exactly! The glass is always sticky. But the tables and floors are usually clean."

"Same packs of hot mustard and soy sauce and chopsticks."

"They understand everything you order perfectly."

"And they're super fast at the register."

Joy laughed in delight. "I love everything about Chinese takeout. Which is why I need to find a gym."

"You could just walk every evening."

Joy considered the residential area with its old, cracked sidewalks and towering trees. She'd either walked or ridden her bike along these streets all the time as a kid. She never gave a moment's thought to how much exercise she got. "Nope. I need weights and spin classes and kickboxing and anything else they have to offer. Gotta fight the effects of aging. Not to mention my wine intake."

"You're not that old. And you look like you're in pretty good shape."

"Because I go to the gym. *Duh.*" She turned to smile at him when she said it. "What do you do to stay in shape?"

"Sex."

"*What!*"

Granger smirked at her. "And lots of it."

"Uh-huh."

"You'd be surprised at the number of lonely housewives here in Liberty. Not to mention the widows and divorcees. Oh, sorry."

"No need to apologize. I've been widowed for a very long time."

When Granger didn't respond, Joy continued. "Sometimes it feels like I was never married. Mike died before Devonny was born and I raised her on my own."

"That's your daughter?"

"Yes. And I have a baby granddaughter, too. Lucy."

"You sure as hell don't look old enough to have grandchildren."

"Damn right."

His smile encouraged her. "What about you?"

"What about me?"

"Any grandchildren?"

"Oh, man, you're making me feel old, reminding me I could have them. But no, none yet. And no prospects on the horizon as far as I know."

"Cassie is a little young, I suppose."

"She has an older brother. I certainly hope he leads the charge, so to speak."

"Oh. I didn't realize."

"Cameron. He lives in Cincinnati."

"Oh."

They reached the outskirts of the business area and turned toward it, leaving the homes and most of the trees behind. "Go ahead and ask. I know you're dying to," he said dryly.

"Ask what?" Joy feigned ignorance. Even as she did, she wondered why. Wasn't she too old to play these games? "Okay, I'll bite," she said before he could answer. "Marital status? Yours, not your son's."

"Divorced. Dumped. Left. Abandoned. And yes, I have issues about it." He pulled open the door to Wing Lu's. "Ready for some moo goo gai pan?"

Wing Lu's turned out to be just as they'd described. There were no other customers, but activity filled the kitchen nonetheless, and several bags were set up for takeout or delivery orders.

The young woman behind the counter said, "Help you?"

"Yes," Joy said, seeing no reason to look at a menu. "I'd like chicken with mixed vegetables and fried rice."

"And for you?"

"Mongolian beef with fried rice."

"For here or to go?"

Granger and Joy looked at each other. They hadn't discussed it. "Here?" Granger asked.

"Why not?" They each ordered a bottle of Kirin and split the bill. They took seats at a Formica table near the smeared window.

Granger seemed to have done an about-face since that first meeting where he'd hardly said two words to her and nearly undone her with the penetrating stare tactic. She hadn't expected him to open up, go for a walk, eat a meal, or anything else with her. She'd imagined he saw himself as an island and behaved as if he didn't need or want the company of other human beings.

"You're not what I expected," she told him.

He raised an eyebrow which she took as encouragement for her to elaborate.

"The day you showed me the apartment, you barely said two words to me."

"Yeah."

"And when I saw you at my parents? Basically, the same thing."

"I don't like to waste time."

"Waste time?"

"On people. Sometimes they're not worth it."

"A lot of the time."

He tilted his head in agreement. "So, I don't make much effort at the beginning."

"That silent, brooding thing...that works for you? With women, I mean?"

He gave her a genuine grin. "Worked with you, didn't it?"

"Hey, this isn't..." She waved a hand back and forth between them. "A *date*. We're not dating. We went for a walk. We bought food. Separate checks."

"Lots of women pay on dates now."

Joy liked his smile. She picked up on his attempt to bait her, how he tried to get a rise out of her. Trying to gauge her interest level, perhaps.

Oh, I'm interested, she wanted to tell him. *But I've been warned away. And I don't know how long I'm staying. And the last thing I want to do is hurt you.*

Their order came and they dug in. Joy found the food as good as that of China Star back in LA.

"Are you going to tell me what criteria made me worth the effort?" she asked.

"Oh, I always knew you'd be worth the effort. I just couldn't decide if I wanted to make the effort." That wasn't the answer she'd expected. Granger Sullivan confused her.

"You're going to have to explain."

He cut up some of his beef. "I remembered you. I knew who you were the minute I saw you."

Joy set her chopsticks down and sat back. She spun her beer bottle around in its ring of condensation. "You remembered me. Seriously? After all this time?"

He pointed his fork at her. "Yes."

"How is that possible? I had no idea who you were." *I still don't, apparently.*

"Easy. I had a crush on you."

"Okay. I'm going to need another beer." She stood. "You want one? I'm buying."

He gave her a mischievous look from beneath his brows. "Even though it's not a date?"

She tapped her toe on the relatively clean linoleum, waiting for his answer.

"Sure. Thanks."

She went to the counter, trying to regain her equilibrium. She couldn't believe Granger remembered her. That he'd recognized her. She hadn't even recalled his existence. Of course, she'd been in her own orbit for a long time, so busy being defiant and caught up in her own life she'd had little time to notice much of anything else. Or anyone else.

She paid and brought the bottles back to the table. She resumed her seat but pushed her food away and concentrated on her beer. She had a feeling she'd need it. Granger appeared unperturbed by his pronouncement or that she'd stopped eating. Finally, he looked up at her, and she signaled him with her fingers. "Tell me about this supposed crush."

"Oh, there's no supposed about it. First time I saw you in church. You were eleven, I think." He squinted. "Probably more like twelve. You had blond hair. A bow. A plaid dress with a white collar."

"Oh, my God. How *old* were you?"

"Nine."

"Nine!" Joy laughed, delighted. "That's adorable."

"So was I, but you didn't know I existed."

"Well, sure, but three years." She shrugged, letting herself off the hook.

"I knew I'd never catch up to you." Granger drank some beer and returned his attention to the last of his food. He'd apparently done some thinking on this.

Well, here I am. The thought appeared in Joy's head before she could stop it but saying it aloud would be entirely too flirtatious. And they both knew he *had* caught up with her. They were now adults in their forties, and a three-year age difference meant nothing.

But the many other differences in their life experiences? Those might mean something. Widowhood. Divorce. Granger's teenage daughter, and her own being a former adult film actress. LA vs. Ohio. Maybe it wouldn't take much to bridge the differences. But Joy wondered if it would be worth it to Granger. Or to her.

Her thoughts brightened when she realized they didn't have to become romantically involved. They could simply remain friends.

Couldn't they?

Chapter Ten

M onday morning, Joy came down the apartment steps in yoga pants and a long-sleeved tee just as Granger crossed the yard to his truck. He stopped momentarily when he caught sight of her but then continued on.

"Good morning," Joy called in an extra cheery tone just to see how he'd react.

"Morning," he returned. He unlocked the truck and stood by the door without opening it, watching her approach.

"I wondered if you could steer me to a reputable car salesman?"

His almost smile gave Joy a small spurt of triumph. Like his daughter, the man needed to smile. Maybe he just needed a reason.

"That's kind of an oxymoron, isn't it?"

"Probably, but I need to unload my rental car for something permanent."

Granger held up a finger, opened the truck door, ducked inside, and set his insulated coffee mug in the cupholder. When he reappeared, he began scrolling through his phone. "I know a guy at the dealership out on Route 29. Seems like a straight shooter. Probably won't help, but you can mention my name." He gave her a lopsided smile and looked at her expectantly.

It took Joy a minute to realize what he wanted. "Sorry. I don't have my phone with me. I was just going for a walk. But I can go get it."

She took half a step away before he said, "It's okay. We can do this the old-fashioned way." He ducked back into the truck.

Joy studied what she could see of him, while he unearthed a pad of paper and a pen. He wore the same uniform she'd seen him in before. He evidently saw no reason to shave every day. The slightly too-long hair and scruff worked for him.

So lost in her thoughts of what else went into Granger Sullivan's appeal, it took her a moment to realize he stood in front of her once more holding out a slip of paper.

She took it automatically, feeling a tingle at the touch of his fingertips against hers. She hoped she wasn't blushing. "Thank you. I appreciate it."

"No problem."

He got behind the wheel, started the truck, and backed out. She tucked the slip of paper into the pocket of her shirt and set off for her walk.

From the kitchen window, Cassie watched Joy until she turned the corner. She wasn't sure exactly what she'd seen during that exchange between Joy and her father, but she didn't like it.

She didn't like Joy being Pastor Art's daughter, either. Pastor Art and Miss Marcy were like another set of grandparents to her. How dare Joy just barge back into their lives and expect to be their daughter again? And how dare she barge into her father's life and—and what? Expect to be his—what? Girlfriend? *Lover*?

Cassie made a gagging sound and turned away from the window. Her dad was too smart to be taken in by an LA phony like Joy Laurence. Besides, she wouldn't stick around here for long. Who would, given the choice?

On the way to visit her grandparents, Joy's phone burbled from the side pocket of her purse. She looked at the screen to see a number with the local area code, but Joy didn't know who it could be. She answered anyway.

"Joy?"

"Brian?"

"Hey, you left your card and told me to call. I'm calling."

Joy laughed in delight. "I'm glad you did."

"Are you free for dinner?"

Joy glanced Marcy's way to see her concentrating on the road. She could probably hear everything Brian said.

"When?" Joy asked.

"Tonight?"

"Sure. Why not? What time and where?"

"My place? Say, seven or so?"

"Perfect. What can I bring?"

"I'd say just your sweet self, but if you come attached to a bottle of wine, I wouldn't be disappointed."

Joy laughed again. "I promise not to disappoint. Text me your address, okay?"

"Will do."

Seconds later, the phone pinged with an incoming text message. Joy glanced at the address but didn't recognize the street name.

"That was Brian Crowley," Joy said as she slipped the phone back into her purse.

"I gathered," Marcy said.

"We used to be good friends. I hope we will be again."

Her mother said nothing for a moment, and then, "I envy you."

"Envy me? Why?"

"You get a chance to start over. With everyone. You have a clean slate."

"Hardly. They all remember the way I left. Why I left. And that I shut them out. I stayed away all these years."

"They remember you as a child. You're re-entering as an adult. A lovely, successful woman who forged her own path and raised a daughter on her own. Your history with almost everyone you ever knew here starts all over. You managed to set a rewind button." Marcy sounded wistful.

"I never thought of it like that," Joy said. "I kind of thought I'd have to make amends somehow, that everyone would hold a grudge against me. I don't expect it to be easy to rebuild my relationships. Not even with family."

"Joy, the ones who are worth it will be happy to have you back. They'll overlook everything else. Ignore the rest of them."

"Even Dad?"

Marcy made the turn into the retirement village. But she didn't answer Joy's question.

"Welcome!" Brian said, when he answered Joy's knock. He enveloped her in a bear hug. "I'm so glad you're here."

"Me too."

"Very nice," he said when she handed him the bottle of wine she'd brought. "Come on back."

She followed him down a narrow hallway where she got a glimpse of a cozy sitting room and framed photographic prints scattered along a wall painted the color of chocolate milk.

She paused at the threshold of the kitchen to take in a space as pleasing to the eye as any she'd seen in home décor magazines. Here she saw exposed brick, thick butcher block countertops, and the way French farmhouse accents blended with California coastal.

This end of the house had been opened up to accommodate a large dining area with a beautiful knotty pine table and an equally large seating area boasting a modern entertainment center and sectional sofa.

"Brian, this is fantastic. Don't give me any more of your 'the old ladies of Liberty buy wallpaper from me' bullshit. You're obviously the crème de la crème of interior designers in the area."

Brian laughed as he extracted the cork from the wine. "If I'm the crème de le crème, that's only because I have so little competition."

Joy approached the counter and Brian held one of the glasses out to her. "Same old Brian. Never one to toot his own horn."

"Same old Joy. Always calling me on it. What should we drink to?"

"New beginnings?" Joy asked.

Brian grinned. They clinked their glasses and took a sip. Brian let the wine roll around on his tongue. "Very nice, indeed. You've learned a thing or two since high school."

"I did. No more wine coolers for me."

"I'm having a hard time with how quickly we ended up in our forties," Brian said. He nudged a charcuterie board in her direction. "Help yourself."

"Wow. This is exquisite," Joy said, studying the meats and cheeses, nuts, olives, and crackers.

Brian snitched a small square of cheese. They took seats at the counter.

"I think you're too—what do I want to say? Hip? Sophisticated? Stylish? For this town," Joy told him. "I'm surprised you didn't land somewhere more cosmopolitan."

"Like LA?"

"Or New York. Atlanta, maybe?"

"I did spend some time in LA, actually. Right after college."

"Really?"

"You know the old story. Boy meets boy. Boy falls in love with boy. Boy follows boy to California. Boy proceeds to break boy's heart."

"Oh, Brian. I'm sorry."

"Yeah, well, what are you going to do? I can look back now and say it was a great experience. Certainly influenced my design aesthetic. I came back home to lick my wounds and what can I say? I guess I didn't have the guts to venture anywhere else."

"Or maybe you belong here. Maybe this is where you're supposed to be."

Brian drank some wine and snitched another bite of cheese.

"Forgive me for saying this, and maybe I'm wrong, but you don't exactly seem unhappy," Joy said.

"Honestly? I'm not. I've got some good friends here. I take a decent vacation every year. Never the same place twice, I might add. Business is good. I'm looking to expand. I've about got this place the way I want it, although you know me, I'm never completely satisfied. As soon as I think I am, it means something needs to be changed."

"I wish I'd known you were in LA," Joy said. She looked into her glass of wine before meeting his eyes. "Especially if you were there with a broken heart."

"I wish I'd known where you were in LA. I'll admit, I could have used a friend at the time. And I bet you could have as well."

Joy blinked. She covered Brian's hand with hers and squeezed. "You've got one now. And I promise not to leave you in the lurch ever again."

"You better not." He got up and moved behind the island. "Okay. No more talk of our distant pasts. Tell me what you've been up to since you got back."

Joy caught him up, and then she thought of the visit to Granger's garage. "By the way, do you know a guy by the name of Granger Sullivan?"

"Granger Sullivan. Doesn't ring any bells. Is he an actor? A tennis player? My type?"

"He's an artist."

"Local?"

"Mmhmm. He's also a handyman. Has his own business here in town."

"Okay, yeah. I might have heard of him. What kind of artist?"

Joy explained how she'd discovered Granger's pieces hidden in his garage. "They are like nothing I've ever seen before. So whimsical, almost poetic. Cleverly done."

"What do they sell for?"

"That's just it. He doesn't sell them. He seemed surprised when I suggested anyone would even be interested in them."

Brian regarded Joy with curiosity. "And what's your angle? Are you going to represent him?"

"Me? No. But I think you should take a look at them. You're the one with the art expertise. You might want to take a few on consignment or something. I feel sure they'd sell."

"Are they lawn art?"

Joy tilted her head to one side. "Maybe." She drew the word out. "Honestly, I think the possibilities are endless."

"You're not looking for a job, are you?" Brian asked.

"Why? Did you have something in mind?"

Brian looked sheepish. "I had this thought if you'd want to work with me. Even if it's part-time. It could be fun."

"Are you kidding? Brian, I'd love it. I'll help you any way I can."

"I've got a couple of part-timers. Warm bodies to keep an eye on things when I'm not there. It'd be great to have someone around who's interested in the business."

"I'm interested. I could come in tomorrow. How would that be?"

Brian clinked his glass against hers. "Perfect."

Chapter Eleven

The tingle of excitement still hadn't left Joy when she arrived back at the apartment. She couldn't wait to show Granger's sculptures to Brian. She knew she wasn't wrong about how special they were. Brian would flip over them.

She headed to the stairs, but she noticed the kitchen light still on in Granger's house. She saw him framed in the window, head down, as if concentrating on something.

No time like the present. She crossed the lawn and knocked. A few seconds later, an outside light came on and the curtain covering the door's window twitched. The lock clicked and Granger faced her through the screen. He finished drying his hands on a towel, slung it over his shoulder, and crossed his arms as he regarded her.

"Hi," she said, wondering why she sounded nearly breathless. His lack of greeting didn't surprise her. She found a man of so few words refreshing. Many men could probably learn something from Granger. Namely, when to keep their mouths shut.

Those eyes of his pinned her, and he finally drawled a response that sounded like, "Evening."

"I uh, I had dinner with Brian Crowley. Do you know him?"

"I know *of* him," Granger said. "Runs that interior design place downtown, right?"

"Oh, well, yes. He's heard of you, as well." Joy hesitated in the face of Granger's less than welcoming stance. Perhaps she'd overstepped the unmarked boundaries of their, what? Friendship? Relationship?

She forged ahead anyway. "I mentioned your sculptures to him. He'd like to see them. Perhaps, take a few on consignment. That is, if you're interested in selling them."

Granger's expression went from surprise to thoughtful to uncertain. He scratched the back of his head, then smoothed the hair down and looked at her once more. His shoulders lifted and fell. "I guess he can see them if he wants. I'm not agreeing to anything else."

"Of course. He can probably stop by one afternoon this week."

"I'll be working. Bathroom remodel."

"Could I? I mean, would you trust me to show them to him? I promise we won't disturb anything else in your garage."

This earned her a calculating look. He chewed the corner of his bottom lip for a moment before he said, "I guess that'd be okay. Hang on."

He stepped away from the door and she heard him open a drawer. He came back, cracked the screen door, and handed her a garage door opener. She smiled in relief. "Thanks. I'm sure Brian will be in touch."

"Right. Night then." He closed the door and the lock clicked behind her.

You're being ridiculous, she warned herself. She couldn't remember the last time she'd had a crush like this. High school? With Mike? She'd dated some over the years, but no one had made all her nerve endings come alive the way Granger Sullivan did without even trying. How could he deny this weird chemistry between them? Surely, he felt it too, but he didn't act all that interested, which was a shame. Because she was.

But it probably wasn't a good idea. No sense getting entangled in something if she didn't plan to stay. No sense further antagonizing her father further, either, when her initial goal was to make peace with him.

So, Granger Sullivan was off-limits. She'd crush on him in private and that would be that. But his sculptures? They were going to go places. She just knew it.

Art stared at the food on his plate once he'd offered the usual blessing before a meal. He picked up his fork. But then he put it down again as he contemplated the conversation he needed to have with his wife. A conversation he didn't want to have because it would start an argument which he was certain to lose. But he couldn't just let it go on. Let this kind of behavior go by unchallenged. He knew it. Marcy knew it.

Marcy showed no awareness of his disquiet. She cut up her chicken and speared the small bites, adding rice and green beans to her fork before eating it. He'd always been amused by Marcy's eating habits. She liked to combine little bits of everything on her plate. He, on the other hand, didn't like his food touching. He finished one thing before he started on the next.

He picked up his fork and his knife and cut into the chicken breast. He tried for a nonchalance he didn't feel. And why should he? Why should he have to playact with his wife of more than forty years? Why couldn't they be real with each other?

Art knew the answer. *Joy.* He hadn't had a moment of peace since her birth. And since her return to Liberty? Even less. But still. Marcy's behavior could not go without comment.

"I saw Bonnie Camden this afternoon. She mentioned you missed the Women's Bible Study. She said Evie Hawthorne subbed for you."

Marcy glanced at him. He couldn't be sure, but he thought he saw a challenge in her eyes. "Evie's subbed for me before. She knows the Bible as well as I do."

"That isn't the point," Art said.

"What is the point?"

"If you weren't at the Bible study, where were you?"

"Joy invited me to go car shopping with her."

"Car shopping? You've never shown any interest in buying a car before."

"And I had no interest in it today. But I am interested in my daughter. I want to spend time with her. Even if it's an invitation to car shop."

Art set his utensils down again, not bothering to hide his consternation. "So, every time Joy says jump, you're going to say how high, is that it?"

"You're being ridiculous."

"You're just going to blow off your responsibilities to the church, to the community, because of Joy?"

"I didn't 'blow off' anything," Marcy sputtered. "I've been heading the Women's Bible Study for more than twenty years. Maybe I don't want to do it anymore."

Art stared at her like he'd never seen her before. "You never said anything about not wanting to do it before." *Before Joy showed up,* hung in the air between them. He speared a bite of chicken, afraid if he put it in his mouth, he wouldn't be able to swallow it.

"Maybe there are a lot of things I don't want to do anymore," Marcy said. The lack of defiance or anger in her tone scared him even more. She appeared calm and thoughtful and almost serene—surer of herself.

"Like what?" he asked, forcing himself through the fear.

Marcy put down her fork and looked at him. He could see a spark of fire in her eyes. "Like doing everything your way. Following blindly along, being the dutiful wife. It cost me my daughter, *our daughter.* I have her back, and I'm not going to lose her again. If you don't like it, too bad. I guess it's your turn not to like the way things are."

"She disrespected me. She disrespected *us*. She went against everything we believed in. Everything we taught her to believe in—"

"Did she, Art? Or did she simply decide to live her own life? She was eighteen and legally an adult even before she left. She made choices we didn't like, sure. But by then, I don't think it was our place to tell her how to live or what to do. Did that mean we, and by we, I mean you, had to cut her out of our lives for all these years? What did we gain, Art? What did you gain? I didn't get to see my granddaughter grow up. And now we have a great-granddaughter." She shoved her plate away nearly toppling her water glass. Her chin came up and her shoulders squared. "And if you think for one minute I'm going to stand by and let you keep me from either of them, you are more wrong than you've ever been before."

"And what are you going to do when Joy decides to up and leave again? You can't rely on her. It took her over twenty years to come home—"

"And that's on you, Art. You know good and well I'd have taken her back in a heartbeat. But you wouldn't let me. You wouldn't tell me where she was. You wouldn't let me look for her. And for that, I have never forgiven you. You talk about Joy disrespecting you? What about the way you disrespected me? You crammed that my-way-or-the-highway garbage down my throat for years until I was choking on it. Joy is back. And I'll be damned—*damned*, Arthur—if I'm going to lose her again."

Marcy pushed back from the table and left the rest of her meal uneaten. She marched from the room and Art could hear her feet pounding up the stairs. He knew she'd find refuge in Joy's old bedroom, which Marcy had turned into a sanctuary for herself. It was where she went to read or sew or talk on the phone. She used Joy's old desk for correspondence and to pay the household bills.

His appetite gone, Art scraped the uneaten food from both plates into the trash. He looked blindly around the kitchen, not sure where to go or what to do now. Marcy was his anchor. He'd be rudderless without her. But he could feel the riptide Joy's presence created, tugging his wife farther and farther away from him. And he didn't know how to stop it.

Marcy closed the door to her space without making a sound. She wasn't given to displays of anger like slamming doors. Maybe she'd feel better if she did. But she'd also feel like a two-year-old in the middle of a tantrum, which wasn't an attractive quality for a woman in her sixties. No, when angry or upset Marcy did a slow simmer. She kept the emotion under control. Mostly. Usually.

Joy had been the door slammer. Looking back to her teenage years, it seemed Joy had stomped up to her room and slammed the door daily.

Marcy had been a dutiful child. She'd grown up to be a dutiful wife. She abided by the rules, and rebellion hadn't been in her nature. She'd been, she saw now, a timid mouse, afraid of consequences, first of incurring her parent's wrath or disapproval, and later Art's.

But Joy? Joy had spunk. She had spirit. She wasn't easy to intimidate. She might have once sought Art's approval, but by the time she reached adolescence, she'd given up. Because, Marcy knew now, Art had never approved of his daughter. She wasn't even sure he'd ever loved her. Not the way a father should.

Marcy'd had a difficult pregnancy for which Art had blamed Joy. He'd come too close to losing his wife, and he'd never gotten over the fear. It had taken Marcy years to figure this out, much longer than it should have, and by then, the damage to Art and Joy's relationship had been irreparable.

Marcy had secretly admired her daughter. Perhaps even, in some ways, encouraged her rebellious nature. Joy was everything Marcy was not, but perhaps had secretly wanted to be.

Not that Marcy had approved of Mike Laurence. She'd hated his motorcycle, his long hair, his cigarettes, and his attitude. Still, she would have given him a chance, but Art wouldn't hear of it. He forbade Joy having anything to do with Mike. Joy had given her father a calculating look after he'd issued that ultimatum, and for once, she glided up the stairs without making a sound and closed her door softly. The click of the lock echoing down the stairs somehow sounded more ominous than any of Joy's previous outbursts.

Marcy picked up a framed photo from the shelf. Joy's high school graduation picture. Marcy smiled, remembering her with her long blond hair, taking her shopping for a graduation dress, watching her walk across the stage to receive her diploma. The explosion afterward when Art had physically barred Mike from the party at the house.

Joy became very quiet after that. She didn't speak to her father at all, and to Marcy in only the most subdued tones when absolutely necessary.

Two weeks later, she was gone.

Marcy had been heartbroken, frantic with worry. She'd hired a private investigator to track Joy. When Arthur learned what she'd done, he hit the ceiling. He'd canceled the detective agency's contract, and the only thing Marcy knew by then was that Mike and Joy had married in Las Vegas and were likely in California.

Marcy was torn between loyalty to her husband and concern for her daughter. She had no money of her own. Everything of hers also belonged to Art, provided by him since their marriage. She'd been the supportive pastor's wife all her adult life. And where had it gotten her?

She began to resent Art's control over her, even though it had been her choice to be involved in the church and the community, and to be a stay-at-home mother to Joy.

She'd lost herself, she saw now. Or maybe she'd never really known who she was or who she could be. Maybe not then. But she knew now. She knew she was choking on the decisions she'd made, on the thin threads of her own life. She'd loved Art once, hadn't she? She didn't even know anymore. All she could see now was how he had cost her years with her daughter. And she was sick of paying the price.

Marcy took a photo album from the closet and sat in the padded rocker. She began leafing through the pages, watching Joy grow from a toddler to a middle-schooler. Marcy did this often. She found it relaxed her and soothed her disquiet to think of her daughter in California somewhere. Happy, successful, with a husband and children.

Marcy had dreamt of the day Joy would return. All their years apart would fall away. She'd have her baby back. And now it had happened.

Now Marcy had a new dream. Time with her granddaughter and her great-granddaughter.

Marcy picked up the phone and called Joy.

"Hi, Mom."

"Hi, baby."

"Everything all right?" Joy asked, with a touch of concern in her tone.

Marcy smiled. "Everything's fine. I just wanted to hear your voice."

Chapter Twelve

Joy sat on the top step and stared out into the night, though there wasn't much to see. Mostly shadows. The streetlight at the corner didn't throw enough light into the backyard for Joy to distinguish anything other than Granger's truck parked in its usual spot. Earlier, she'd noticed leaves were sprouting in the giant oak. Spring was in full swing. But the branches were mostly still bare and the night air cool enough to warrant a sweater to ward off the chill.

Evenings were the hardest, Joy found. Harder than they'd been in LA. Not only did the studio apartment lack the kind of space she was used to, sitting here made her miss her fenced deck on the ground floor and the balcony off the master bedroom. It wasn't much, but it was something, and Joy liked escaping to one or the other in the evenings.

Somehow, she'd felt less alone with the city wrapped around her. She picked up the cup of herbal tea and held it with both hands, letting the heat warm her and the aroma of mint and chamomile relax her.

Not that she had anything to be stressed about, she assured herself. What she had was a feeling of not being settled. A mild discontent, perhaps. After years of setting her own course, of establishing domination and control over her own life, she'd set herself adrift with this trip.

It began when Devonny abruptly left LA. For a long time, her daughter had been her only family. Even though the two of them had been at odds before Jack's death, Joy had assumed they had each other's back. But Devonny was made of stronger stuff than Joy realized. She'd cut Joy off, leaving Joy no recourse but to track her down and insist she see reason. She'd be forever glad she'd done so, happy they'd reconnected, delighted to be a grandmother. She could have missed it all. And it would have been her own fault.

Just like her estrangement from her parents, her extended family, her hometown, and the friends she'd had here was her own fault. She could admit that much at least.

But still, if her father had even tried to understand her, if they'd ever had a reasonable conversation, if he'd ever given Mike a chance, maybe she wouldn't have left the way she did. Twenty-five years should have been enough for her to get over her father's behavior. She should be able to be the bigger person and apologize for what she'd done. And if she thought for one minute she was in the wrong, she'd like to think she would. But she didn't and she couldn't.

Had she expected too much? She didn't think so. From Devonny she'd learned a parent didn't have to agree with a child's choices in order to respect the child's right to make them. That's what her father didn't understand. Because she didn't choose what he wanted her to, he saw her rebellion as disrespect. She saw it as living her own life.

They'd probably never agree. She'd never apologize. He'd never forgive her. In which case, maybe she'd made a mistake returning to Liberty.

No, she hadn't. She had her mother back, and Brian, and maybe some of her other extended family. The ones who wouldn't hold a grudge because of her father, at least. In that way, her return had been a blessing.

Joy sipped the tea, which had reached the perfect temperature. A breeze picked up just as she saw a shadow cross the edge of the lawn near the road. Joy leaned forward, watching as it moved behind Granger's truck. She set her tea aside. Her sneakers made hardly any sound against the wood stairs. She reached the bottom and tiptoed alongside the truck, trying to minimize the sound of her footsteps on the gravel.

She peeked around the back of the truck in time to see a car parked at the far corner, its brake lights glowing. The door opened, and the interior light came on long enough for Joy to see who got into the passenger seat. The car accelerated and disappeared into the night.

Joy made her way back up the stairs knowing Granger had no reason to sneak out of his own house. But apparently, Cassie did.

Joy picked up her mug and went back inside. She'd made the tiny space as comfortable as she could, and the effort pleased her. The reading lamp cast a warm glow over the padded recliner. The light above the stove reflected the neat-as-a-pin countertops and coffee maker standing at the ready.

She set her mug in the sink and got ready for bed, even though it wasn't late. As she smoothed night cream into her skin, she regarded herself in the mirror and considered cutting her hair. She'd worn the chin length bob for most of her adult life. It was classic and easy to style, but now she wanted a change. Maybe something short and spiky, or maybe not spiky, not so drastic. But definitely shorter.

She looked good, she thought, for being a few years into her forties. She'd tried to take care of herself, partly for her and partly because of Devonny. As a single parent, she took her health seriously. Because if something happened to her, what would happen to her daughter?

Once Joy got into the habit of working out, doing yoga, and eating a pretty healthy diet, it stuck with her. She had good genes, too, she decided because her mother also looked younger than her years.

She switched off the bathroom light, then the other lights, and climbed into bed. She fell asleep thinking about Cassie. She'd have to do something about what she'd seen. She just wasn't sure what.

By the next morning, she was nowhere nearer to an answer. Probably she should tell Granger. He deserved to know what his 15-year-old daughter was up to. But Joy didn't want to be cast in the role of tattletale. If she hadn't been sitting outside, she wouldn't have seen Cassie at all. She couldn't be held responsible for coincidentally being a witness.

But Joy knew she'd have to do something. Tell Granger or confront Cassie. Joy didn't like either option. If things were already not great between Granger and Cassie, she didn't want to add to that. It didn't take much self-examination for Joy to admit she saw quite a bit of her teenage self in Cassie. She could hear Cassie's scoff of disbelief if Joy said something like, "I know exactly how you feel. I felt the same way at your age."

Joy knew the last thing a teenager wanted to hear was that their parents or their parents' peers had gone through the same experiences. The same emotions. The same difficult transition into adulthood.

Still, Joy decided to approach Cassie first. Depending on how that went, she could always inform Granger later.

Chapter Thirteen

D orothy Laurence lived in a single-wide mobile home in a run-down trailer park. The structure sagged on one side and rust crept like a vine around the bottom and corners. The skirting was cracked in some places and missing entirely in others. The unfortunate paint choice of avocado made Joy think of that particular fruit gone bad. Even the few weeds struggled for survival in the lot's unhealthy soil.

Joy pulled off the dirt road and parked in the small space next to the portable steps. She saw a curtain twitch in the window of the place next door. She suspected there were few secrets in this neighborhood. The residents wanted to know when trouble arrived and most likely would then look the other way.

Joy didn't know how many lots there were in the inaptly named Sunny Days Park. Twenty or thirty, she guessed. All looked like close relations of the Laurence place.

She climbed the concrete steps, holding on to the metal rail. A small pot in the corner opposite the door held a red geranium. It might have been the only bright spot in the entire area.

She knocked and didn't have to wait long before the door on the other side of the rickety screen opened. There stood her deceased husband's mother.

She'd met Dorothy here only twice before, as a teenager, and they'd had minimal interaction since.

Joy arrived without giving the other woman a heads up. She didn't know what she'd find. During Mike's childhood Dorothy had a drug and alcohol problem. Joy didn't know if she still did, but if Dorothy wasn't coherent, Joy planned to turn around and walk away.

"Yes?" The woman who answered the door did not seem to be under the influence, but her appearance bore the ravages of past addiction. Veins were visible on her nose and in her deeply lined face, but perhaps that was to be expected as Dorothy would be well into her sixties by now. Gray now streaked her once dark hair, and the dry, frizzy mass would have benefited from a good conditioner. A pot belly pressed against the loose top she wore, and beneath a pair of ragged denim shorts, her legs poked out like two pieces of freckled kindling.

"Mrs. Laurence? It's Joy. Mike's wife." Joy hadn't thought of herself as Mike's wife in years. Didn't think of herself as his widow either; it had been so long since he'd died. But she couldn't expect his mother to recognize her after all this time.

Dorothy's eyes, however, bugged in recognition. "Joy Harmon? I declare. This is a surprise. Come in. Come in."

Dorothy unlatched the screen and pushed it open allowing Joy to step inside. The scent of cigarette smoke coated the interior. A worn and stained sofa set along the far wall along with two wobbly-looking end tables, each sporting sad mismatched lamps with crumpled shades.

A recliner, its leatherette cracked in strategic places, angled in the adjacent corner to face a small flat-screen TV on a rusty metal stand.

Dorothy waved a hand toward the sofa. "Have a seat."

Joy sat gingerly, knowing she'd have to shower and change clothes once she left to get rid of the smoke that already seemed to soak into every fiber of her clothing.

"You want a cup of coffee?" Dorothy asked. "There's some left from this morning. It's cold now, but I can nuke it."

"I'm fine, thank you."

Having performed her hostess duties, Dorothy sauntered to the recliner. She got comfortable, kicked the footrest out, and reached for a cigarette. She lit up and blew smoke toward the ceiling. "So, what brings you by? You fixin' to cut me off?" She gave Joy a shrewd, assessing look.

"No. Of course not." After Mike's death, Joy used some of the settlement money to set up an annuity for Dorothy. She'd been receiving a few hundred dollars monthly ever since.

"Wouldn't blame you if you did. You didn't owe me anything, that's for damn sure."

"You were Mike's mother."

"Not much of one," she said derisively. "Didn't deserve your generosity, but I was glad to have it just the same."

"How are you? How have you been?"

Dorothy puffed on her cigarette and seemed to consider her answer carefully before she spoke. "I been getting along all right. Part of that's your doing."

She'd lost Joy. "I didn't—"

"Yeah, you did. You let me know what happened to Mike. You set up that 'nuity for me. You done more than anyone else ever did for me. Mike's daddy ran off and left me high and dry, the bastard. I had this young'un to look after. No money. No family. No job." She cackled sadly which gave way to a bout of coughing filled with the sound of phlegm deep in her chest. "I was in a bad place. Didn't know how to get myself out of it." She shook her head. "And then my son died." She sniffed and stubbed her cigarette out before looking back at Joy.

"Then those checks started coming like that lawyer of yours said they would." She picked up her lighter and tapped another cancer stick out of the half-empty pack. "Took me a few years to believe them checks were going to keep coming." She held the lighter in one hand and the cigarette between the fingers of the other. She looked at Joy with her son's eyes. "You were the only person who ever took care of me. I know it's just money, and you didn't want nothing to do with me as a person."

Joy made a sound of objection, but Dorothy ignored her. "Don't blame you. I wasn't much of a person to know. But what you did, it made a difference."

She lit the cigarette. Joy waited, sensing Dorothy wanted to say more.

"I went to meetings, gave up the booze and the pills. All of it." She regarded her cigarette. "Except for these." She took another puff and smiled grimly through the smoke. "We all got our vices, though, don't we?"

"Yes," Joy said, breathing shallowly through her nose. "I suppose we do."

"You're back in town now, that it? How long you staying?"

"I don't know exactly." Joy glanced around at the rest of the living space. A compact kitchen and miniature dining area took up the front portion of the trailer. The cabinets were missing some of their knobs and the wood veneer had peeled off most of them. The kitchen faucet dripped steadily into the sink. But the place looked as clean and tidy as a place in this condition could be.

When she turned her attention back to her mother-in-law, she found the other woman studying her with that same shrewd gaze.

"You were the best thing ever happened to that boy."

"Oh, I don't think—"

"I remember the first time he brought you around. I was half in the bag at the time—hell, maybe more like three-quarters of the way in, but I remember. He stood up a little straighter, tried to act like a gentleman, even if he didn't have any idea what that looked like."

"We were here for all of five minutes. How could you—"

Dorothy pointed her cigarette at Joy. "He wanted to do better, be better than what he was, because of you."

"Ironic then, isn't it, that he died because of me?"

Dorothy frowned. "What are you talking about?"

"If we hadn't taken off for LA, if he hadn't married me. If I hadn't gotten pregnant, he wouldn't have felt like he needed to get a second job. That's where he was headed when he was killed."

Dorothy leaned back and lit up. She lowered the footrest and set the chair to rocking. A breathy squeak emitted from the chair's hydraulics with each backward movement. "That been eatin' at you, has it? All these years?"

"I don't know. Maybe."

"Who's to say the same thing wouldn't have happened if ya'll had stayed here? Maybe even if you'd dumped him and he found some other girl."

Joy couldn't answer. She hadn't expected such directness or thought-provoking insight from Dorothy Laurence.

"You're not God, you know." Dorothy's tone held no admonishment. She merely stated a fact as she saw it. "You ever hear that Serenity Prayer?"

Hadn't everyone? "Of course."

"Plenty of blame to go around if that's what you're lookin' to do. If I'd been a better mother, if he'd had a better life, maybe he wouldn't a been so hell-bent on leaving when he had the chance."

"I didn't mean—"

Dorothy waved a hand. "It ain't your fault Mikey died. It ain't mine. It happened. You got no choice but to accept it, try and make peace with any part you think you played in it, and move on. Otherwise, you'll get sucked into a black hole you'll never get out of. That's all I'm saying."

"Thank you."

Dorothy blinked. "For what? I didn't do nuthin.'"

"For spending time with me. For inviting me in."

"Well, that ain't much. But you're welcome."

"Would you like to see a picture of your granddaughter?"

"Oh, I surely would."

Joy reached for her phone and brought up the photo gallery. She found a picture of Devonny holding the baby. "That's Devonny," she said, handing the phone across to Dorothy. "And the baby is your great-granddaughter, Lucy."

Dorothy unfolded a pair of drugstore reading glasses from the end table and settled them on her nose. She peered at the image on the screen. "Well, lookie there. Look at that baby." She stroked her finger across the screen then looked up in dismay. "Oh, no. I made it disappear."

Joy smiled and reached for the phone to bring the image back up. "Smartphones are a little touchy," she explained.

Dorothy studied the image once again. "It's so small. I wish I had a bigger picture." Joy noted the wistful tone of her voice and promised herself she'd get prints made and bring them by. "Such pretty girls. Mikey would have been proud." She drew a crumpled tissue out of her pocket and pressed it to her nose before she handed the phone back. She slipped the glasses off and swiped at her eyes. "I wish..." she began. "Oh, never mind. No sense wishing for what never happened. Won't happen."

"My mother wants to plan a family reunion this summer. I'm not sure when, but Devonny and Lucy, and I think Devonny's husband, Luke, will be there. I'd love it if you'd come, too."

"Oh. Oh, I don't know. I'd love to meet them, of course, but your family...they're not my kind of people."

Joy couldn't think of a good response to that statement. "Tell you what. I'll let you know when it is, and if you'd prefer not to come, I'll make sure to bring Devonny and the baby by so you can meet them. How's that?"

Dorothy didn't look any happier with that suggestion. "I don't know if that's such a good idea. This place..." Her voice trailed off, her gaze fixed on her lap.

The squalor in which she lived meant nothing to her, but Joy could understand how she might be embarrassed by it in such a circumstance. "We'll figure it out," she assured the other woman. "Maybe a picnic at the park or something. I know for a fact Devonny is looking forward to meeting all of her extended family, and that includes you."

Dorothy brightened. "Haven't been to a picnic in a long time."

"I should be going." Joy stood and so did Dorothy. "I'll be in touch, okay? And here." She reached into her purse for a card. "My cell number is on there, if you want to call. I might stop by again, if you wouldn't mind."

"Wouldn't mind at all."

"Take care, Mrs. Laurence."

Joy opened the door.

"You can call me 'Dot,' you know. Being we're family."

Joy reached the car and turned to wave. "See you soon, Dot."

Chapter Fourteen

The following afternoon Brian confirmed Joy's initial reaction to Granger's art. When she found the light switch for the half of the garage she hadn't seen clearly before, she found it a bit overwhelming. Granger's creations reminded her of guests jockeying for space at an overly crowded cocktail party. Carefully, she and Brian rearranged them and assessed each one.

They weren't all human-like, either. He'd created a spotted dog, a whimsical cat, and a rooster, along with a bicycle and a funny little garden gnome. Somehow Granger managed to combine the abstract with realism.

After Brian examined them all with a critical eye, he agreed with her about their marketability. They decided she would approach Granger initially and determine whether he'd be receptive to selling his work.

After Brian left, Joy decided she could no longer put off the inevitable and there wouldn't be a better time to catch Cassie alone. Familiar enough now with Granger's work routine, Joy knew he often returned to the house for lunch, but usually didn't end his workday before five.

She knocked on the back door and waited, not terribly surprised when she had to knock again. Cassie might be holed up in her room blasting music in her earbuds to tune out the world. If necessary, she'd walk around to the front and ring the doorbell.

She knocked a third time, rewarded with a curtain twitch. Cassie knew she was there, but it was anyone's guess whether she'd open the door. Joy figured she would because as her father's surrogate landlord, Cassie wouldn't want her father to know she'd ignored the tenant.

When the deadbolt shot back Cassie yanked the door open just enough to frame herself in the opening, her expression stony. "My dad's not here." She started to close the door.

"Wait," Joy said, putting up a hand as if she could block the door through the screen.

"What?"

"I'm not here to see your father. I want to talk to you."

Her expression turned wary but also held a touch of defiance. "About what?"

"About the other night."

Cassie stared her down.

"Around ten-thirty?"

"Fine."

She moved away. Joy opened the screen and stepped inside. Cassie went to the counter where she'd been in the process of fixing herself a snack.

Joy stood near the table and watched her. She reminded her not only of herself at the same age, but also of Devonny. She remembered how her daughter would defy her in small ways, searching for independence, a way to get out from under Joy's thumb. Jack had been the perfect vehicle for that. Joy believed Devonny would never reach her potential as long as she was with him. But Devonny was in love, and Joy couldn't hang on to her or make her see reason.

Devonny had been lucky. Joy wasn't so sure Cassie would be.

Cassie turned from the counter with a plate and a glass in her hand. "So? You're going to tell my dad. Are we done?"

Joy waved to the table. "Could we sit down for a minute?"

Cassie offered up a put-upon sigh, set her snack down, and plopped into a chair. She picked up the peanut butter and jelly sandwich and began picking at the bread crust. She didn't look at Joy.

"Cassie?" Joy said. She waited until the girl glanced up. "I'm not your enemy."

"You've got something going with my dad."

Joy tried to hide her surprise. She hadn't expected Cassie to take this tack. "Actually, I don't, not beyond having a few conversations with him."

Cassie didn't look convinced. She continued to pull the crust off her sandwich.

Joy plunged ahead. "I saw you crossing the lawn. You got into a car—"

"Yeah. Thanks for spying on me."

Boy. Granger had his hands full with this one.

"I wasn't spying. I happened to be sitting at the top of the stairs drinking tea. I enjoy fresh air, and there's nowhere else to be outside. *I* wasn't doing anything wrong," she pointed out, needlessly stating an irrelevant fact.

"So? Go narc to my dad. I don't care."

"I think you do." Joy kept her tone gentle. She wasn't going to allow Cassie's attitude to get to her. *Been there, done that.* Devonny had taught her well.

"He thinks I'm a child." Cassie reminded Joy of a sulky two-year-old.

"I'm sure he doesn't. Not unless you act like one."

Cassie flashed her a look of pure dislike.

"Your father wants to keep you safe, that's all. It's what all parents want for their kids."

"I can take care of myself."

Joy could have argued that point, but she decided not to. Instead, she said, "Do you know who you remind me of?"

Cassie didn't answer. She pinched off a bit of bread and peanut butter and popped it in her mouth.

"My daughter," Joy went on, not caring if she wasn't getting through to Cassie. If Cassie didn't want to work with her, she'd tell Granger and leave it in his hands.

Cassie sighed and pinched off another bite.

"And you also remind me of myself when I was your age."

"A hundred years ago," Cassie muttered under her breath, but loud enough for Joy to hear.

Joy laughed. "Closer to thirty, actually. My parents, especially my father, didn't understand me. They didn't listen to me. They didn't like my boyfriend. In fact, my father forbade me to see him, so you know what I did?"

Cassie looked up.

"I sneaked out to meet him. I got caught, but it didn't stop me." Joy remembered her father's anger, her mother's tears, and her own determination to free herself from her parents' restrictions. "Things were so bad at home, I left."

"You made Miss Marcy and Pastor Art sad."

"I'm sure I did, but all I knew at the time was they were making me sad. What about me? Don't I get to be happy?"

Cassie looked down at her plate. Her hair fell forward, and Joy couldn't see her expression. She didn't know if she was getting through or not.

"Cassie."

The girl looked up, her expression stony.

"I won't say anything to your dad about it this time. But if I catch you sneaking out again? All bets are off. I will go directly to him and tell him exactly what I know, exactly what I saw. You want to be treated like an adult? This is the kind of decision an adult has to make. You and me? We don't have to be friends. As I said before, I am not your enemy. And if you ever need anything, I'd be happy to help you if I can."

Joy stood. "Enjoy your snack."

The moment the door closed behind her, Granger's truck turned into the drive. She couldn't avoid him and no way he wouldn't see her. She raised a hand in greeting as he stepped out of the truck.

"I was wondering when you'd be home."

Granger glanced toward the house before settling his attention back on her. "Is there a problem?"

How could he tell? Joy didn't want to lie to him. In her experience, lies always came home to roost. Besides, the "problem" was with his daughter, not with her as a tenant. She justified answering his ambiguous question just as ambiguously. "I don't think so." A light bulb came on in her head. "I'm just overly eager to talk to you about placing your work with Brian."

Granger crossed his arms, tucked his thumbs beneath his armpits, and waited.

Joy stopped a couple of feet from him, thinking once again how much she liked what she saw. The tee shirt. The faded jeans and work boots. The dark hair. And those eyes that never missed a trick. She hoped he couldn't tell she'd fudged a bit on the truth of why he'd caught her leaving his house.

"He wants to take a few of the pieces on consignment. The hitchhiker, for sure. The clown. A couple of others. Initially, he wants to price them between fifteen and twenty-five hundred. He'll take a fifteen percent commission. He's confident if he—"

"Fifteen to twenty-five hundred *dollars*?"

"Of course. What did you think I meant? Pesos?"

Granger grinned. Chuckled. He laughed. And once he got going, it seemed like he couldn't stop. She liked how genuinely amused he seemed to be, even if she didn't understand what he thought was so funny. He stood to make some decent money off the things he'd been hiding in his garage.

"I want to hear the rest of this. Let me get cleaned up and I'll be over in a few minutes. Okay with you?"

"Sure."

Less than ten minutes later, Granger knocked, and Joy let him in. He smelled like soap, his hair was damp and his tee shirt clean. He had an open bottle of beer in one hand and an extra in the other.

She couldn't help but smile. "I guess this means you're celebrating."

" *We're* celebrating. Although you probably don't want a beer."

"No, but I'll put this in the fridge and have a glass of wine."

"More for me, then." He gave her a devilish smile which made her laugh.

She set the extra beer in the fridge and poured wine for herself. She turned to find him watching her. "Please," she said, indicating the table. "Have a seat."

He pulled a chair out for her and took the one adjacent for himself.

"I'm going to go out on a limb here and say you seem...pleased?"

Granger drank some of his beer and shook his head as he set the bottle on the table. "I can't believe anybody would pay that kind of money for what's essentially junk."

"But it isn't junk. It's art."

"Made of junk."

"It's no different than a blank canvas and a supply of brushes and paint. No one would page huge money for those things by themselves. But what the artist creates using those things? That's what they'll pay for."

"I never thought of it that way. I saw this dented, rusty, curved perforated panel with two screw holes near the top. Came off a boiler, I think. It kind of looked like a face to me. I played around with it. Made it look more like a face."

"An artist sees what others don't. You're an artist."

Granger still didn't look convinced, but he said, "So tell me the rest of it. How exactly does your buddy think he can sell my *art*?" He grinned and drank some more beer.

"Social media, websites, designer showcases, word of mouth. Marketing is a multi-faceted process."

"And he gets fifteen percent of whatever he sells them for."

"It's fair. He's the one getting them to a place where they can be sold."

"More than fair. Plus, I'm running out of room in the garage."

"You need to come up with a name."

"A name?"

"For your work. Granger Sullivan Creations. Granger Works. Art by Granger. Something like that. You should consider creating your own logo."

"How about BS by GS?"

Joy giggled. Granger Sullivan, Entertainer.

Granger's good humor evaporated. He sat forward, picking at the beer bottle label with his thumbnail before he looked up at her. "Seriously, though, can we keep this between us?"

"Us...you and me?"

"And your art buddy. What's his name? Brian?"

"He's a professional. I'm sure he'll handle the business any way you want."

He lifted a hand and let it fall. "I'd rather no one knew that it's me."

Joy sensed he wanted to say more. She took a sip of her wine and waited.

Granger sat back and ran a hand through his hair. "I mean, what if it's a big flop? If no one buys them? As it is, no one even knows I make them. I'd like to keep it that way."

Granger wanted to save himself the embarrassment of rejection. Joy could certainly understand that. Stepping out of one's comfort zone was never easy.

"What about Cassie?"

"She knows I go out to the garage and tinker, but she's never shown any interest in what I'm doing."

And you've never invited her into your world to share it.

Fathers and daughters. It was so easy for that divide to happen. She wondered how Mike would have been as a father. Would he and Devonny have been close? Would his influence have changed any of the decisions she made as an adult? Would he and Joy have lasted as a couple?

"Let me set up a meeting between you and Brian to iron out the details. How does that sound?"

"Okay, but..." Again, the hand went through the hair. "Can you be there too? Would you mind?"

"Of course, I can be there. And no, I wouldn't mind at all. She reached across and covered his hand with hers. "I believe in your talent. You should too."

"Talent. Hah!" He picked up his beer, drained it, and stood. "I'm going to get out of your hair. Let me know about the meeting."

Joy stood as well. "I will. I'll see you later."

The moment the door closed behind him, Joy thought of the perfect name for his art. GS Designs.

Chapter Fifteen

G ranger opened the overhead garage door and turned on the lights. Everything was in its place, just as Joy promised. He stared at his "people" trying to see what someone else might see—Joy, Brian, and lots of others if he agreed to Brian's proposition. Social media. A website. *Everyone* could see it. Judge it. Laugh at it. Find it wanting or ridiculous.

He wasn't an artist, no matter what Joy said. He just messed around with stuff.

And yet...hadn't he always thought there was something about the figures he created that made them, if not exactly life-like, possessing personalities in a way? His hitchhiker, for example, wore a woebegone yet hopeful expression. The clown searched for a laugh. The cyclist wanted more than anything to win the race.

Still, they weren't art. He didn't know what they were. All he knew were the moments of pleasure he found while he created them. And these past few years, pleasure had been hard to come by.

Until Joy showed up, that voice in his head reminded him. He closed the lights, lowered the door and headed for the house. Hard as he tried to fight it, he couldn't argue with the voice, dammit. That damn childhood crush remained and refused to be dislodged.

He knocked on Cassie's door. He'd dismantled the lock after the last time he'd caught her sneaking out. It was the only way he could occasionally check at night to make sure she was there. But he never entered without knocking and getting the okay to open the door. When she ignored his first knock, he knocked louder. "Cassie!" *Damn earbuds.*

The door popped open, and she yanked one of the earbuds out. "What?"

He should be used to her sullen demeanor by now, but he continued to wonder where that little girl she used to be went. The one with pigtails and freckles and a grin a mile wide so she could show off her missing teeth. He missed that girl. Missed her delight at being taken out for ice cream or getting a second ride on the carousel at the fall festival.

Now nothing he did or said pleased her or made her smile. But the glare, her annoyance with him? Those he'd become excessively familiar with.

His earlier mood faded away. He thought of the beer in Joy's refrigerator. He should have stayed over there. He didn't think Joy would have minded. At least she seemed to welcome his intrusion into her space, while his daughter resented his presence near hers.

"You haven't started anything for dinner yet, right?"

"No, Dad, geez. What are you? The kitchen police?"

"Do you think maybe just once you could speak to me in a pleasant tone? What's your problem, anyway?" His idea for making French toast and bacon and home fries faded away. Cassie used to love breakfast for dinner. They used to prepare it together.

"Oh, sorry, Daddy dearest," Cassie simpered. "How may I be of service to you today?"

Granger clenched his fist. He'd never raised a hand to either of his children. He'd come up with much more inventive ways of disciplining them. But right now? He understood, as only a parent could, the desire to wipe that snotty look off a teenage girl's face and the sarcasm out of her tone.

"You know what? Forget it. Don't bother with dinner."

He walked away, seething. He made himself unclench his fingers, but the tension settled between his shoulders and shot up his neck. Living with Cassie was like being in a war zone, and he knew he was losing the battle. He chose to retreat before a bomb went off between them and did damage beyond repair.

Back in the kitchen, his stomach growled. He'd barely taken a break today so he could finish a job and knock off early. He knew it'd be too late to start another job.

He'd go out to eat. Alone. It wouldn't be the first time.

He glanced up at Joy's apartment. Even though he told himself it was a bad idea, he thought, *why the hell not?*

When she opened the door, he said, "You want to go grab dinner?"

She glanced over his shoulder for a second. "Just you and me? What about—?"

"She's fine. She wouldn't come even if I asked her."

"It's kind of early. Do you want to—?"

"I just want to eat. You in or out?"

"Well. Since you asked so nicely..."

Granger hung his head. "Shit."

"What's wrong?"

"I just asked my daughter why she couldn't say anything politely, and here I am with my attitude. Sorry."

Joy bit her lip, trying not to smile. "I guess now you know where she gets it."

"If I'd ever pulled any of the stuff she pulls on me or spoke to my dad like that? He'd have popped me one."

Joy chuckled. "It's too bad beating children when they misbehave went out of style, huh?"

"Let me try again. Would you like to go to dinner with me this evening?" He didn't smile, but his tone fell somewhere between pleading and cajoling. It came as a surprise how much he did not want to eat alone.

"Why, I'd love to," Joy responded with a smile. "Thank you for asking. Can you give me a minute to change? Come on in."

Joy disappeared into the bathroom and Granger wandered through the space, liking what she'd done with it. She'd enhanced the neutral color palette of the few furnishings with navy blue pillows on the bed and touches of aqua here and there. Granger sat in the recliner and picked up the book she'd apparently been reading. An anthology of the writings of Vietnam War veterans.

"I'll drive," Joy said decisively. Granger followed her to her car and took the passenger seat without comment.

"Where to?" she asked.

"Bubba's?"

"I don't know where or what that is."

"It's a hamburger joint out on 289. More of a tavern serving hamburgers. But the food's decent and the beer's cold."

"Burgers and beer. What could be better?" Joy backed out and headed for the highway.

Granger eyed her. She'd changed into a pair of black slacks that tapered to her ankles and a long-sleeved, black and white, intricately woven sweater kind of thing, along with black shoes with a wedge heel and lots of crisscrossing straps. He looked down at his own attire. Not very impressive for a first date.

Come on. It's not a date!

"I guess it's not really your kind of place."

"I'm sure it will be fine."

Granger shut up and pretended to watch the road, but more than once his gaze slid to Joy. Her hands curved around the steering wheel. The swell of her thighs beneath the fabric of her slacks. Her appropriate use of a turn signal. Driving skills as a turn-on were underrated. It seemed like hardly anyone used turn signals anymore. Especially young people. Oh, God, he was old. He made a sound of disgust in his throat.

Joy signaled to merge with the traffic on the highway. She cut a glance his way. "You okay?"

"You use your turn signals."

She shot him another quick look. "Yes. That's what they're for."

"I know. I was just thinking how so many people don't. Especially young people. And as soon as I thought that I wondered when I got old."

Joy laughed. "I'm even older."

"Not by much."

"No. I know what you mean. We're not that old. But sometimes, the younger generation seems light-years away. So much of what they do I don't understand. It's baffling, isn't it?"

"Do you think it's just us?"

"No. I'm pretty sure our parents felt the same way about us. And when today's teenagers are our age? They'll be shaking their heads at the antics of *their* teenagers."

"God, I hope so. I'm starting to feel ancient."

"My dad taught me to drive," Joy said, apropos of nothing.

Granger picked up on the wistfulness in her tone. "I'd have liked to have been a fly on the wall for that."

Joy laughed without humor. "Driver's ed wasn't good enough for him. But then, nothing I did was good enough for him. He wouldn't allow me to use the car until *he* taught me to drive."

"You're a good driver."

"He was a stickler for turn signals. A stickler for everything, in fact."

"I guess I better not say you turned out all right, huh?" Granger flashed her a teasing smile.

"Is that it up ahead?"

Granger knew a subject change when he heard one. "That's it."

Joy pulled off and parked in the gravel lot surrounding the building made of rough-hewn timber. *You're not in LA anymore.* Joy couldn't say she exactly missed the overcrowded freeways and the excess of concrete, the smog, or the palm trees.

She'd been homesick initially, but when her father hung up on her after that fateful phone call? She'd embraced LA with open arms, adjusted to the lifestyle.

Joy supposed, as Granger said, she'd turned out all right. But was it because of her father, or in spite of him?

Inside, the place consisted of an extremely long bar, tables and booths, a raised platform for the nights they had a band, Friday and Saturday, according to the sign outside, and a smallish dance floor. Bubba's was probably a happening place for the locals on the weekends. But at the moment, there were only a few patrons drinking at the bar, and only a couple of the booths were occupied. Of course, it was also barely after five on a weekday.

Numerous flat-screen TVs were placed strategically above and around the bar, many of them tuned to the same variety of sports channels.

They found a booth near the back. A server in worn jeans and a Bubba's tee shirt dropped off menus and took their drink orders. Granger ordered a beer. Joy stuck with iced tea.

The minute Cassie heard the back door slam, she shot down the hallway. She figured her dad would get in his truck and head out somewhere to get something to eat. She peeked through the curtains in the kitchen and saw him taking long strides toward the garage. But he didn't get in his truck. He went upstairs. To *her* apartment.

Cassie ducked down to see the door at the top of the stairs. She saw Joy open it and her father walk in.

"Ewww," she said to herself. If her dad was *with* Joy, *ugh*. Cassie couldn't even think about it. Refused to picture it. Didn't matter what Joy said. *Something* was going on between them.

She stood at the sink, contemplating the situation. Her mom had left. Maybe now her dad would leave too. Maybe he'd go to LA with Joy. Realistically she knew her dad wouldn't do that. Not after he quit his engineering job so he could be here for her. But the only reason he went over to Joy's place now was because she'd been a jerk to him earlier.

Cassie didn't know why she couldn't be nice to her dad. He wasn't her enemy. Joy claimed she wasn't either. But why did it feel like every adult she knew ganged up on her? All she wanted was to have a *life*. Pick her friends. Hang out with them. Have a boyfriend. It didn't seem like she was asking for much.

Cassie saw movement and watched as her dad and Joy came down the steps and got into Joy's car. She focused on the car until she couldn't see it anymore. Her dad must have asked if Joy wanted to go eat with him. And he'd only done that because she'd been such a brat earlier. Cassie wished she hadn't been. She missed her dad the way he used to be, taking her out for ice cream or making breakfast with her on Saturday mornings. She didn't know where the dad he used to be went. But then, she didn't know where the little girl she'd once been had gone either.

Chapter Sixteen

G ranger couldn't get his mind off Cassie. He knew he was screwing up. He should have found a way to reach his daughter instead of walking off in a huff. He should have invited her to join him for dinner instead of Joy.

Too late now, though. And truth be told, something about being with Joy both calmed and excited him. Those old feelings he'd had for her rose to the surface every time he saw her. He'd been invisible to her back then, and he almost couldn't believe she returned his interest now.

"Tough day?" she asked after their drinks arrived and their food orders were taken.

Granger took a fortifying drink of his beer before he answered. "The toughest part is when I get home."

"Ah," she said. She dumped a packet of sweetener into her tea and stirred it with the straw. "No one survives raising teenagers unscathed. You know that, right?"

"No, actually, I didn't. My son, Cameron." Granger waved a hand as if that would explain his thoughts. "It wasn't this hard. I know it wasn't."

"Maybe boys are easier?"

Granger drank more beer. "The moods. I'm sure he had them. But not like Cassie's. I'm almost sure Cameron was less complicated. I knew what made him happy. Sports. Video games. Pizza. So much pizza."

"With Devonny it was books, movies, and chicken quesadillas." Granger smiled at that, but Joy grew pensive. "Maybe it's easier with dads and sons than it is with dads and daughters. Although, as a mother of a daughter, I can't say I always had it easy with her, either."

Granger's smile faded. "I'm pretty sure if Cassie's mother was still around, things would be easier for both of us."

"Really? But—never mind. It's not my business."

"No. Go ahead. I'd like to hear your thoughts."

Joy gave him a look full of doubt. "Obviously, I have no knowledge of your ex-wife."

A smile played around Granger's lips. "Obviously."

"But for whatever reason, she must have been unhappy in the marriage."

Once again, the smile lessened. "Obviously."

Joy squirmed. "Being in a home with two parents who are miserable would have affected Cassie, too. Maybe not as much as her mother leaving, but..."

"For the record, *I* wasn't unhappy."

Joy tilted her head intrigued. "But you knew she was?"

Granger drank more beer before he answered. "Who's guaranteed happiness?" Joy must have thought his question rhetorical because she waited a beat, so he repeated himself. "I'm asking you. Who's guaranteed happiness?"

Joy didn't hesitate. "No one."

"Exactly." Granger sat back, more relaxed than before. "You're asking if I knew Adele was unhappy. What I knew was we had an agreement—a commitment. I also knew I couldn't make her happy. She was the only one who could do that."

"You're saying she chose to be miserable. At least in the marriage."

Granger thought about it. "Maybe not consciously. I think she thought someone else might make her happy. Being somewhere else. Doing something else." He spun his glass around on its cardboard coaster. "I don't know what she thought. She left me. Left Cassie."

"What about Cameron?"

"He was in college by then. I don't think it impacted him as much as it did Cassie."

Their food arrived. A burger and fries for him, grilled chicken sandwich and coleslaw for her. Granger ordered another beer.

"For the record," Granger informed her after they'd sampled the food, "I don't usually talk about this stuff."

"This stuff?"

"My marriage. My divorce. My kids."

"What do you talk about?"

"Honestly?" He chuckled. "As little as possible."

Joy grinned. "I did notice you're not a fan of conversation."

"Better to remain silent and be thought a fool." He looked at her expectantly.

"Than to open one's mouth and remove all doubt?" she finished, delighted.

"My dad used to quote that all the time when I was a kid. I guess it sunk in."

"Maybe a little too much," she teased.

Granger didn't know if it was the two beers or the company or the unexpected break from Cassie's brooding, but he knew he felt lighter than he had in a long time. He'd also decided he was going to do something he'd probably regret when they got back home. He was going to kiss Joy, date or no date. He wanted to know how she'd respond. Did she want to keep this on the friendship level, or could she want more? Which was what he'd concluded he wanted.

Did it matter so much whether she stayed in Liberty? Couldn't they have a...what? A fling, for lack of a better word? Even as he thought it, Granger admitted to himself he wasn't wired that way. When he fell, he fell hard, as he had with Adele. And when she'd left, he'd been like a faithful old dog not understanding the disappearance of its master.

Could he stand to have his heart broken again? He hadn't enjoyed it the first time, but he'd survive it a second time, he supposed. He'd discovered four years was a long time to go without female companionship. No guts, no glory, as his high school baseball coach used to say. And who knew? Maybe Joy would decide to stay.

"Thanks for inviting me to dinner," Joy said. "I enjoyed it."

They were out of the car, meandering toward the stairs to her apartment. "Me too," Granger said. "Does that mean maybe we can do it again sometime?"

"Sure. I'd like that."

Joy made no move to head up the stairs. Granger tried to recall how he knew lingering and fidgeting with her keys meant she wanted a goodnight kiss. From a movie, maybe? The comedy with Will Smith as a dating coach to an inept Kevin James. He'd caught parts of it a few times when channel surfing.

Granger reached for the hand holding the keys and closed his around it, stilling the movement. He leaned in, waited a couple of seconds, leaned a few millimeters closer, and it worked. Just like in the movie. Joy's lips touched his. They were both tentative at first, neither sure of the other, he supposed. Then he remembered something else from that movie—Will Smith shouting, "This is the woman of your dreams." Something like that, anyway, as he encouraged his client to take definitive action to win her.

Joy was the woman of Granger's dreams. The one he'd resigned himself to never having. But she was here now, kissing him.

Another line from the movie flitted through his mind. *What is our objective? Shock and Awe.*

Granger deepened the kiss while simultaneously trying to block out Will Smith's voice in his head. Joy responded with an encouraging little sigh. Her arms locked around his neck as he drew her close enough to feel every curve of her body pressed against him. *Wow.* That thought was all his.

Kissing Joy was everything he'd ever dreamt it would be. Holding her like this, the way she responded to him, exceeded every expectation he'd ever had. They fit, somehow, the way he'd always been sure they would. He finally came up for air, but they were still locked together.

"Wow," he said. He smoothed his hand through her hair, finding it as silky as he thought it would be.

She opened her eyes and smiled. "I agree."

"We're definitely doing dinner again."

She laughed, and he released her. After she started up the stairs, he headed across the lawn, but he turned when she said, "Hey, Granger."

He waited.

"It wasn't the dinner. It was the company."

He stood in the yard with a smile on his face until she reached the door. She waved before she went in and closed the door. And still he stood there grinning like an idiot.

Cassie glared at the closed door of her bedroom, disgusted by what she'd witnessed. Her father. And Joy. *Kissing!*

All she'd done was take her ice cream bowl to the kitchen sink when she heard the car, and there they were when she glanced out the window. It was too dark to see much, but she saw enough thanks to the security light on the corner of the garage.

The idea of her father being happy pissed Cassie off. Why should he get to be happy when she was miserable? Presumably, her mother was happy now, too. God knew she hadn't been when she'd been here.

Cassie'd got used to her father being her only parent. He wasn't like her mother. She knew he'd never just up and leave her. He'd always look out for her, be there for her if she ever needed him. But she didn't know how to tell him what she needed from him. She wasn't even sure she knew what that was.

But she didn't need another female competing for his attention. Especially when it seemed there was so little of it to go around.

Cassie turned away from the door, onto her side and stared at nothing as the little voice in her head reminded her that he had tried to pay attention to her earlier. Maybe he was going to ask *her* if she wanted to go get dinner somewhere. Maybe that's why he asked if she'd started anything yet.

And what had she done? Hit him with her attitude. Maybe him asking Joy out was all her fault.

God, she was screwed up. She didn't know what was wrong with her. But she knew one thing. Being in her own skin, in her own head, was not a fun place to be.

Chapter Seventeen

The next morning Granger woke up in a good mood, which wasn't surprising because he'd spent the time before he fell asleep reliving every moment he'd spent with Joy. He knew himself well enough to know he was half in love with her already, and for him, that was a dangerous place to be. She hadn't decided to stay. Already he tried to imagine what it would be like if she up and left the same way Adele did.

He didn't want to think about it, so he decided not to. He put coffee on and got ready for work. He leaned against the fridge and studied the calendar on his phone to refresh his memory about the jobs scheduled for today and the rest of the week.

Cassie appeared in the tee shirt and baggy shorts she slept in, wearing her usual wary expression, and waited for him to get out of her way so she could open the fridge. He didn't. Instead, he put the phone away and looked her in the eye. She stared right back at him, not in a friendly

way, either. What he'd been doing with Cassie wasn't
working. He had to try something different. He knew
better than to expect or wait for an apology from her.

"How about we declare a truce?"

"Fine." Nothing but annoyance in her tone.

"We could make breakfast for dinner tonight like we
used to."

He thought he saw a flare of surprise, perhaps even
pleasure, in her eyes but it was gone so fast he couldn't
be sure.

"Okay," she said, with a slight drop in hostility.

"I'll make the bacon if you do the pancakes."

"Fine. Can you move?"

This time Granger waited. He knew she'd been taught
manners. He'd let last night slide, and that was enough.

"Please?" she finally said.

Granger stepped out of the way.

"Do we have everything we need? Or should I stop at
the store?"

"We have everything." Cassie said with her head inside
the fridge.

Granger topped off his travel mug and screwed
the lid on. Cassie reappeared, holding a container of
yogurt and closed the fridge door. She crossed to the
silverware drawer. Granger wanted to say something or
do something to bridge the distance between them, but
he wasn't sure what that something was or how it would
be received.

While he stood there thinking, Cassie found a spoon,
and started back to her bedroom, breakfast in hand.

"I'll see you later, then," Granger called after her.

She waved a hand behind her, leaving him no choice but to head out to his truck.

It didn't feel much like progress to Granger, but at least they'd spoken a few civil words to each other.

When Granger got home that evening, he found Cassie in the kitchen frying potatoes. A bowl of pancake batter stood ready for the griddle.

"You didn't have to do the potatoes. I would have helped."

She lifted a shoulder and let it drop. "It's okay."

He saw the oven pre-heating for the bacon. "I'll get washed up and do the bacon."

"That works."

Sadly, even her innocuous responses encouraged him. He changed his shirt, too. Not something he normally did, but he wanted to make some kind of effort. To show Cassie he was trying while telling himself she probably wouldn't notice.

Rather than attempt conversation, he laid out the bacon strips in silence and set the pan in the oven. He set the timer even though he wasn't going anywhere and could keep an eye on the progress.

He got down plates and put butter and syrup on the table. The potatoes were done, and Cassie kept them warm while she started ladling batter onto the griddle.

Granger's stomach growled loudly. He probably should eat more for lunch because by dinner time he was almost always hungry. He appreciated Cassie's willingness to tackle the evening meals. He tried to recall if he'd told her how much it meant to him to come home at the end of the day and not have to think about what to eat.

He poured water for himself after seeing Cassie's full glass. He laid out the silverware and took a peek in the oven to find the bacon browning nicely.

Cassie set the first of the pancakes on a platter and ladled out four more.

Granger leaned on the pantry door and watched before forcing himself to say what he wanted. "I really appreciate you cooking dinner."

"It's part of the deal," she reminded him.

"I know. But I can still be appreciative, can't I?"

Again, the one-shoulder shrug. "I guess."

Granger wanted to sigh, but he held it back. He couldn't reach her. Couldn't scale the walls they'd built between them. All he could do, he supposed, was keep chipping away and hope they'd fall eventually.

The timer for the bacon beeped. He laid the crispy strips on paper towels and turned off the oven. Cassie dumped the potatoes into a serving bowl and set the pancakes on the table.

They loaded their plates and dug in, the silence stretching between them, broken only by the sounds of fork tines against plates until Granger couldn't stand it any longer. "You know," he said, "I was going to suggest we do this last night."

Cassie flashed him a quick look before focusing on her food once again.

Then she said, "Instead, you went out with her."

Granger froze, his fork halfway to his mouth. He set it back on the plate, trying to decide if Cassie had emphasized the word *her*, trying to gauge her feelings about last night.

"You have a problem with that?"

"It's none of my business what you do."

Definitely an undertone of resentment there. Granger had heard enough of it to know. "Of course, it's your business. We're a family."

Cassie snorted in disbelief. She might as well have stabbed him in the heart.

"Sorry if you don't feel the same way." He stared at his plate, appetite gone.

"You kissed her."

His head came up at Cassie's accusing tone. "So?" He knew he sounded defensive even as he tried to wrap his head around the fact that Cassie must have been spying on him.

"You like her." She sounded defeated.

"You don't?"

Cassie raked her fork through the puddle of syrup on her plate. "I don't know her."

"I don't know her very well, either, but what I do know, I like."

"Good for you." Cassie pushed her chair back and took her plate to the sink.

Granger couldn't think of what to say, but knew he had to say something. "Why is this a problem?"

She paused on her way out of the kitchen and gave him one of her glares. "It's not. Do whatever you want."

Chapter Eighteen

Art sat in his car outside his one-time mentor and now spiritual director's house, tapping his fingers on the steering wheel in trepidation of the forthcoming meeting. He'd known Tyrone Winslett for forty years. In fact, Art began his ministry career as assistant pastor several years before Ty retired and made Art his successor.

The Winslett house always made Art think of a miniature mansion, with its white columns and wrap-around porch. Potted ferns hung intermittently above the railings and lace draperies crisscrossed the windows on either side of the double front door. Impeccably well-maintained, there wasn't a hint of dust on the white clapboard or a speck on the glass panes.

Ty insisted every minister needed a spiritual director because being leader of hundreds of faithful parishioners could not only be exhausting but could skew one's thinking. Therefore, upon retirement, Ty decided to offer his services to ministers in the area. He insisted on meeting with them every month, every two months at a minimum. Otherwise, as he knew from experience, things could get out of hand.

Usually, Art approached these meetings prepared with a few church issues he'd already dealt with but asked Ty's advice anyway to placate him and make him feel useful. Once in a while there really was a problem Art needed outside input on, and Ty's advice had proved invaluable on those occasions.

Art would then offer a few tidbits from his personal life, but he'd never liked talking about his marriage, family, home life, dreams, or emotions with Ty. Or with anyone else, other than Marcy. There'd been a time when he'd told her everything, where they'd dreamed together.

But Joy's birth changed all of that. And once she left, a wall came up between him and Marcy. They went through the motions and routines they'd become accustomed to. Anyone on the outside looking in would think there were no problems between them. Even Art sometimes fooled himself into believing that. But Joy's return had stripped away any illusions he and Marcy might have had about their relationship. Like a rocket that had lost contact with ground control, he feared their marriage might spiral down and crash. And when it hit, he knew it would be ugly.

Which was why Art wanted to be anywhere else but here. Still, he made himself walk to the door and knock. Ty answered and ushered him into his study, a formal room featuring a pair of antique leather sofas, built-in bookshelves filled with a variety of tomes, and a giant desk positioned in front of French doors which led out to the side porch.

As always, they sat across from each other on the sofas, the old leather making breathy sounds as they settled themselves. Ty began by offering a short prayer over both of them and the session. When it concluded, he gazed directly at Art.

"How have things been?" he asked in a way that made Art think he already knew the answer. Though pushing 85, Ty's body might have slowed down, but his mind remained sharp as ever. His eyes, too, behind the wire-frame glasses, didn't miss a trick. His linebacker's body had lost most of its muscle and gained a sizeable paunch, but still he exuded strength.

Art surprised himself by saying, "I suppose you've heard my daughter is back in town."

Ty neither confirmed nor denied that he'd been privy to rumors or gossip. "And how's that going?"

Art shifted his position on the sofa, coughed, uncrossed then recrossed one leg over the other, his ankle resting on his knee, his foot twitching. "It's been difficult."

"Difficult in what way?"

In the way that I don't want her here. "I find her presence disruptive."

"Disruptive in what way?"

Ty's tone held no judgment and even though he knew of Art's struggles with his daughter, knew of her disappearance all those years ago, he seemed more curious about Art's reaction to her return than anything else. Art uncrossed his legs and sat forward. "Disruptive to my normal routine. To our daily lives."

"And why is that?"

"She and Marcy have grown thick as thieves, that's why. Marcy is shirking her duties at the church, running off with Joy to shop or have lunch or do whatever every time Joy calls."

"I imagine Marcy is happy to have her daughter back."

Art glowered at him.

"It's only natural for a mother to want to spend time with her child."

Art glanced over Ty's shoulder at a row of Bibles in various versions. A concordance took its rightful place at the end of the shelf.

"And you?" Ty asked. "Have you spent time with your daughter?"

"No," Art growled with a glare at Ty.

"Still carrying that grudge, I see."

"It isn't a grudge," Art insisted. They'd had this discussion more than once.

"You don't like my definition? You pick one."

"She disrespected me. Defied me."

"Over twenty years ago."

"She never tried to make it right. Never apologized. Never asked for forgiveness."

"Maybe she doesn't want forgiveness. Maybe she hasn't apologized because she doesn't believe she's done anything to apologize for."

When Art made no comment, Ty said, "Have you considered forgiving her anyway? For these perceived slights?"

"They aren't *perceived* slights. I know what she did. How she behaved."

"But you still refuse to consider that your own behavior might have precipitated hers?"

When Art remained mute, Ty said, "Oh, come on, Art. Deal with the plank in your own eye, before—"

"I'm well aware of the passage."

Ty quieted for a moment, obviously seeing he wasn't getting anywhere. "You know a few years ago, Erica had the TV tuned to Dr. Phil," he said referring to his late wife. "She always enjoyed that pop psychologist, always quoting his tidbits of wisdom." Ty got lost in his recollections for a moment as he often did at the mention of the wife he'd loved and lost. "I happened to be passing by and something Dr. Phil said has stuck with me ever since. His guests were a couple whose marriage was in trouble, and he looked at the husband and he said, "Would you rather be right? Or would you rather be married?""

Art slunk down slightly in his seat, splaying his legs and crossing his arms. "I don't see what that has to do with me."

Ty raised an eyebrow. "You don't? Then let me ask you this, Art. Would you rather be right? Or would you rather have peace and harmony in your household?"

"I *am* right," Art ground out. How did Ty not get such a simple fact? He'd never understood. Maybe because he didn't have children. Maybe he couldn't understand.

"Ah," Ty said, steepling his hands beneath his chin. He smiled his clever, angelic smile, eyes crinkling behind the lenses. "Something else old Dr. Phil once said. There is no reality. There's only perception."

"You know, Ty, I didn't come here so you could spout pop psychology at me."

"Why did you come?"

"Damned if I know," Art said, surging to his feet. "I know what's true and I know what's right. I sure as hell don't need you or anyone else trying to convince me I'm wrong. I won't take up any more of your time. You and the good doctor should expend your efforts on those who really need you."

"Art!"

Art didn't give Ty a chance to get to his feet or to see him out. He didn't care about the mild epithet he'd used which had probably shocked his old mentor. Using the word felt strange on his tongue but satisfying as well. The mini explosion allowed him to vent some of his anger and frustration.

He didn't slam the door behind him, but he shut it firmly enough he knew Ty would hear it. Art nearly sprinted to his car, and by the time he got it started he could see from his peripheral vision Ty framed in the doorway, watching him. Art refused to look back. His heart rate accelerated as did the car and his hands weren't quite steady on the wheel. He'd held onto his convictions for all these years and if Ty thought he was going to let go of them now just because he and Dr. Phil McGraw thought it was a good idea, he could think again.

Chapter Nineteen

J oy found herself in charge of arranging a meeting between Brian and Granger for late the following Saturday afternoon in Granger's workshop. Brian wanted to take another look at the pieces and, if Granger agreed, take the ones he'd chosen with him afterward.

Joy came downstairs five minutes early to find Granger already there. Instead of his usual jeans and tee shirt, he wore navy blue slacks and a white button-down shirt open at the collar.

He'd made an attempt to style his hair, although the thick dark waves were intent on defying that effort. The ends curled over his collar, and Joy thought once again that somebody should tell him to get a haircut.

He'd been looking over his creations but turned when she greeted him. His eyes lit up. A slow smile curved his lips. "Hello."

She smiled back. She couldn't help it. She was ridiculously glad to see him, even if she hadn't heard from him since their impromptu dinner earlier in the week. She told herself not to expect anything, not to even want anything where Granger was concerned. But that helpless attraction she felt every time she saw him wouldn't budge. Granger got to her in a way no other man ever had.

She stepped closer. "How are you?"

"Honestly? I'm a little nervous."

"Are you?"

"This whole thing." He gestured at his finished work. "Putting them out there. Putting myself out there. I can't say I'm comfortable with it."

"And you don't have to unless you want to. You haven't signed anything yet. It's not too late to back out."

Granger winced. "True. But in my head, I'm already adding thousands to Cassie's college fund."

Joy laughed. "I guess there's always a trade-off, isn't there?"

When Granger didn't answer her rhetorical question, she said, "By the way, I thought of a business name for you. GS Designs."

"Hmmm."

"Personally, I think it's pretty perfect. It reflects both your product and you as the creator."

"I'll definitely keep it in mind," he said. "Thank you."

Brian pulled his van to the curb, and Joy and Granger turned to greet him.

Joy got a chance to see Brian in full-on professional mode. She stood back while he and Granger rearranged the finished work so Brian could get a better look at each piece, remarking on the originality and the workmanship.

They were consistently impressive. Granger imbued metal and wood, nuts and bolts, with personalities. One in particular stood out to her. Two children, a boy and a girl, holding hands. The slightly taller boy appeared to be a step ahead of the girl and Joy wondered if Granger had his own children in mind when he created it.

Granger himself grew more animated as he answered Brian's questions and discussed his process. In the end, Brian decided he wanted to handle six of the sculptures to begin with. He produced a straightforward contract ready for Granger to sign once he'd filled in the details.

Brian's van held straps and moving pads. He made sure to secure everything before he closed the door and turned back to them. "I've got space reserved at a design expo in Dayton next weekend. It would be a good opportunity to display your work. Any chance you're free to attend Saturday?"

Granger glanced at Joy. "Me?"

Brian's lips twitched as he sent a look Joy's way. "Both of you. But be warned, I might put you to work while you're there."

Pleased to be included, Joy said, "I'd love to go."

"I guess I could do Saturday." Granger didn't sound nearly as confident or enthusiastic as Joy.

"Great. I'll be there all weekend, but I'll get the details to you before then." He stuck out his hand to Granger and they shook. "Joy," he said, "I'll see you soon."

Chapter Twenty

"**I** like it when you smile. You should do it more often." Joy grinned at him before returning her attention to the road.

"I *am* doing it more often. Whenever I'm with you, in fact."

Joy glanced his way again, her eyes soft, as if what he'd said touched her deeply.

"I've noticed that I also feel like smiling whenever you're around. If I'm not mistaken, I spent most of the day smiling."

True that. Granger might have experienced a few nerves when they'd arrived at the design expo, but after the first hour or so, she noticed he relaxed into it. Brian's booth featured two of Granger's figures and, no surprise to Joy, they attracted attention. Granger hastily printed up business cards using her idea for the name GS Designs, handing them out along with the info about Brian's business. Since her presence wasn't really needed in the booth, she spent a good part of the day browsing the other vendors and indulging her love of art and design.

The show ran from ten until five and they'd joined Brian for dinner before heading home. All in all, a pleasant and successful day. The best part was the amount of time she spent in Granger's company.

Granger drew a finger along her thigh. "Maybe we like being around each other," he said, as if he could read her thoughts.

She felt his touch everywhere. A stab of desire like she'd never experienced before shot through her. She couldn't wait to get back home, where she planned to haul him upstairs and find out what else his touch could do to her.

"Maybe we do," she agreed, finding her voice breathy from excitement.

Granger shifted in his seat.

"Can I ask you something?" she said.

"Sure."

"Are you as turned on as I am right now?"

He turned his head to look at her straight on. His fingers slid along the nape of her neck, his thumb sweeping along that sensitive place behind her ear. Joy sucked in a breath.

"What do you think?" he asked.

"I stopped thinking about thirty seconds ago."

Granger responded with a low and sexy chuckle. "Maybe when we get back, you could invite me up to your place."

"I could. I definitely could. But you should stop touching me now."

Granger stilled. "Why?"

"Because if I'm distracted, I can't stay in my lane."

He crossed his arms over his chest but twisted in his seat as far as the restraints would allow in order to face her.

After a couple of minutes of silence, Joy said, "What are you doing?"

"Using my imagination."

"Tell me." Her voice taking on that breathless quality again.

"I'm imagining undressing you. Slowly."

"Why slowly?"

"Undoing each button on your blouse. One by one." Granger's voice mesmerized her.

"I figure it will take ten minutes per button."

"Ten?" Joy squeaked.

"There are only five or six, right?"

"But, but, that's like an hour."

"It's my imagination," he reminded her, sounding delighted.

She flicked a quick glance his way. "Not reality, in other words."

"That remains to be seen."

"Granger, I swear if you take an hour to unbutton one blouse—"

"I know. Just imagine the possibilities."

This time she saw not only his smile in her peripheral vision, but a wicked gleam in his eyes as well.

"Besides, you don't know what else I might be doing while I'm unbuttoning you."

"Like what?" Parts of her were aching at the thought of being with him. She hated to admit she couldn't even remember the last time she'd been with a man like that. The last time she'd even been interested in being with someone.

"Use your imagination," he suggested as she took the turnoff for Liberty.

"Are you sure you want me to do that?" she teased. "I've been known to be pretty inventive."

Granger groaned which made Joy smile in response. Oh, she looked forward to the rest of the night.

Joy eased her car into the driveway next to Granger's truck. They wasted no time exiting the vehicle. Joy grabbed his hand, and they hustled up the stairs. Once inside, Granger locked the door behind him.

The light over the stove, burned just bright enough for them to see each other. His back against the wall, Granger slid his hand into her hair and drew her toward him. Their lips met and they both sighed. Joy's arms slid around his neck and the kiss deepened. Granger really didn't want to hurry. He'd waited years for this. He didn't want to rush through it, no matter how turned on he was or how long it had been since he'd been with a woman. He wanted to savor every moment of being with Joy, especially this, their first time.

He slipped a hand between them and undid the top button of her blouse and felt her muffled laughter, though their mouths were still exploring each other. She drew back for a moment and looked into his eyes. "Want me to set a timer?"

He tapped the side of his head. "No need. I've got one going up here."

"Five minutes per button, max," she said as her lips drifted back to his. "That's all you get."

"Don't be so bossy."

In answer, she began unbuttoning his shirt before she pulled out of the kiss. "I think I need to show you how it's done."

He tilted her chin up and said, "No, you really don't," before he silenced her with his mouth. He drew her as close as he could, molding her body against his, feeling every one of her curves and hollows, letting her feel every one of his.

She yanked the button-down and the white tee shirt he wore under it out of his waistband and slid her hands underneath and along his sides up to his chest, exploring the shape and texture of him.

He undid another of her buttons to reveal the deep vee of her cleavage. His lips drew a hot path along her throat to where her pulse leapt against his tongue. He found that place just below and behind her ear, pressing his tongue against it, brushing along the nerve endings, sensing her knees weaken. Her head dropped back, exposing more of her for him to feast on.

He undid another of her buttons and lowered his head to run his tongue along the top of her breasts just above her bra.

"Granger," she gasped.

"What?" he whispered. "What do you want? Tell me."

"You," she said. "Bed."

"Not yet."

"I can't stand up."

"I've got you." His arms were secure around her. All that muscle, she thought, those calloused hands, rough and yet so gentle. She wanted to melt into the floor, knowing he could pick her up and shape her once again into who she was.

She stopped trying to direct things. Gave up control. She'd never done it before. She'd never trusted anyone enough.

She started to unbutton the cuffs on his shirt. Granger lifted his head to watch. She tugged the shirt off and dropped it. When she lifted the tee shirt, he let her help him out of it.

"Who invented buttons anyway?" she muttered. She pressed her lips against his chest Everywhere her mouth explored, her hands followed until her lips came back to his.

He undid another of her buttons and traced his fingers along the top of her bra, then down across each cup. Her nipples stood at rigid attention, and he circled each with his thumbs teasing them, toying with them. Joy sagged with desire, and he caught her once again.

He settled her securely against him, his crotch nestled just above hers. He undid the last button. Her eyes glittered up at him. "Finally," she whispered, her smile hot and sexy.

"How are we doing on time?" he asked.

"We've got all night, don't we?"

All night. It seemed an eternity. He'd always been fascinated by the way time seemed to both slow down and speed up during intimate encounters.

He pushed the blouse over her shoulders and she let it drop. She filled the lacy black bra beautifully. He should torture himself longer, he thought, torture her too. But why? They had all night.

He found the clasp and released it and the bra went the way of the blouse. He stared, mesmerized, at what he could see of her breasts in the dim light. But he wanted to see more.

"Okay. Bed."

She laughed in delight and led him to it. She turned on the small bedside lamp and drew back the covers before he brought her down with him. He dipped his head to taste, to suckle, first one breast then the other, stroking her, teasing her, while she writhed in delight, her hands feverishly touching every part of his torso she could reach.

Joy unbuckled his belt, pushed and shoved until he relented and sat up to remove shoes, socks, slacks.

"You might as well take those off too," she said, giving his boxers a tug.

"I'm shy. Turn over."

"Ooh," she said as she complied. "Now who's being inventive?"

"Hush." He unzipped her skirt and tugged it off. She wore a satiny slip under it. He pulled that off too, taking his time, drawing it down over her thighs and calves and feet to discover black silky underwear. He let his fingers trail down her spine and along her panties, using his thumbs to explore the vee between her thighs.

She quivered at that final touch. "God, Granger. You've got some moves."

"Yeah?" he asked in delight.

He repeated the move, pausing a little longer to draw his finger along the damp crotch of her panties. She reacted the way he hoped so he rubbed some more. "Granger," she said, in a tortured voice.

"I kind of want to take these off."

"Good idea."

He drew the panties down, enjoying the view of her bottom, firm from all those workouts she talked about, over thighs and calves and ankles. He tossed them aside.

She turned to her back, and he paused to view her naked, her skin flushed with desire, lips plump from his kisses, nipples erect, moisture pooling between her thighs.

He touched her there. "Open for me."

Her thighs parted to reveal everything that made her a woman, the moist deep pink of her. He stroked her, watching for her reaction, seeing she'd closed her eyes. He watched the rise and fall of her chest as her arousal increased with each stroke. He spread her further and lowered his tongue to her, easily finding the swollen nub, tasting, teasing, caressing until she came violently, shock waves rocking her, gasping cries of pleasure emitting from her throat.

She watched through slitted eyes as he wiped his mouth on the back of his hand and removed his boxers. He lowered himself to her, pressing her into the mattress, propping himself on his elbows.

"Now what?" she asked, twisting a strand of his hair around a finger. His cock strained against her as she drew him down for a kiss that never seemed to end. Somehow she drew him in, there, where he wanted to be. Her knees hiked up nearly to his shoulders, cradling him, cushioning him, stretching to accommodate him.

He plunged again and again, lost inside her, lost to himself, blinded by the pleasure of being with her. She met him, she matched him, pushed him to his limit and he let go, flying, soaring, until he crashed, collapsed against her.

He rolled away and they lay there panting. Joy tried to remember a time when she'd felt this soul-deep sense of satisfaction after making love and again, she couldn't because she knew it had never happened before.

She waited for Granger to say something as their breathing calmed and their bodies cooled, but when she turned her head to look at him, her finger playing along his bicep, she saw that his eyes were closed. She propped herself on an elbow and looked at him. He didn't move. He appeared to be asleep.

She fell back against the mattress. Why, she wondered, when a woman wanted to share a sense of rapture with the man who had caused it, was he likely to be asleep? It didn't seem fair. But she couldn't bring herself to wake him, either.

In the bathroom she got ready for bed as she always did, with the exception of nightclothes. She wanted to be prepared for an encore performance. She nudged him over to make room for herself and turned off the light. Granger shifted, his arm seeming to naturally curve around her. Somehow, she too fell asleep.

Chapter Twenty-One

J oy didn't know how long they slept. An hour? Two? She wasn't going to get up and check her phone to find out. Not with Granger's arm around her, his fingers exploring her breasts, teasing her nipples. Her butt was tucked firmly against him and she could feel every silky steel inch of his hard-on.

She smiled without opening her eyes. She planned to enjoy every dreamy moment of the encore. The way his body felt against hers, his front to her back. The gentleness of his calloused hands against the soft skin of her breasts. His teeth tugging on her earlobe, his tongue snaking out to play along that sensitive place just below.

She wondered how long she could pretend to be dozing, how long she could control her physical reactions to all the sensations being this close to him, naked, ignited.

His fingers raked through her hair, drawing it away from her face. He followed the line of her temple with the tip of his finger, drawing it down past her earlobe and around the curve of her jaw, as if memorizing her. The feather light touch against her lips surprised her and he traced the line and shape of them, then up the bridge of her nose to her eyebrow and back again to her lips.

He rubbed his finger against them more insistently this time, and she couldn't resist. She nipped him with her teeth. She grabbed his wrist and suckled his finger and when he offered her another one, she took it into her mouth, thinking how much she'd like to repeat the treatment on another part of his body.

He turned her toward him and withdrew his fingers, but not before she pressed a heated kiss to the palm of his hand. His mouth found hers and he kissed her with the kind of intensity she'd come to expect from him. He undid her. She wanted everything he had to offer. Mind. Body. Soul. Spirit. She wanted to give the same back to him.

He kept her wedged tight against him while they kissed. It seemed to go on forever, this exploration of each other's mouths. This went beyond sex. *Making love.* She'd heard the term hundreds of times and always suspected it was merely a blunted way of saying "they had sex." Yes, but it was much more than that. At least for her. She hoped for him. A connection on every level.

She breathed in his scent, the musk of his skin, which still held a faint trace of a spicy cologne. The heat of his mouth still held the tang of rosemary and lemon used to season last night's meal.

She wanted her mouth on him but didn't want to rush through whatever else he had in mind. Feverish with desire she touched him everywhere she could and eventually worked her hand between them. She explored the length of his cock before curling her fist around him. He throbbed in her hand until she wiggled her way down to take him in her mouth.

"Joy." Her name passed his lips in a strangled whisper. She took him deeper, as deep as she could, using her fingers to stroke the base of his cock while she sucked.

When he shifted away from her, she scrambled up to straddle him, lowering herself until he was deeply, satisfyingly inside her. He laced his fingers with hers. She could almost see him in the murky light from the kitchen. There was something freeing about the near darkness. It opened her up to feeling and sensing without seeing.

She untwined their fingers so she could stoke his chest while she rode him and reach back to cup his balls.

He, in turn, tortured her breasts, his thumbnails scraping erotically across her sensitive nipples in a way that sent a signal directly to her clit. Almost as if he sensed what had happened, he squeezed his thumb between them, putting pressure on that swollen nub every time she moved.

She got lost in her own excitement, searching for that touch that would send her over the edge, picking up the pace, moving in a rhythm that he matched until they fell over the edge in unity, breathing hard, crying out as they crashed.

There aren't words. Joy lay collapsed against his chest. *But if he falls asleep again, I'll kill him.*

He wasn't asleep, though. He stroked her back and along her thighs in a sweeping motion. She listened to the steady beat of his heart beneath her ear.

What if I had stayed? It wasn't the first time the thought had popped into her head since she'd been back in Liberty. But now she wondered if she and Granger would have ever found each other before now. What if she could have had this, had him, all this time?

No use thinking that way. They had each other now.

I love you. The words were on the tip of her tongue, but she didn't say it. She needed to explore how she felt to make sure she wasn't just saying the words in the heat of the moment. Or, technically, in the moment after the heat. But for the first time, maybe ever, she could envision a future with a man. A long-term future. She just didn't want to be the only one in this bed with that vision.

She moved to his side, into the crook of his arm, where he continued brushing his hand along the curve of her elbow. His lips pressed against her hair.

He didn't speak, which she'd bet a thousand dollars was typical for Granger after sex. Correction. Making love. She curled her fingers against his chest and drifted off once again.

Granger knew almost the exact moment Joy fell asleep. Her movements stilled. Her breathing leveled out.

He wanted to sleep too, but he stared up at the ceiling, fighting it. He feared he was heading straight for a fall. An abyss he might not be able to climb out of. Somehow, he'd managed to carry on after Adele left, like a wounded soldier who must make it back across enemy lines to save himself. He'd trudged through the past few years one step at a time until he'd recovered from the hurt of her abandonment. At least, that's what he told himself.

He'd jumped the gun with Joy, in spite of all the warnings he'd given himself. If he took a hard fall, he couldn't blame anyone but himself. She wasn't committed. To him. To staying in Liberty. To anything, really, as far as he knew. Joy was a free agent. She had nothing tying her down to any place, anything, or anybody.

He wished he was one of those guys who could have sex with a woman and walk away without any lasting connections. But he wasn't. He'd tried a couple of times, fleeting encounters where the women had no expectations beyond a night where both parties scratched an itch.

He didn't like sharing himself like that. It seemed pointless, and it made him disappointed in himself. Like he couldn't wait for something that at least had the potential to be real and lasting.

He'd put himself in a position with Joy now, where he had to decide to go all in or take a giant step back. But he might be headed for a fall either way he went.

The quality of the light when he woke told him it was just before dawn, which meant he'd dozed for a couple of hours at least. He sat up and swung his feet to the floor, feeling content but weary.

As quietly as he could, he gathered his clothes.

"What are you doing?" Joy asked, her voice full of sleep.

"Getting dressed. Going home."

"You don't have to. I'll make coffee."

He considered the offer. Nothing he'd like better than to share coffee with her. Maybe while it brewed, they could try for round three. "You go back to sleep. I've gotta get ready for church in a while, anyway." He sat on the edge of the bed to put his socks on.

"Church? Why? You need to ask for forgiveness?" Joy's tone held a note of amusement.

"Church because it's what I do on Sunday mornings." He located his shoes half-kicked under the bed and slid his feet into them.

"Seems kind of hypocritical. It's been a while, but I doubt God has changed his stance on this." She gestured to indicate the bed and the two of them.

"Yeah, well. The world is full of hypocrites and sinners. As are the churches."

He bent to kiss her, circling the tip of his finger around her nipple. "For the record," he said, his voice husky, "I don't regret anything about last night." *Yet.*

"As you may remember, I did warn you," she said, her tone matching his as she pulled him in for another kiss.

"And I told you I'm not afraid of you."

Joy trailed a finger down his chest and smiled up at him. "Maybe you should be."

He grabbed her hand and pressed his lips to her palm. "I'll call you later, okay?"

"Okay."

Unlikely any of the neighbors were awake and alert enough to notice him crossing the lawn to his back door. At least he hoped not. There were few secrets and a lot of loose lips in the neighborhood.

He set coffee to brew and took a longer than usual shower. Padded back to the kitchen for a cup of coffee to drink while he shaved.

He wished he could escape church this morning, but he'd been going since childhood. If he didn't show up, questions would be asked, and he wasn't a liar by nature. He couldn't imagine admitting to his father, to Art, to Cassie, to anyone, that he'd spent the night with Joy. Besides, the Sunday service was the one hour of the week where he felt somewhat at peace. The time when he often zoned out and stopped worrying about Cassie and the turmoil in his home, where he let the petty problems and anxieties of the rest of the week slip away and he could just be.

Cassie had stayed overnight with her friend Lindsay, and Lindsay's mother would be bringing both girls to church. It might be one of those mornings when his father suggested breakfast out for the whole family. Granger found himself looking forward to the prospect because he was starving.

Chapter Twenty-Two

When Joy woke, the sun shone, and it promised to be a beautiful morning. She stuck her head out the door and made a quick decision to go for a long walk. She could head downtown and stop for coffee and enjoy the walk back.

She dressed quickly, figuring she'd shower when she returned. A buoyant sense of well-being put a spring in her step, and enthusiasm for the future filled her in a way it hadn't for a long time.

Happiness. That's what she felt. Apparently, it had been so long it took her awhile to recognize the emotion. Because of Granger? Partly, she admitted to herself. If she were honest, she could also admit while she hadn't been miserable being single for so long, a part of her still wanted someone to share life with. It wasn't hard to see Granger fulfilling that role even though she knew she was jumping the gun even having such thoughts.

But it was her fantasy, so she could think whatever she liked. She enjoyed what-if scenarios. What if Cassie didn't hate her? Or what if they simply waited a couple of years until Cassie left for college to make things permanent between them? Maybe Cassie would mature by then and not find the idea of her father and Joy so objectionable.

For all Joy knew, Cassie might be the smallest of obstacles. Granger's divorce had impacted him deeply. Joy wasn't sure he'd healed completely after four years. But it sure hadn't kept him from going all in last night.

Joy sighed as she walked along the sun-dappled sidewalks. The mature trees overhead showed off their new leaves. The home gardeners did their part and everywhere she looked there were flower beds and vegetable gardens.

In no time at all, she arrived downtown. She crossed to Brian's gallery, seeing it as a passer-by would, checking the window displays and peeking beyond them for a glimpse into the interior. Brian wisely kept the windows clear, so the space glowed with light. The neutral colors of the art, furniture, and plush, fringed throws at the front would appeal to a broad range of potential customers.

"Well done," she said to herself. She turned to glance across the street and noticed a For Lease sign in the window of a ground floor storefront kitty-cornered from the gallery. She crossed over and cupped her hands around her eyes so she could see into the interior through the plate-glass windows. Joy didn't know what the space might have been used for in a previous incarnation. Now the interior held nothing but dust.

"A blank slate," she said to herself, as the germ of an idea began to take shape in her mind.

"What if," Joy began, "we renovated the space available across from the gallery?"

Brian looked up from the Bistro's brunch menu. Joy had called him when she got home and insisted on taking him out. "Why would *we* want to?"

"Okay," Joy leaned forward, "I have an idea. We create a retail space for local artisans."

Brian laid his menu aside. "I'm listening."

"I figure there have to be people like Granger," she said. "Creating art in their own private spaces who might be interested in a bigger audience for their work. All we have to do is find them and make them an offer. Maybe work with them on a consignment basis. The point is, we find handmade, homemade, *real*, one-of-a-kind pieces. We give them exposure they wouldn't otherwise have. We'll set up some kind of commission or consignment percentage so everyone's happy. It's brilliant, right?"

"I'm not sure brilliant's the right word," Brian said cautiously.

"Really?" Joy said after the server took their orders and left. "You don't like the idea?" She sat back, crossing her arms, feeling her lower lip protrude like a five-year-old who wasn't getting her way.

"I didn't say that. In fact, I've got a file folder filled with the kind of people you're talking about. I just haven't had the time or opportunity to do much with it."

"Until now."

Brian held up a hand. "Hang on. You're saying *we*. Are you thinking about a joint venture? Because renovating that space is not going to be cheap. And I'm not sure it's something I can commit to right now."

"We could be partners, though, right?" Joy found it impossible to hold back her enthusiasm. "There's a contract pending on my condo in LA. If it sells, I'll have enough to invest in the renovation. We can design the space together. I can contact the vendors and set up the retail side."

The server swung by to refill their coffee cups and assured them their food would be out shortly. Joy pushed the coffee away. Her excitement gave her enough of a buzz. Plus, she'd stopped for a double skinny latte on her walk.

"I already looked around online. There are weekend craft fairs all summer long. I can go check them out. Pick the best of the best. Things that might even dovetail with the gallery and your design business.

"Everybody's flipping these days, too. Buying up used furniture and repainting it, repurposing junk they find at flea markets. Brian, the possibilities are endless. It'll be like a creative outlet in a concrete way."

"A lot of those artists are probably selling online, though," Brian pointed out. "Retail is tough these days."

Joy didn't like him playing devil's advocate, but one of them had to and Brian knew way more about running a business. "True. But I also think shoppers miss the in-store experience. They want to see and touch. Examine before they commit. Plus, we're giving the artists more exposure. There's no reason we can't have a website, too. Maybe include links to the artists' sites as well.

"So they can cut us out of our percentage?" Brian said in a teasing tone, but one of his eyebrows went up in an *are-you-serious?* kind of way.

"Maybe that's not the best idea," Joy conceded. "Could we set up our site with affiliate links so we still get like a referral fee or something? I admit I don't have all the details worked out yet. I only came up with the idea this morning."

After their food arrived, Brian pointed his fork at her. "I'm open to the possibility of some sort of cooperative. But we have to get one thing straight between us before we move forward."

"What's that?"

"Starting a business like this, running any business really, can be stressful and divisive. Whatever we do, we should agree right now it won't affect our friendship."

"That's an easy promise to make," Joy assured him. "I'm not dumb enough to let go of what we have a second time."

"Good." Brian tried some of his food before he said, "Does this mean you've decided to stay in Liberty?"

Joy'd been so carried away with her brainstorm she hadn't stopped to consider what it would mean long term. Was she committing to staying in Liberty? All things seemed possible now. She'd renewed her relationship with her mother and some of her extended family and had a potentially serious relationship with Granger. Of course, she didn't know where Granger stood, but after last night, her intentions were definitely on the serious side. She could see a future in Liberty start to take shape.

"Honestly, Bri, I wasn't thinking in those terms. I got so caught up with my ideas. My vision. But if we go ahead with it, of course I'll stay."

"Good."

They went on to discuss possibilities for the business. Brian agreed to call a contractor he'd used before first thing Monday so the three of them could tour the space together.

When they parted, Joy took off for Cedar Mill, which, according to Google Maps, was about an hour away. After a bit of research earlier she found a craft fair scheduled there this weekend. She figured if she got there in the afternoon, she might get some good deals, if there were any to be had, as the vendors might be more inclined to bargain to make a sale rather than haul the merchandise home.

Besides, Joy had nothing else to do today. She didn't know what Granger's plans were after church, but thought it likely Cassie would be around, and he wouldn't want to ruffle her feathers. Joy hadn't made plans with Marcy, but Sunday was kind of a sacred day. Her parents often joined her father's side of the family for an afternoon meal, her aunts and uncles taking turns hosting it. Both Joy and her mother knew Art wouldn't welcome her presence, and Joy assumed her mother would defer to his wishes.

She didn't mind. She'd reconnect to the extended family in her own way and in her own time. If Marcy had her way, they'd all attend the reunion, and she could meet up with them then, if not before.

Joy drove to the fair, her brain humming with visions of the retail space she wanted to create. A comfortable, welcoming space inviting shoppers to browse, to touch, to sit, to buy. She hoped to have a mix of furniture and a way to display it in a functional manner. Hand woven throws over the backs of rocking chairs, pottery pieces displayed on rustic coffee tables. Refinished china cabinets filled with whatever struck her fancy—no two items alike.

Everywhere customers looked, there'd be something new and interesting to catch the eye. Or, she supposed, something old and made more interesting with renovation.

She found the fair set up next to a co-op farmer's market. There wasn't a huge crowd, so Joy took her time, lingering longer to examine the things she found truly interesting and meeting the vendors.

She came away with even more ideas. Hand-woven baskets for one. And a variety of items made from reclaimed wood, including several pieces of furniture.

Joy decided against carrying jewelry unless they were truly unique pieces. It seemed there were just too many crafters into beads and wire. But she definitely wanted a children's section and a kitchen section. She'd also seen a couple of neat storage ideas.

Chapter Twenty-Three

Back in Liberty, she shopped for a few groceries. When she got home, she saw the overhead door up and Granger in the garage. She stepped just inside the door with her purse and her grocery bags. "Hello."

Granger stood near his workbench, but he'd watched her the whole time.

He gave her one of his almost smiles. "Hi, there."

They stared at each other, their connection like a live wire between them. "Working on something new?"

"Just screwing around. Seeing what I could start with."

"You inspire me," Joy blurted. She knew it was because of Granger, his art, the art show, maybe even their intimacy last night, that she'd been so inspired today.

Granger came around the bench toward her, his smile definite now. "I do, huh?"

"You've given me ideas." Joy's voice took on that breathless quality again, like it had last night. "I'll tell you all about it sometime."

"Tell me?" he asked, a devilish glint in his eyes. "Or show me."

A giggle escaped Joy's lips. He couldn't know they were talking about completely different things. "Both."

"Think we can get together again?" His eyes never left hers, but he ran the tip of his finger along her arm, and she felt the light touch everywhere.

"Oh, God. I hope so."

"Maybe next weekend...?"

"You can't sneak away before then?" Joy wondered if he heard the note of desperation in her voice. If he touched her again, she might drop everything and tear his clothes off right here in the middle of his garage, in broad daylight on a Sunday afternoon. Maybe her father had been right about her all along.

"I don't know." He'd lowered his voice to just above a whisper. "I could try."

"You've got a key," she reminded him, as if he needed reminding.

His eyes widened at the open invitation. "I do."

She leaned closer, her mouth next to his ear. "Use it."

Joy turned and made her way out of the garage and up the stairs, her gait unsteady. They hadn't kissed, and barely touched, but Joy felt undone in a way she never had before.

Had she ever flirted like this? No. This went beyond flirting. This was—was—blatant seduction. At least to her it was. She hoped Granger got her message loud and clear. Oh, how she hoped he would act on it soon.

She forced herself to act normally. Put her groceries away. Straighten the apartment.

She regarded the box of condoms as she set it in the top drawer of the small cabinet she used as a nightstand. They'd been irresponsible last night, neither of them even thinking about birth control. She hadn't, at least. She supposed Granger hadn't either.

But they both should have behaved more like responsible adults as opposed to giddy teenagers. Joy's only excuse was that she'd stopped thinking altogether. And that was no excuse at all.

Even if, as her doctor has suggested on her last check-up, perimenopause had begun, Joy knew the possibility of pregnancy still existed. She'd thought of herself as being so far beyond childbearing, it hadn't really entered her head until today. Chances were good she wasn't pregnant, but she wasn't taking any more chances, either.

She uploaded the photos she'd taken at the craft fair and created a file for the contact information she'd gathered.

By the time he normally went to bed Granger knew he should be tired. Was, in fact, tired. But energized at the same time. He lay on top of the covers, fully dressed, hands beneath his head, and stared at the ceiling of the bedroom he'd once shared with Adele and thought about Joy's invitation. In truth, he'd thought of little else since she'd issued it.

Thinking he could sneak into her place any time he wanted to made him smile. The thought of having to sneak anywhere made him smile first, but then he frowned. Because sneaking around made it seem like he was doing something he shouldn't be. Except he was a grown man and had every right to visit Joy. The only reason he'd be sneaking out would be because of his daughter.

Ironic, he supposed, because the only reason she sneaked out was because of him. Again, he wondered how they'd come to be so far apart. But he wasn't so stupid as to think that Cassie would be happy if she became aware of how far things had progressed with him and Joy. Bottom line? He wanted to protect his daughter. And if that meant keeping things a secret for now, it seemed for the best.

Still, it didn't seem like a fatherly thing to do. It seemed like a cowardly thing. Granger didn't like viewing himself that way. He'd caught Cassie sneaking out. She'd probably catch him too if he kept up this pretense.

Granger rolled to his side, trying to decide if going to Joy's in the dead of night was worth it. No, he knew it would be worth it. But was it a good idea to keep it from Cassie? He knew the answer to that, too. It wasn't. He'd be setting a bad example and going against everything he'd tried to teach her.

He rolled to his other side and bunched the pillow beneath his head. A great way to have a moral debate with himself. But where had the moral code he'd tried to live by gotten him? He'd been a faithful husband, someone who tried always to do the right thing. And after all those years of living that way, he had a marriage that hadn't stuck, an ex-wife, and a daughter who would barely speak a civil word to him. He'd given up the frequent travel his high-paying engineering job required to make way less as a handyman, so he could be closer to home.

Screw it.

He slipped his shoes on and made his way through the dark and quiet house. He unlocked the door and opened it, trying to ease the clicking sounds as best he could, and made his way up the stairs to the apartment. He tried the door and smiled when he turned the key.

He locked up and stood for a moment, letting his eyes adjust to the dim light in Joy's less familiar place. Once they did, he moved up close behind her, pressing his lips against the back of her neck.

She woke with a gasp and turned to her back. In a sliver of light from the window, he could see her eyes sparkling up at him. She pulled him in for a kiss and he sank against her softness. He wanted to kiss her for a long time and touch her everywhere he might have missed last night. He pushed the covers down and kicked them out of the way. She wore some kind of filmy nightgown that felt like silk beneath his fingers.

Things heated up fast. She drew his shirt up and he helped her by yanking it over his head and tossing it aside. Shimmied out of his jeans and boxers as fast as he could. But it wasn't fast enough, for she put her hand flat on his chest and said, "Stop."

He stilled and collapsed on his back, already breathing hard, his arousal pulsing madly.

"Sorry," she said. "But we need to think about birth control."

He turned to look at her. "We didn't last night. But, yeah, we should have." He rolled to his side toward her and took her hand, linking his fingers through hers. "Honestly? I was married so long, I didn't have to think about it. Adele put herself in charge after Cassie was born."

"I understand," Joy said. "But—"

"Do you think it'll be a problem? Last night, I mean?"

"Probably not. There's this thing called perimenopause. Maybe you've heard of it."

Granger's teeth gleamed when he smiled. "Believe me, I've tried not to. But I have a vague idea."

"Well, I'm there. But I'd feel better if we took precautions from now on."

"I've got condoms," they said at the same time. They stared at each other for a moment before they started to laugh.

"They're in my pocket," Granger said. "Let me just find my pants."

"There's a whole box in the drawer there by the side of the bed."

"A whole box, huh?" he said, looking back at her from where he'd grabbed the jeans he'd shoved aside. "We probably won't need all of them. Not tonight, anyway."

Joy giggled.

Granger set several foil packets on the nightstand and came back to her. "Now where were we?"

Chapter Twenty-Four

"The family reunion is set for the first weekend in August," Marcy said. "Devonny will be arriving with her family the Wednesday before—"

"No," Arthur said.

Marcy heaved a put-upon sigh. "Art, this is happening whether you like it or not. Joy deserves a chance to reconnect with our families."

"She most certainly does not. Are you forgetting she's the one who left? She's the one who turned her back on all of us?"

"Do you really want to do this? Now?"

"Do what?"

"Have this conversation about who turned whose back on whom?"

"You think it's my fault. You've always thought it was my fault. Go ahead. Tell me again how I should have welcomed her home with open arms after she disrespected us. After *she left us*!"

"It's been twenty-five years, Art. When's it going to be enough? She's here now. And that's all we have. That's all we ever had. *Right now.*"

"I don't want anything to do with that girl."

"She's no longer a girl. Joy's an adult."

"I don't mean her. I mean the daughter."

"Devonny?"

"I won't have anything to do with a porn actress."

Marcy's mouth dropped open. "What? What are you talking about?"

"That's what she does. Who she is. A sinner. A pornographer. A fornicator."

"Devonny isn't—she has a baby. She's married."

"I know what I know."

"But how? You haven't had anything to do with Joy all this time. How could you know anything about her daughter?"

"I know."

"How. Do. You. Know?"

"It doesn't matter how I know."

"It matters to me." Marcy looked at him as if seeing him for the first time and not liking what she saw.

"If you don't believe me, ask *her.* Ask your daughter."

"I'm asking you."

"And I told you what I know."

"Tell me *how* you know." Marcy's stern tone, one she rarely used, got Art's attention. Animosity between them stirred the air. Prickles of awareness tickled his nerve endings.

He remained silent, standing at the crossroads of the before and after, looking both ways, trying to see the consequences before he chose, knowing he'd already made a decision, and nothing could stop it now.

"Tell me how you know!" Marcy's wrath bubbled to the surface and so did his.

"Because I had her followed!"

In the face of his thunderous response, Marcy shrunk back. Her tone became one of wonder. "What do you mean? Followed?"

"The investigator you hired."

She stared at him. "The investigator you fired. The one you told me I couldn't use."

Art stared back at her, a stony expression on his face. He turned to head into the office.

"Oh, no, you don't." Marcy scooted after him and grabbed his sleeve. "Arthur James Harmon, you'd better explain yourself right now, or else." He saw the fire in Marcy's eyes, and Art knew she wouldn't back down.

"Explain what?" he asked tiredly, his earlier burst of anger and frustration gone. Having Joy back in their lives bred nothing but discontent and chaos as he knew it would.

"Arthur." His name came out of her mouth covered in broken glass.

"You want to know about your precious granddaughter?" He spat the words like dirty rain. "Your daughter's child whom you've elevated to sainthood without ever having met her? Is that what you want?"

Marcy stood her ground waiting until he opened the closet in the office and rummaged around, coming up with a locked metal box. He opened the second desk drawer on the right and felt beneath it, coming up with a key. Marcy watched in growing horror as he unlocked the box and withdrew a sheaf of file folders. He tossed them on his desk.

"It's all there," he said. "Look for yourself."

Marcy opened the top folder. Inside she found a copy of Mike and Joy's Nevada marriage certificate. An address in Los Angeles. Employment records for each of them. A phone number.

The next folder contained a report a year later. A copy of Mike's death certificate. Devonny's birth certificate. Information about a pending lawsuit. Financial records.

The much thicker third folder contained copies of a court ruling in favor of Joy. A hefty settlement in a wrongful death claim. A new address.

As quickly as she could, Marcy scanned the contents of the other folders. She almost couldn't take in the enormity of the information and the fact that her husband of over forty years had withheld it from her.

"You knew. All this time, you knew where Joy was. How she was." She could barely look at him, but she made herself, in spite of the tears of hurt and anger filling her eyes.

"Marcy, I—"

"I spent years, *years* worrying about Joy. Praying that she was all right. Lying awake nights wondering where she was, how she was. You knew that. And you knew all of this."

"Marcy, if she'd needed us, if anything had happened to her, I would have—"

"If anything happened to her? Her *whole life* happened to her. Without us."

"That was her choice."

"No. Not entirely. It was *your* choice. One you made without me."

"And you never forgave me for it, did you?"

"You never asked for my forgiveness. You just told me this was how it was going to be. You wouldn't forgive Joy until she apologized. But you think I should forgive you when you never have."

"Marcy, I was afraid if she came back, it would all start again. We'd be right back where we were when she left."

"So, it was all about you. You didn't care how I felt. How Joy felt. You only cared about yourself and whether your life was the way you wanted it."

"Marcy, I wanted to protect you."

"I didn't need to be protected from my child."

Marcy began pulling the file folders back into a stack, then she picked them up and turned to leave.

"Where are you going?"

"To see Joy."

"Marcy, it's late. Don't. Let's talk about this."

Marcy whirled on him. "I have nothing to say to you." She picked up her purse from the entry table.

"Marcy!" Art called as she tore down the front steps. He heard her car door slam and watched her back out of the driveway. He closed the door, but it couldn't block what he'd always feared would happen if Joy came home.

Chapter Twenty-Five

J oy wanted an early night. She'd put on her pajamas already and settled into her comfy chair with a cup of chamomile tea and the remote and a romcom on Netflix she'd been meaning to watch.

But someone clattered up the steps making zero effort to be quiet. For a second, she thought it might be Granger, but it didn't sound like his tread. How, she wondered, could she be attuned to his *footsteps*? A series of rapid knocks followed. Also, not his style. She went to the door, which offered no peephole or side window.

"Who is it?" she asked.

"It's me, Joy."

Joy unlocked the door and yanked it open. "Mom?"

Her mother, chest heaving, hair wild, and face ravaged, barged past her and dropped a sheaf of file folders on the table. She covered her face with her hands and began to sob.

"Mom!" Joy didn't try to hide her alarm. She put her arms around her mother, which only seemed to increase Marcy's agitation. "Mom, what is it? What happened?"

"Your father," came out in a voice choked with tears and a lot of emotion Joy couldn't decipher. Anger? Grief? Disappointment?

Whatever her father had done, Joy knew she wouldn't like it. For her mother to be this upset, it must be bad.

Marcy shook her head against Joy's shoulder and finally stepped back. She swiped at her face with her fingers. Joy went to the kitchen and handed her a paper towel.

After Marcy cleaned herself up and blew her nose, Joy pointed to the table. "What's all this?"

"It's—" Marcy looked away and gave another brief headshake, as if an explanation was beyond her.

Tentatively, Joy opened the top file. Then the next, and the next, before she glanced at her mother, who stood like a statue, fists clenched. "He knew," Joy said. "He kept tabs on me all this time." She couldn't believe it. For all his claims of wanting nothing to do with her. "And he never told you."

Marcy's lips were pressed into a tight line. She jerked her head in the negative once again. "Oh, Mom." Again, Joy embraced her mother, trying to comprehend the kind of betrayal she must be feeling. But she couldn't. It was one thing for her father to turn his back on Joy. But for him to keep this kind of secret from her mother? His wife of over forty years? Unbelievable.

Once again Marcy broke the embrace. "He said terrible things about Devonny."

"Oh, Mom." Somehow, Joy had hoped to spare Devonny her family's judgment, especially that of her grandfather. But she guessed it was true. Honesty truly was the best policy.

"Let me make you some tea. We can talk."

"It's true, then? About Devonny being in those films?"

Joy could see her mother desperately wanted to hear some other explanation. "It's true," she said quietly.

"You didn't tell me."

"No, Mom, I didn't. And honestly, even if we'd stayed in touch all these years, I probably wouldn't have told you. If Devonny wanted you to know, I'd have felt it was her place to tell you. She was an adult when she did those films. It's part of her past now. As for why I didn't tell you when I came back, my reasons are the same. Her past is Devonny's to share or not share. I wanted you to meet her without pre-judgments, get to know her for the person she is."

"Surely you weren't supportive of her decision."

"Of course not. Nor did I have any say or sway for that matter." Joy smiled, remembering her conversation with Dot. "You're familiar with the Serenity Prayer, aren't you?"

Marcy sipped her tea, eyeing Joy over the rim of the mug.

"Especially the part about accepting the things you can't change. That's not easy. Parenting isn't easy.

Parenting adult children isn't easy. I love Devonny. I don't have to agree with everything she does, but I realized I had to let her live her life and accept her choices if I wanted to have a relationship with her. I wasn't willing to lose her because she didn't do what I wanted her to do."

Marcy set her mug down and leaned her chin into the palm of one hand. "Your father was, though, wasn't he? Willing to lose you."

"Was he?" Joy asked, uncertain. "He kept track of me all this time. Why would he do that if he didn't care about me?"

"I don't know." Marcy's eyes flashed behind her glasses. "I don't know why he didn't let me in on his secret, either."

"I think you do."

Marcy's head dipped. "I'd have wanted you back in our lives. You and Devonny."

"I'm sure that's it."

Marcy reached across and covered Joy's hand with her own. "I missed you so much. I ached for you. Made myself sick over it. He *knew* that. Yet he never said a word."

Joy clasped her mother's hand. "Mom, I want you to do something for me, please. While all of this seems inexplicable, selfish, and just plain *wrong*, don't judge Daddy too harshly just yet. Don't do anything rash and in the heat of the moment. Give yourself a little time to think on it. To pray about it. Will you do that?"

Marcy squeezed her hand. "For you. Not for him."

Joy squeezed back. "All right then. It's getting late. Do you want to stay here tonight?"

"Oh." Marcy gave a little laugh. "I didn't even think about that. I left in such a rush. I don't have any of my things."

"I can lend you some night clothes."

"Oh, dear. I don't have my prescriptions. My eye drops. My phone. What was I thinking?"

"Mom, I can get your things for you. I can go right now."

"But your father—"

"What's he going to do? Deny me entry? You have your house key, don't you?"

"Yes, it's on my key ring."

"Let me deal with him. I don't think there will be a problem, but if there is, I'll handle it. He's not going to deny you your prescriptions, surely."

In the bathroom, Joy changed into jeans and a tee shirt. She grabbed Marcy's keys and wrapped her arms around her mother's shoulders from behind. "I'll be back quick as I can."

For a fleeting moment, Joy thought about asking Granger to go with her. She glanced at his dark house. It was late. Joy didn't think they'd reached a point in their relationship where she could heap her problems on him.

For all her bravado in front of her mother, Joy felt nothing but trepidation as she drove the nearly deserted streets to her childhood home. Her father literally had not spoken one kind word to her since her return. True, she avoided him whenever possible, but on those few occasions when they'd crossed paths, he had not been kind. Or even civil, for that matter.

Now she felt like she was about to walk into the lion's den, and she was woefully unprepared. But she had told her mother the truth. She didn't think her father would ban her if he knew she'd come only to retrieve some of Marcy's things.

She parked the car on the street and sat looking up at the darkened house. Almost all her memories of home and family occurred here. In her mind's eye, she saw Easter dinner spread out on the dining table for grandparents, aunts, uncles, and cousins. The Christmas tree that always stood in the living room near the front windows so the lights would be visible from the street. Her father putting out the nativity scene on the front lawn and hanging colored lights from the porch eaves. Her mother winding greenery around the railings.

The birthday slumber party she'd invited all her friends to when she turned twelve. The afternoon snack her mother always had ready while she shared her school day happenings at the kitchen table.

Overlaid by it all was the presence of her father, who never seemed as interested in her or as excited by her childhood achievements. She'd sensed a coldness in him aimed directly at her, but Joy could never figure out a reason for it. What had she done to alienate him?

Maybe all along she'd been trying to get his attention. Since none of her positive endeavors worked, she searched elsewhere to get a reaction out of him. Challenging him after his Sunday sermons, stepping over the line when it came to curfews and what he considered "acceptable behavior." Finding the one boy at school she knew her father would object to.

She got a reaction out of him, but Joy hadn't counted on him cutting her out of his life. Perhaps it would be best not to anticipate his behavior now.

Chapter Twenty-Six

J oy climbed the porch steps and discovered the door
wasn't locked. She stepped inside and closed the door
without making a sound. In the darkened entryway she
paused, listening. If her father was already in bed, she
couldn't sneak in there. She'd have to knock, face him,
and request access.

She heard a noise she couldn't readily identify. Alert
for any new sounds, she crept along the familiar path
through the living room, where the furniture placement
never changed, into the dining room. Light spilled from
the office, allowing her to see the outlines of the table and
chairs, china hutch and sideboard. She inched forward
and peeked through the open French doors.

Whatever this room off the dining room had originally
been intended for, her parents used it as a shared office
space. Her mother's desk was tucked into the far corner
where it overlooked a window that offered a narrow view
of the backyard. From here she kept track of her church

and community activities and filed household bills and documents. She used to keep a giant calendar filled with important dates for Joy's school and extra-curricular activities.

Her father's massive roll-top desk faced the opposite wall closest to the doors. From here he conducted church business, wrote his sermons, counseled parishioners, and meted out punishment when Joy tested his rules.

A couple more careful steps brought both him and the desk into view. Photo albums Joy recognized as ones from her parents' wedding and their early years together were spread open across the desk. They were usually stored on a bookshelf just to the left of the doors.

Her father sat hunched over them, his head buried in his hands. His shoulders shook and Joy now understood the source of the sound she'd heard earlier. A sound of such anguish erupted from him that her eyes widened in alarm. Her strong, stern, unforgiving father sobbed as though his heart was broken.

Joy froze at the sight of him, not sure whether she should approach or simply back away, retrieve her mother's things and slip out the same way she'd come in. Her father need never know she'd seen him.

She must have made some sound or movement because he turned slowly toward her, his face a mask of grief. For the first time, she didn't see contempt in his eyes. She saw vulnerability and possibly fear.

"Daddy?" she whispered from a mouth gone dry.

"Don't call me that. I haven't been a father to you," he croaked.

"I haven't been much of a daughter." She could admit that much, she supposed.

An open bottle of the fine Irish whiskey he favored but drank only on rare occasions, sat at the edge of the desk. A highball glass with a quarter inch of amber liquid perched next to it.

His attention returned to the photo albums, one of which held her baby pictures. "It wasn't your fault. None of it was your fault. Still, I blamed you."

Joy moved a bit closer. "Blamed me? For what?"

He gave a harsh laugh. "For being born."

Joy stared at him. He turned a page in the book. Then another. Surely, he wasn't going to stop his explanation there. "Why? I don't understand."

"I wasn't unhappy when we learned we were expecting a child. I always knew we'd have a family. I welcomed the start of one, but..." He trailed away and turned another page to a large studio photo of her mother holding her. Joy had seen the picture many times and knew she was no longer an infant when it was taken, but closer to a year.

"But what?" she asked, her voice louder than she intended.

"She got sick."

"Who got sick? Mom?"

He traced a finger around the image of her mother. "She almost died, but she wouldn't give you up. The doctors warned her..." Again, he trailed off.

This was news to Joy. She'd never questioned her single child status. With plenty of friends and cousins she'd never really longed for brothers and sisters.

"I couldn't bear the thought of losing her." Her father swallowed hard. "She's all I ever wanted. All I ever needed."

"You saw me as a threat." She couldn't keep the bitterness out of her tone.

A sudden turn of his head and his watery eyes pinned her.

So much became clear to Joy all at once. "If you lost her, it'd be my fault."

"She nearly died when you were born. And yes, I blamed you. It took her months to recover. I was afraid I'd come home one day to find her gone."

"And you'd be stuck with me."

"It was never the same after that. You took so much of her time and her energy."

"Her love," Joy inserted before he could. Because now it all started to make sense. "You resented it. You resented *me.*"

She gave him credit; he didn't deny it. "I knew it was wrong. I knew I should love you. But I couldn't. I was so afraid of losing her."

"Wow." Joy slumped into the visitor's chair near the desk trying to absorb her father's words.

"I tried," he said, "to do right by you, to raise you right. Because maybe that would make up for...for..."

"For not being able to love me." Joy's eyes filled with tears. Her sense that her father didn't love her was one thing. To have that belief confirmed was another. She grabbed the bottle of whiskey and splashed some into his glass and tossed it back. Whiskey wasn't her thing and she coughed once. Twice. But in seconds a bit of warmth spread through the chill inside her.

"I drove you away." More tears leaked from his eyes, and he swiped at them as if annoyed with them or with himself for displaying such weakness. "But when you left, I was glad you were gone."

Joy stared at him. "Fuck you."

His eyebrows raised but he let the profanity pass without comment. "Your whole life you'd done nothing but drive a wedge between us. You'd been gone for months and there was finally peace in the house. When you called that time, I knew if you came back there'd be nothing but discord. Chaos."

"And you'd have to share Mom with me again."

Again, he didn't deny it.

"I knew it would be hard at first. But I thought over time, she'd get over you leaving."

"I guess you know better than anyone she never did."

He inclined his head, allowing her the point.

"But why the investigator? The yearly reports? You wanted me gone, and I was gone. You didn't want me to come home, and I didn't. So why bother?"

"By the time I learned your mother had hired the investigator, he'd already traced you to California. He'd already been paid. He offered an annual update and report for what I thought was a reasonable fee."

"That still doesn't explain why you bothered," Joy pointed out.

"For my own peace of mind. I'd banished you. That's how I thought of it. But I didn't want you to suffer. If at any time any of those reports had indicated you needed help, I'd have offered it."

"Wow. Even for a minister, you've got quite a God complex."

He dropped his head, his fingers plucking at the edge of the open album.

"So, what?" Joy went on. "You didn't think me being alone, and pregnant, and broke was suffering enough to warrant a rescue from my almighty father?"

He peered up at her, head still bowed. "I expected there'd be an insurance settlement. Social security benefits for the child." He lifted his shoulders and let them drop as if that were an adequate explanation for his behavior. He'd been right on both counts but in Joy's book that didn't justify what he'd done. Nothing could. Perhaps he knew that now.

Joy stood. "You see the irony here, don't you? All this effort to get rid of me so you wouldn't lose Mom. You lost her anyway."

He nodded. "I know," he said, his voice barely there.

For even more irony, Joy discovered she didn't have it in herself to hate him.

"After her heart attack, I was just so, I don't know. Overwrought, I guess."

"Wait. What heart attack? Mom had a heart attack?"

Art nodded. "Not too long after you left. The doctor said it was likely from the stress. At the time, that was one more thing to blame you for. Easier than blaming myself."

"She never mentioned it."

Art almost laughed. "Probably didn't want you to worry. She recovered. There weren't any lasting effects. They call it broken heart syndrome."

Joy could understand why. "I'm going to get some of Mom's things for her. She wants to stay with me for a few days."

He lifted a hand in acknowledgment.

Joy waited a beat before she turned and went upstairs to her parents' bedroom. She found an overnight bag where her mother said it would be and rummaged through the dresser drawers and closet for clothes, then the bathroom for toiletries and medications.

The short drive back to the apartment gave her time to contemplate her father's behavior. All these years when she'd lived under the assumption, the *belief*, that he'd turned his back on her. That he wanted nothing to do with her. She'd held that nugget of knowledge close to her heart. She'd allowed his behavior to nourish the seeds of bitterness between them and ultimately influence every decision she made.

But in some misguided way, he'd also thought he was protecting her mother. Even though it sounded to Joy like what he did made things worse.

Her father had been a fool, but perhaps she had been a bigger one. She'd gone it alone all these years, depriving Devonny of an extended family who, if they'd known her, would have loved her as much as Joy did. Who's to say whether Devonny would have made different choices if she'd been surrounded by family.

Accept the things you cannot change. Joy didn't have a choice. She couldn't change the past. Couldn't change what she'd done or the choices she'd made *then*. All she could do was move forward and try to do better.

Inside, her mother had tidied the kitchen. Her eyes were full of questions Joy didn't feel ready to answer tonight. She set the bag she'd packed near the table.

"I think I got everything," she said, hoping her mother didn't notice the quaver in her voice.

"Did it go...all right?"

"It's fine. Let's talk about this tomorrow, okay?"

Marcy looked as if she wanted to say more, but she capitulated. Something, Joy now knew, her mother had always done too easily. "Of course."

Joy didn't think her mother slept, although she remained quiet and kept to her side of the bed with her back to Joy. But Joy couldn't sleep. Seeing her father earlier seeming so broken, his confession, kept playing through her head as she tried to make sense of it.

Did her mother even know how important she was to her husband? Joy supposed she could understand her father being so besotted, so in love, even though she didn't think she'd ever felt that depth of emotion for a man. She could understand the fear he must have felt at the thought of losing her.

What she couldn't understand was how he could blame an innocent child. Surely God hadn't sanctioned such behavior?

For all his knowledge of theology, for all his piety, her father was still a man. A fallible human being. Being a member of the clergy didn't guarantee perfection. It couldn't protect one from twisted logic or a determination to take the wrong course of action.

Her mother reached back and patted her hip, which answered the question of whether she'd fallen asleep.

"You could pray for him," she said into the darkness. "That's what I'm doing. Pray for me too, okay?"

Joy reached down to clasp her mother's hand and didn't let go.

Chapter Twenty-Seven

J oy texted Brian first thing the following morning to let him know she'd be in late. Hashing out the events of last night with her mother would take some time.

When Joy left the bathroom, she found her mother seated at the table, her head propped in her hands while she stared into a cup of coffee. Joy squeezed Marcy's shoulder as she went to pour her own. She took a seat. When Marcy's head came up, Joy thought she'd never seen her looking worse.

"How are you doing?" Joy asked. "Did you get any sleep at all?"

"Not really." Marcy took a sip of her coffee. "I spent the night trying to wrap my head around what your father did."

"I know you're hurt—"

"Hurt?" Marcy repeated, incredulity tinging the word. "I'm so far beyond *hurt* there isn't a word for a how I feel. Hurt is when someone forgets a birthday or leaves the wet towels on the bathroom floor when you've asked a hundred times for them to be hung up. Your father didn't forget to hang up a towel, Joy. He neglected to tell me that he knew where you were. *For twenty-five years.*

"Honestly? I don't know where to go with how I feel. I'm not just beyond hurt, I'm beyond angry. I'm appalled that the man I've been living with for most of my life would do something like this. He's been lying to me. All. This. Time."

"I know, Mom, but—"

"But what?" Marcy snapped. "Surely you're not going to make excuses for him?"

"No. What he's done is inexcusable. That doesn't mean it's unforgiveable, though, does it?"

"You think I should forgive him?" Marcy sounded appalled at the very idea.

"I'm not saying you should or shouldn't," Joy said, choosing her words carefully. "But, Mom, from what he told me last night..." Joy hesitated. The revelations her father had shared were too recent, and the way they'd made her feel too raw.

Marcy's eyes narrowed. "Go on. What did he tell you?"

It wasn't her place, Joy realized, to explain her father to her mother. This was between them. "You need to talk to Dad about it."

"What did he say to you?"

"That's between him and me. Your relationship with Dad is a separate thing. Talk to him."

"I'll do no such thing. Why won't you tell me what he said?"

Joy backed away. "It's not my place, just like it wasn't my place to tell you about Devonny's films."

Marcy seemed to deflate. "I thought I had you back. That we'd grown so close. He wouldn't have a thing to do with you, but now it seems like you're cutting me out and trying to protect him even though he doesn't deserve it."

"Mom. I'm not protecting him or taking sides. I'm not putting myself in the middle of this. You two will have to hash it out."

"There's nothing to hash out," Marcy averred. "What he did was wrong. He betrayed both of us and there's no excuse that will make it right."

"When I got there last night he was crying."

"What?"

"He had all the old photo albums out. He'd been looking at pictures and crying." Joy saw no reason to mention he'd also been drinking.

Marcy's expression didn't soften one iota. "Good. After all the tears he's caused, he should shed a few of his own."

"I think you should hear his explanation before you judge him too harshly."

"The very last thing I want is to speak to him."

"Why didn't you tell me you had a heart attack after I left?"

Marcy looked away. "He told you about that? It was so long ago. It didn't do any permanent damage."

"I think it made Dad feel like he needed to protect you, though."

Marcy slammed her hand on the table making the coffee mugs jump. "I don't need to be protected from my own child! Why can neither of you get that through your heads?"

Joy knew a losing argument when she was in the middle of one. Retreat was the best plan of action. "Mom. I can't tell you what to do. Maybe you'll feel different in a day or two, but it's up to you. I've got to get ready for work. You know you are welcome to stay here as long as you like, right?" Joy hugged her, but Marcy remained stiff as a board.

The moment Joy left, Marcy called her sister, Ginny. After a brief explanation, Ginny assured her she'd be welcome to stay with her as long as she wanted. Ginny's children were all grown with families of their own and her husband, Don, had passed five years ago. Ginny still lived in the home they'd been in for almost fifty years.

She packed her few things and, rather than call or text Joy, she left her a note. Marcy didn't feel like having more conversation with her daughter. For so long, Marcy's life had followed a routine. Very little had changed in the years since Joy left. Marcy knew herself to be quietly discontent, but she hadn't known how to change it.

But now? All bets were off. Her husband's betrayal freed her in a way she never expected. Although terrified of stepping out on her own, she knew she needed distance from both Art and Joy to help her see things more clearly. Especially since it seemed to her she could no longer count on Joy's loyalty.

How could she? *I'm the one who missed her. I'm the one who welcomed her home.* Shouldn't Joy be as righteously outraged as Marcy? Yet it seemed the two most important people in her life were against her.

She needed time to reflect, to analyze, to pray, and get in touch with her own feelings. Ginny would give her that time. Her big sister had her own life and activities. She wouldn't pry, no matter how curious she was. But she'd also listen if Marcy needed to talk.

Ginny would stand up to Art, too, if the need arose. And Marcy had a feeling, once he found out where she was, there would be a need. Because right now, she wanted nothing to do with him, and she didn't know when or if that would change.

On the drive over, she contemplated the possibilities. Divorce? She couldn't conceive of such a thing. Even through all the difficult years, she'd never considered breaking her marriage vows. But hadn't Art broken them with his lie of omission? His betrayal?

Her heart already had a brittle shell around it, built up over the years of Joy's absence. But overnight it seemed to have hardened to impenetrable rock, and she began to think about what her life would be like without him.

Chapter Twenty-Eight

J oy saw it was Devonny calling and swiped to connect, feeling relieved. She didn't have anyone else to talk to about what had happened. Well, Brian, maybe. But Devonny was her family, and right now she needed to hear her daughter's voice.

"Hi, Mom. How's it going?"

"Not great, if you want to know the truth." Joy's voice reflected her tiredness. Probably her confusion as well.

Devonny's tone changed in response. "Why? What happened."

Joy gathered herself to explain. "My father? He knew where I was all along. Where we were. He used a private investigator to send him yearly reports."

"What?" Devonny sounded no less surprised than Joy had been by this revelation.

"Yes. My mother brought up the reunion with him last night and, from what she said, he blew his stack. Said he didn't want you there. He knew about your film career. When Mom asked him how, he basically threw the reports in her face."

"Oh, Mom."

"Mom walked out. She stayed with me last night. Of course, she wanted to know why I hadn't told her."

"You could have, you know. Maybe you should have."

Joy said, "It's not my story to tell, it's yours. If you even want to share it."

"I guess it doesn't matter now," Devonny said in a matter-of-fact tone. "They know. If they don't want me at the reunion, I guess that's that."

"It most certainly is not! I want you there. This is your family, too, Devonny. Your grandfather may never be on board, but that doesn't mean we can't still do the reunion."

Devonny didn't sound a hundred percent certain when she said, "I don't know, Mom."

"There's more," Joy said. "After my mom showed up and told me what happened we decided she'd spend the night with me. But she'd left without anything but the files. So, I went back to pack a bag and grab her prescriptions. I talked to my dad."

"That couldn't have gone well."

"If things were surreal before, they got even more so. He had a bunch of old photo albums out. He was crying when I got there."

"Crying?"

"I couldn't believe it, either. My tough, stern father in tears. Mom leaving devastated him. He explained a little about why he did what he did, although I'm still not sure I understand his motivations."

"What did he say?"

"He thought if he kept track of me, if anything truly awful happened, he'd be able to step in and help."

"But otherwise, he wanted nothing to do with you." Joy could hear the contempt in her daughter's voice. "As if being a widowed and pregnant teenager wasn't truly awful."

Misplaced loyalty surged to the surface just as it had when Joy'd spoken to her mother. The last thing Joy thought she'd ever do was defend her father's behavior. But for some reason she didn't want Devonny to judge him too harshly.

"Dev, I know it's a lot to ask and I don't know if all of us will ever work as a family but try to keep an open mind. Don't let my past relationship with my father color yours."

"I'll try," Devonny said after a long pause. "For you. Not for him."

Brian offered his usual support when Joy told him family problems had contributed to her lateness. He invited her to dinner at his place, and grew even more concerned when she declined, explaining that her mother was staying with her.

But when she got back to the apartment and found her mother's note, she texted him to see if meeting for dinner was still a possibility. His enthusiastic yes made her smile for what seemed like the first time all day.

She quickly changed and stopped to buy a bottle of wine. She walked through the door and into Brian's bear hug happy to absorb his genuine warmth and caring. He followed her to the kitchen, where two wineglasses were already waiting on the island counter.

"You sit yourself right down"—he instructed as he opened the wine— "and tell me everything." He pushed a glass of the New Zealand Sauvignon Blanc toward her. He lifted his own glass up before he drank, and she tapped hers against it. "To solving problems," he toasted.

Joy felt her lips curve as she took a sip. If only life were so easy that problems could be solved with a toast and a glass of wine.

Brian pushed a small plate of cheese, crackers, and fruit in her direction while he began chopping and sautéing.

"What would you say if I told you my father has been keeping tabs on me the entire time since I took off?"

Brian's knife stilled, and he stared at Joy. "Frankly? I'd be shocked. Is it true?"

"It's true." Joy sipped more wine to fortify herself and placed a square of Havarti on a cracker, knowing if she didn't eat something, the wine would get the better of her.

Brian returned to his knife work. "I guess it makes a certain kind of sense. He knew he'd driven you away, but he'd feel terrible if something bad happened to you because of it. Right?"

"That's kind of what he told me. He said if he knew I ever needed his help, he'd be there for me."

Brian gave her a quick glance. "Out of love, do you think? Or obligation?" He paused to sample the wine again. "Or guilt?"

"I don't know. Maybe a combination of all three," Joy mused. "The thing is, he never told my mother."

"Ah. But she found out."

"Yes. Because Dad lost it last night and said he didn't want Devonny there or in his house. Then he threw the yearly updates the investigator sent him at her."

"Oh, wow. Poor Marcy. Hang on a sec."

Brian unwrapped chicken breasts and began pounding them until they were thin enough for his liking. "Go on." He measured out flour and breadcrumbs in one bowl and beat an egg in another.

"Mom's beside herself when she gets to my place. I go back to the house to get her things and find my dad sobbing." Joy drank some more wine, feeling its soothing effect on her agitation. Brian abandoned his chicken prep and stared at her. "You're kidding."

"Nope. He's got all the old family photo albums out and he's absolutely wrecked."

"Pastor Arthur Harmon in tears. I can't picture it."

By the time Joy finished telling him about the conversation with her father and the one this morning with her mother, dinner was ready. They poured more wine and adjourned to the table.

"I should be too upset to eat, but this looks delicious," Joy said, cutting into the chicken before she realized she didn't need a knife. "I love it that you're such a good cook," she told him after she swallowed the first bite.

"I love it that I have someone to cook for."

Sadness washed over Joy. "What did I do without you all these years, Bri? What was I thinking?"

"No looking back." He wagged a finger at her. "Remember your Serenity Prayer. Accept what you can't change and all that."

"I know." But Joy couldn't help it. For so long, she'd been so sure about everything, the choices and decisions she'd made, the reasons for the estrangement from her family and friends. Faced with the possibility that she'd spent so many years being *wrong* wasn't something she could easily let go.

"So before, your dad wasn't speaking to you. Now it sounds like your mom is mad at you."

"She thinks I'm taking his side or something. Which I'm not. I told her she needed to talk to him. It isn't my place to explain what he did. But this morning she was pretty insistent about not wanting to have anything to do with him." Joy stared at her plate. "I feel like I came back here and screwed everything up."

"The all-powerful Joy Harmon, er, Laurence."

"Meaning?"

"Meaning you know you don't have that much influence or control over anyone but yourself. Your parents' relationship is between them. To quote some wise philosopher or psychologist or whoever, 'everything is as it should be.'"

"You think so?"

"Don't you think you and your mother deserved to know what your father did?"

"I suppose in some ways it's better that it's out in the open."

"Let's be real. What if he'd never told her, or you? When he died, you'd find those files. And then what? You can't ever ask him about it or what his reasons were. At least now there's the possibility of understanding why he did what he did."

"I hadn't thought about that."

"And honestly, Joy," Brian said, "I think you have to consider the possibility that on some level at least, your father loves you. Otherwise, why would he have bothered to make sure you were okay all this time?"

"My father loves me." Joy drained the rest of the wine into their glasses. "Now that's a concept I have a hard time wrapping my head around."

"He wouldn't be the first parent who has a funny or bizarre way of showing it," Brian pointed out.

Joy knew this to be true. All she had to do was think of some of the things she'd said and done out of love for Devonny, often misunderstood by her daughter.

"One other thing," Brian said as they stood and began to clear the table. "At the risk of sounding like a commercial for 12-step programs, all you can do is take it one day at a time and see where things lead."

"I know, right?" Joy set the plates in the sink and opened the dishwasher. "It's not like any of us have a choice, anyway. We can't leap forward or step back in time."

"Exactly." Brian scraped the leftovers into plastic containers. "Speaking of leaping forward, have you approached Granger about when he might have some more pieces ready?"

"Honestly? No, I haven't. In fact, I've hardly seen him the last week or so."

"Uh-oh. Trouble in paradise?"

"No. At least, I don't think so. He's kind of tiptoeing around Cassie, and I don't think sneaking over to my place is setting very well with him, either."

"Oh, what tangled webs we weave," Brian said as he drained the last of his wine and handed the glass to Joy to wash.

"It's really stupid, isn't it? We're adults, but we behave like children. What are we so afraid of?"

"You know what's interesting?" Brian asked, leaning against the counter while Joy continued to clean up. "There's a correlation here between your father and Granger."

Joy paused and gave him her full attention.

"The dishonesty, for lack of a better word. The sneakiness. The secretiveness."

"You're right." Joy tossed the sponge into the sink. "Oh, my God, Brian." She gave him a horrified look. "I'm right back where I was at eighteen. Sneaking around. Defying my father, who, as you may recall, told me to stay away from Granger. Afraid of getting caught by a 15-year-old."

Brian giggled. And once he got started, he couldn't stop. The absurdity of it got the better of Joy as well, and she joined him.

Chapter Twenty-Nine

"**Y**ou're making this too easy for me."

Joy turned her head to look at Granger. They were naked, their skin cooling after a frenzied bout of lovemaking. It had only been a little over a week since they'd been together, and Joy's depth of desire surprised her. Maybe she shouldn't be so willing to accept Granger on whatever terms she could have him.

"What do you mean?"

Granger turned on his side and yanked the sheet up to their waists. "I should be wining and dining you. Trying to win you."

Joy smiled. "We're in Liberty. Where might this wining and dining take place?"

"You let me sneak over here whenever I want. It doesn't seem right."

"I like having you here." She poked him in the shoulder. "I like having *you*."

He grabbed the finger she poked him with and kissed the tip. "I like being here." Joy found herself once again drowning in the intensity of his gaze.

"I'm not going to expect more than you can give. If I'm not happy with this," she waved her hand back and forth between them, "I'll let you know. So, what's the problem, again?"

"You deserve better."

Joy could see Granger meant what he said. Believed it. She turned to her side to face him, scrunching her pillow under head. "Well, let's see. You're unapologetically heterosexual. Sexy. A fantastic lover." She ignored Granger's splutter of disbelief at the adjective she'd chosen. "Employed. Artistic."

Granger rolled his eyes. "Stop."

"A family man who goes to church. Intelligent. I'm pretty sure there's a sense of humor lurking in there somewhere, too. A guy who always tries to do the right thing."

Granger moved closer and buried his face in her neck. "Please stop."

"Did I mention what nice manners you display when you're so inclined?"

Much later, Granger tracked Joy as she returned to bed from the bathroom. He yawned before he drew her in close to him, spooning her, hearing her sigh as she got comfortable. "You never did tell me why Miss Marcy stayed here the other night," he reminded her, even though he sounded exhausted.

"They had a fight."

"Your parents? No, that can't be right. They never fight."

Joy laughed without humor. She turned to Granger even though she could hardly see him in the dark. "This was more than a fight. A major blow up."

"About what?"

"My daughter. Me."

"What's your daughter got to do with anything? They've never met her, right? Isn't that what this family reunion is for?"

As succinctly as possible, Joy outlined what had happened between her parents and how Devonny's history played into it. "I wanted it to be her decision to tell them about her past. But my mother didn't understand. She's staying with my Aunt Ginny now."

"That sucks."

She waited for Granger to say something else, but he didn't. Nor would he unless he started talking in his sleep. She swallowed her disappointment, wishing she had a partner she could truly share with. Someone to offer perspective or at least sympathize with what she was going through. She turned away and closed her eyes. But right now, at least, Granger wasn't that partner. Maybe he never would or could be. He'd been right earlier. She deserved better.

Chapter Thirty

C assie and Kye were smushed together in the worn and torn back seat of Zak's van. Guitar cases, mikes and stands, amplifiers, a toolbox, and another box filled with connector cords crammed the cargo area behind them. Only Farley— Cassie didn't know if that was his first name or his last—traveled alone in his own ancient Jeep, the entire vehicle filled with his keyboard, Kye's drums, and anything else they couldn't fit elsewhere.

Cassie wanted to gag at the combination of body odor and cigarette smoke, along with the dirt and spills that had sunk into the seats and mashed down the carpeting. The windows in the back weren't the kind you could open. On the road for five minutes and all she longed for was a breath of fresh air. Even though Zak's window was partially down, smoke from his cigarettes fouled the late spring air. The only part of the trip she planned to enjoy was Kye's thigh pressed against hers, their hands clasped in his lap.

Kye had showered earlier, she could tell. He smelled clean and his Imagine Dragons tee shirt still held the scent of laundry detergent and dryer sheets, which was more than she could say for the rest of the band.

Cassie congratulated herself on her ruse working. Her dad had called Lindsey's mom earlier to double-check the arrangements for Cassie to spend the night and that Lindsey's mom knew about it and planned to be home.

Cassie went to Lindsey's after school and stayed just long enough to silence her cell phone and hide it in the bathroom linen closet before inventing a mysterious illness involving a headache and nausea. As soon as Cassie suggested the possibility of food poisoning, Lindsey's sympathy outweighed her disappointment. Lindsey's mom worked until five, but Cassie insisted she'd be able to walk the few blocks home. Kye picked her up before she made it halfway.

It was only a little lie, and Cassie knew the chances of getting caught were minimal. After the gig, Kye would drop her off on the corner and she'd go home. If her dad woke up or when he discovered her there in the morning, she'd tell him Lindsey hadn't felt well, so Lindsey's mom had brought her home.

Another little lie. It hurt no one, and she got some freedom. The chance to go somewhere. Do something. And hang out with Kye outside of school.

She and Kye hadn't done anything except hold hands and exchange a few kisses. Cassie loved that Kye was kind of shy. He didn't know how cute he was. All the girls at school thought so.

Kye wasn't like other guys, not that Cassie had much experience, but she knew girls who didn't mind sharing theirs. Mostly guys only wanted one thing. Sex. A hand job. A blow job. Whatever they could get. If a girl let a guy touch her boobs, that was a major score. Some of the girls Cassie knew had lost their virginity back in seventh or eighth grade. They acted so sophisticated and uncaring about it now. Cassie didn't think she could pull that off.

She'd talked a bit about it with Pastor Art one day when she'd been helping him with the rosebushes and flower beds around the church. She couldn't remember how they'd even got on the subject. Oh, maybe because she'd been telling him about Diane Fitzgerald, a girl a year ahead of her at school. Diane was pregnant, and the rumored father of her baby, Johnny Antonelli, was nowhere to be found.

Pastor Art shook his head. "I'm sorry to hear that. That's not what God intended, that's for sure."

Cassie looked up from patting the soil around the plants he'd set into the ground. "What do you mean?"

Art took another petunia from the flat and set it in the hole he'd dug. He sat back on his haunches and looked at Cassie directly. "I guess you're old enough to talk to plainly about this. Young people always think they know everything. Not just your generation, that's not what I'm saying. Every generation, including mine. They always want to experience everything as soon as they can. Even sex. They forget they've got their whole adult life ahead of them."

He went back to work, setting the petunias in place, while Cassie scooted along next to him, replacing the dirt he'd dug up and securing each plant in the ground.

"God intended sexual relations between a man and a woman to bond them together, for one thing," he went on. "To create children, too, to carry on the generations to come. Ideally, those things occur between two people who love each other and plan to spend their lives as a couple once they're married. It's not meant to be a one-time thing in the backseat of a car."

Cassie thought Pastor Art could be right about a few things, but not about the wait until you're married part. No one did that anymore.

She liked Kye, but she wasn't planning to climb into the back seat with him any time soon. That didn't sound comfortable at all. Or romantic either.

Not only was Kye in no hurry, but she got the sense that he wouldn't be rushed into something he didn't want to do or wasn't ready for, no matter what it was. He was methodical that way. He liked to study things, think about them, before he made a decision. Maybe it would drive other girls crazy, that lack of spontaneity, but Cassie found it attractive. It reminded her of her dad a little bit, not that she'd ever admit that Kye was anything like her dad. Ever.

But she'd seen how her dad took his time with things, whether it was a leaky faucet or paint choices for the living room. He couldn't be rushed, but once he'd decided, he was all in.

She wondered sometimes if that's how it had been with her mother. If he'd taken his time, got to know her, went out with her a whole bunch of times before he decided to ask her to marry him. And once he did, he was all in. Committed. Sticking, even when, young as she was, Cassie had sensed the wheels were coming off her parents' marriage.

And since the divorce, it was like her dad couldn't move. Although she'd been anticipating something bad happening, Cassie hadn't known how it would feel for her mother to rip herself out of their lives. To just leave like that. Cassie had been sad for a long time. So had her dad.

Lately he'd seemed a little happier. She'd heard him whistling the other morning in the kitchen. Her father. *Whistling!*

She knew the reason. Joy.

But Cassie didn't trust Joy. Joy didn't seem like someone who would stick. She'd been gone for years and hadn't ever called her own parents. Who did something like that? She'd made her parents sad. Now she was back, and Miss Marcy was so happy.

Cassie tried to imagine leaving her dad the same way her mother had. Just leaving and never speaking to him again. She knew she couldn't do it. No matter how mad he made her. No matter how unfair he was. She could walk off in a huff and give him the silent treatment for a couple of days. But not speak to him for years? No. She knew she couldn't do that. Wouldn't do that.

She didn't like to think her dad was getting attached to Joy. What if he had sex with her? Bonded with her like Pastor Art said? The thought made Cassie's stomach churn. And if Joy left, her dad would go back to being sad. Maybe even sadder than he'd been when Mom took off.

Kye squeezed her hand. "You okay?"

She turned his way and gave him a smile. "Sure."

He drew his forefinger down between her eyebrows and gave her his lopsided grin. "You were thinking awful hard about something."

Cassie mustered a smile. "Not really."

The two girls Cassie had met before were at the festival. Cassie wasn't surprised. Wherever the band was, they were there. Holly and Ash were their names. Not Ashley. Just Ash. That's how she introduced herself. Holly was the one with the blonde hair and the dark roots. But now all her hair had big streaks of neon pink in it. Cassie didn't think it was such a good look.

Ash wore a pair of faded overalls over a tank top. Her hair was cut pixie short, and she wore it kind of spiky. "You can hang with us, if you want." Her voice was low and husky, sort of like a guy's.

Cassie saw Holly roll her eyes, but she didn't care. *Safety in numbers.* Her dad had drilled that into her head. Cassie hadn't really thought it through. What had she planned on doing? Wandering around the festival by herself? Waiting near the stage for the band's set to end?

They weren't scheduled to go on until nine. Cassie figured what? An hour on stage? Then getting the equipment packed up and the drive back. So maybe by one o'clock she'd be home.

But until then... "Okay. Thanks," she said to Ash.

Cassie hadn't known what a music festival entailed exactly, never having been to one in person. The Internet could only tell you so much, but apparently, it was an excuse to party with a massive number of people. Listening to whoever took the stage seemed secondary to everything else going on. Holly and Ash were charged with hawking the band's one and only homemade CD and tee shirts. They had a folding table, but chairs were in short supply.

If she hadn't been so fascinated people-watching, Cassie would have been bored out of her mind. She'd never seen so many tattoos, for one thing. Such a variety of clothing choices. There were couples with children, babies in strollers even, wandering from stage to stage. There were three stages and the bands rotated. While one was performing on one stage, another was setting up on the second stage, and at the third stage, a band was breaking down their equipment.

"Tomorrow and Sunday are the real draws with the bigger names," Ash informed her. "But even being invited to perform on Friday is a big deal. This is one of the hottest festivals in Ohio."

"If Stomp Freaks' lead singer hadn't gotten appendicitis, we wouldn't even be here," Holly put in. She looked at Cassie. "They got turned down, just like last year. They're a replacement band."

"But still," Ash said.

"But still," Holly mimicked in a high-pitched whine. She addressed Cassie again. "Ash thinks she's dating the next Kurt Cobain." In a loud whisper, Holly informed Cassie, "She ain't."

Cassie glanced at Ash, who seemed unperturbed by Holly. "Everyone has to start somewhere," Ash said. "Zak has a great voice."

"Yeah, and it gets better the more weed he smokes and the more Jameson he downs," Holly muttered.

Both girls had giant go cups crammed with ice and clear liquid. Cassie didn't know what they were drinking, but she suspected it wasn't pure soda. She shifted her attention to the stage where the band was almost finished setting up. She looked at her burner phone while pretending to scan her text messages. It was nearly ten. No one cared about sticking to performance schedules.

She studied the crowd again. The same flow of people as before, just the faces and the ink had changed. A couple of uniformed cops patrolled the perimeter. She'd seen them once before. A lot of people camped overnight and stayed the entire weekend.

Portable toilets were set up in a line on either end of the field where the audience milled. Although each performance seemed to have its own group of diehard fans clustered at the base of the stage, a lot of the crowd were simply hanging out, talking, drinking, sharing weed. Cassie didn't know what else they might be sharing.

Some were moving in a staggering lurch from place to place. A few were passed out on blankets or in the grass. Almost everyone seemed slightly older than Cassie, or considerably younger.

She joined Ash and Holly when they packed up the table and tee shirts and went to listen to the band. For the first time, Cassie thought they weren't bad. Zak appeared to feed off the live audience, if you could call it that, and up his game. In fact, they all seemed to be more into performing than practicing. Although, to be fair, she'd only ever heard them practice one time for about five minutes.

Ash had explained to her that the festival was a good way to get exposure and how it might lead to more live gigs. Cassie remained skeptical. But she enjoyed watching Kye get into performing and allowed herself a brief fantasy of the band hitting it big and traveling the globe. She, of course, would go along as Kye's girlfriend.

After the performance, Cassie didn't try to hide a big yawn as she watched the guys load the last of the equipment into the van. She was kind of sorry she'd sneaked out for this, although she wouldn't say anything to Kye. For most of the evening she'd wished she'd stayed home or spent the night at Lindsey's. At least then, she'd have had some decent food and be asleep by now.

She hadn't been willing to risk a real case of food poisoning from any of the food trucks serving the festival. She'd come close to buying a corn dog until she saw some girl puking one up. Her friends were holding her hair back and Cassie guessed the girl was probably drunk, and getting sick had nothing to do with what she'd eaten. But it put her off the idea of a breaded hot dog on a stick.

She bought a can of Coke and made it last the entire night. She'd used the portable toilet once, enlisting Ash to walk with her. Ash was the friendlier of the two, although Ash said Holly's bark was worse than her bite. Ash linked her arm through Cassie's. "She wants everybody to think she's a badass, but she works in a daycare. She's getting a degree in early childhood education."

Maybe if she scraped most of the makeup off her face, pulled her hair back, and wore jeans and a tee shirt, Holly would look like the average babysitter. Ash worked in a call center for an insurance company and took college classes online.

"That's it. Let's go," Zak called. He opened the driver's door.

"He's not driving, is he?" Cassie murmured to Kye when he indicated for her to get in.

"It's his van," Kye said.

"He's drunk and he's high," Cassie said.

Patrick overheard and shrugged. "He'll be fine. He hasn't had that much." He climbed into the front passenger seat.

Never drive under the influence. And if you ever drink and you're too drunk to drive, call me. Or whoever's driving is drunk, call me. You won't get in trouble, I promise. I'd rather come and get you and know you're safe than risk a DUI on your record. Or worse. Cassie could hear her dad's voice in her head. He'd told both her and her brother Cameron this.

Patrick rolled his window down. "Can we go already?"

"You drive," Cassie said.

Patrick turned and said something to Zak she couldn't hear. The girls were long gone and so was Farley's Jeep.

"Zak's driving. Either get in or stay here. Up to you."

"Cassie—" Kye began.

"Fine." She got in and buckled her seatbelt. She knew she could call her dad. Knew he'd come and get her. And she wouldn't get in trouble for not getting in a car with someone under the influence at the wheel. But she'd get in a *helluva* lot of trouble for sneaking out. For hiding her phone and lying. For being so far away from home. If she called her dad now, she'd have to wait for him for more than an hour. Alone. And there were some scary looking people around. Unless Kye would wait with her. But she didn't know how to ask him. He'd think she was a baby.

She stared at the back of Zak's head, willing him to sober up and get everyone back to Liberty in one piece. His gaze caught hers in the rearview mirror, and he gave her a shit-eating grin before he pulled out onto the highway. She looked out the side window, angry at herself. Kye reached for her hand, and she pulled hers away, annoyed with him for not backing her up. Surely, he could see Zak was in no shape to be behind the wheel. He could have agreed with her, at least.

Zak crossed the divided line and overcorrected, running the van along the shoulder for a quarter mile before he got it back in his lane. "You okay, man?" Patrick murmured.

Zak took a hand off the wheel and patted the air between them. He rolled his window all the way down and Cassie welcomed the fresh air even though it blew right in her face, whipping her hair all over the place. If wind-blown hair meant an alert Zak, she wouldn't complain.

But the window down didn't help. Again, the van drifted into the other lane and Zak jerked the van back into another over correction. Cassie saw a sign for a truck stop two miles away and made a decision. "There's a truck stop at the next exit. Stop there and let me out, okay?" Patrick glanced at her over his shoulder. "I'll call my dad to come and get me."

Zak glared at her in the rearview. His eyes were bloodshot, and he blinked rapidly. "I'm not pulling over. There might be cops around."

"Yes, you are. Let me out there or I'll make you wish you had."

"What's the big deal?" Patrick asked Zak. "Drop her off so we don't have to listen to her bitch."

"Can't leave her there alone, man," Zak said.

Cassie rolled her eyes. Like he cared.

The van's tires bumped along the shoulder again. Zak yanked the wheel too hard, sending it into the next lane.

He straightened it out moments before a semi passed them, horn blaring.

"Jesus," Cassie muttered.

"I'll wait with her. Let us both out at the truck stop."

Kye mouthed to Cassie, *You were right.*

"Oh, for fuck's sake," Patrick threw up his hands. "I don't bring you home, I'll get my ass chewed," he told Kye.

"The exit's coming up. Pull off and let us out, Zak. I mean it."

"She *means* it." Zak mimicked in a high-pitched voice. He laughed before he glanced in the rearview once again. "What are you going to do if I don't?"

Cassie kicked his seat hard. "Pull over, asshole. You don't even have to take the ramp. Just let us out on the shoulder and we'll walk."

"Oh, no, your highness. I'll drop you right at the door. Will that be good enough for you? I don't know where you found this one, Kye, but she's about as high maintenance as they come."

"Shut up and take the exit, all right? That's all you have to do," Kye said to Zak. Even though Kye didn't exactly come to her defense, being pissed at Zak and backing her up counted big time. Cassie's heart swelled.

"This is messed up," Patrick said to Zak. "You going to drop these kids off in the middle of nowhere? Just let me drive, man."

Zak pounded the steering wheel with his fist. "No. They don't wanna ride with me, they can kiss my ass."

He looked over at Patrick, then over his shoulder to glare at Cassie again as he veered off the highway onto the ramp without slowing down. It wasn't a long ramp, and they sped to the top of it. Getting to the truck stop required a left-hand turn. But Zak didn't make it. Instead, he went straight across, heading for the on ramp to get back on the highway. But he'd miscalculated the slight deviation in where the ramp started, which wasn't directly across from the off ramp. The tire dipped as the van missed the pavement and once again Zak over corrected.

"Shit." Cassie muttered certain she could see what would happen next. She shoved Kye forward. "Grab your ankles," she told him, as she grabbed hers and started to pray. She felt the van hurtle down the embankment over the bumpy grassy slope. The seat belt and harness ate into her stomach and her shoulder. The van groaned and tilted and rolled.

She screamed, but she wasn't the only one. Metal creaked; glass shattered. The old van sounded like it was caving in on itself. Cassie's head smacked into the window first and the top of the van second. She had no idea how long it took for the van to come to a stop.

Chapter Thirty-One

G ranger's phone woke him out of a sound, satisfying sleep. It took him a minute to orient himself in the less familiar surroundings of Joy's apartment. Her bed. And another to figure out he'd left his phone in his pants pocket and his pants were...somewhere. He found them on the floor at the foot of the bed and answered before the call went to voicemail.

He stared at the digital numbers of the clock on Joy's nightstand as he listened and tried to comprehend what he was hearing.

"You're absolutely certain it's my daughter?" He listened as anxiety with fear climbing on its back clawed at his insides. "I understand. I'll be there as soon as I can."

Joy turned on the light and sat up, the sheet pulled to her chest. Granger located his shirt and yanked it on. Stuffed his feet into his shoes, picked up his socks. "That was the hospital in Barton. They said Cassie was hurt in a car accident. I have to go."

"Do you...?"

He didn't wait to hear the rest of Joy's question. He was only glad his keys and wallet were still in his pants pockets. He leapt into the truck and drove like the desperate man he was through the deserted streets.

When he reached the state road that would take him to the highway, he instructed his phone to call Lindsey's mother. She wasn't going to like a phone call at four a.m., but neither had he.

She answered, her voice groggy with sleep. "Granger? What's wrong?"

He'd known Sara McKenna since grade school. She'd married and divorced Toby McKenna, his former lab partner from biology class. "What's wrong is Cassie is supposed to be spending the night at your house. With Lindsey."

"Right. But she didn't. She came over after school, but then she told Lindsey she wasn't feeling well, so she went home. I didn't think anything of it. Is she alright?"

"No. I don't think she is." Granger hung up. He'd checked the tracking app earlier. Cassie's phone was where she was supposed to be. It hadn't occurred to him that Cassie herself was not.

Next, he called his son. Unlike Sara, Cameron sounded wide awake and alert when he answered. "Dad?"

"Hey, Buddy." Emotion clogged Granger's throat. Cameron had escaped much of the brunt of his mother's leaving. He'd been almost out of high school by then, almost grown. It hadn't affected him the way it had Cassie.

"What's wrong?"

Granger took a moment to get hold of himself. "Cassie."

"What, Dad. Tell me."

Ah, screw it. He didn't have to be the tough guy with his own son, did he? Tears blurred his vision and leaked from his eyes. "I don't know. She's been in a car accident. That's all I know. She's at the hospital in Barton. They just called. I thought she was spending the night with Lindsey McKenna, but..." Granger sniffed. "Jesus. Hang on."

He leaned over to the glove compartment and found a pile of napkins left from a fast-food lunch. He blew his nose on one and wiped his eyes before he said, "You still there?"

"I'm here. But not for long. I'll meet you at the hospital."

"Cameron, you can't—"

"Bullshit. It's the weekend. I don't have work. I'll meet you there."

He hung up. Granger concentrated on the road. Luckily, at such an early hour there were hardly any other travelers. His thoughts boomeranged from the shock of learning Cassie wasn't where he thought she was. He'd thought himself a responsible father, tracking her phone simply because he knew she was never without it. But she'd fooled him. It made him wonder what he'd done that Cassie would go to such lengths to deceive him.

He only wanted to keep her safe. She didn't realize how young she was, and there was no way he could convince her. In his book, fifteen wasn't old enough to date one on one, no matter what other more progressive parents thought. He needed to know where she was and who she was with.

He shuddered as he recalled following her to that garage, seeing the guys and girls older than Cassie, one of them offering her a cigarette. Turned out she didn't know any of them except for one boy, the drummer, from her school.

He wondered how many other times she'd pulled what she had last night. Faking him out. The other times she'd told him she'd be at a friend's but the only thing at the friend's house was Cassie's phone.

From there, his mind jumped to every bad thing that could happen to a 15-year-old girl in today's world. Even in a rural area like theirs, kids disappeared. Their bodies found weeks or months later. Or they were never found at all. STDs. Pregnancy. Drugs. Drinking. Sex trafficking.

The knot in Granger's stomach grew. Or she could get in a car with an inexperienced driver, or one who was under the influence, and get in an accident.

"We don't know the extent of her injuries," the hospital representative had said. "She did, however, regain consciousness."

He found nothing the woman told him reassuring. Cassie could be brain damaged or paralyzed. He didn't know how he'd cope with such a situation.

One thing he did know. Nothing he'd been doing in dealing with Cassie was working. If she recovered, no, *when* she recovered, they were going to have to figure things out together.

They showed him into a private room in the ER as soon as he got there. Granger stopped just inside the door and stared at the cot where Cassie lay. She wore a hospital gown and a green sheet covered her from chest to toe. Her hair was in disarray, and he could see bits of glass still clinging to the dark strands. Tiny cuts covered her face, probably from the same glass. One arm was in a sling. But there were no machines attached to her. No oxygen masks. No plastic bags of fluids hanging nearby.

He approached slowly. Her eyes were closed, and he thought she must be asleep. A sense of gratitude overwhelmed him. Surely, she couldn't be badly injured if she wasn't being closely monitored. There would be no paralysis or brain damage. He slid his hand beneath hers and noticed the numerous small cuts covering the back of her hand.

"Daddy?" Tears overflowed her eyes and into her hair.

He curved a hand around her cheek and bent low, careful of the scratches. "I'm here, baby." His own tears began to fall. He pressed a kiss to the most uninjured part of her forehead he could locate and straightened. He squeezed her hand. "I'm not going anywhere."

"I'm so sorry I snuck out. I lied to Lindsey and her mom. We went to this music festival, and it was so stupid. I hated it. I only went so I could be with Kye. Zak was drunk, or high. I didn't want him to drive. But he wouldn't let anyone else drive. And you told me never to get into a car with someone who was drunk. To call you. But I was afraid, and Patrick said Zak was okay to drive. But he wasn't. I made him pull over to let us out at the truck stop so I could call you to come get me. He crossed the road to the ramp, and we went down the embankment..." the words tumbled out of Cassie in a torrent, but the more she talked the more agitated she became until she was nearly hyperventilating.

Granger smoothed a hand over her hair, wincing as the glass fragments grazed his fingers. "It's okay, honey. It's all right. Shhh. Calm down. It's going to be all right." Granger reassured her even though he didn't know if he spoke the truth or not.

The door opened and a short man entered and strode to the other side of the gurney. He had black hair, dark skin, and wire-rimmed glasses, behind which his eyes looked concerned but friendly. A surgical mask covered most of his face.

"Hello," he said to Granger. "I am Dr. Patel." His speech had the rhythm of someone born outside the US, but he spoke perfect English. "You are the father?"

Granger introduced himself.

"Very good." He turned his attention to Cassie. "And you, Miss? How are you feeling?" He consulted an iPad he'd brought in with him.

"Everything kind of hurts," Cassie admitted.

"I am not surprised. You have a lot of bruising, inside and out." He looked at Granger. "Partly from the seatbelt and shoulder harness. Especially here." He indicated Cassie's sling. "A fractured clavicle. Your daughter bent forward before impact. Probably a smart move on her part, but the restraints added pressure because of it. The vehicle rolled at least once, so you can imagine what it took to keep her in her seat.

"Expect the discomfort to continue until the bruising dissipates. The fracture should heal on its own if she keeps the arm immobilized." He focused on Cassie. "That means in the sling." He addressed Granger once again. "She has a bump or two on the head as well. Numerous lacerations from flying glass, none of which are life threatening. We'll want to keep her overnight for observation, make sure she has no signs of concussion or internal bleeding. If all goes well, I expect to release her tomorrow."

Granger sighed in relief at those last three words.

"Any questions?"

Granger shook his head.

"How's Kye?" Cassie asked.

"I assume you are asking about one of the other passengers. I can't tell you anything about them except that the three other passengers were all brought in alive.

"Sir, you are welcome to stay until she is moved to a room, okay?"

"Thank you, Doctor."

Granger saw no need to call anyone else until later. He texted Joy because he figured she might still be awake and wondering. He'd wait to call his dad and Art.

After she'd been moved to a regular room, Granger tried to get comfortable in the reclining chair. Cassie finally dozed off. He wished he could as well, but sleep eluded him. His brain refused to shut down as it ran through all the what-if scenarios. If Cassie had died it would have killed him. Somehow, some way, he was going to figure out how to be a better father to her. He thought that probably would start with him stopping being so mired down in his own sadness and confusion.

Adele's desertion left him feeling worthless. Why wasn't he worth sticking around for? He had to admit he'd felt the same way after his mother died. Why hadn't she fought harder? Didn't she want to be there for him? That kind of logic only made sense to a kid who needed his mother. He wasn't a child anymore.

Instead of acknowledging his own pain or even trying to work through it, Granger withdrew further and further. He spent hours in the garage creating his sculptures. Creating his own world, he supposed, of inanimate people who couldn't leave him, unless he decided to let them go.

He'd abandoned Cassie in a way. They could have shared their grief and confusion. Instead, they'd isolated themselves from each other. She resented him and rightly so because she'd needed him, and he hadn't been there. No wonder they'd grown so far apart.

When they got home, when Cassie felt better, he'd talk to her. He'd hate like hell to admit to his mistakes, to share his feelings with her, but he knew he had to do it or face losing her for good.

He opened his eyes when someone gently jostled his shoulder. Cameron stood before him, and Granger didn't think he'd been so glad to see anyone in his life. He stood and they embraced, drawing comfort from their shared concern.

"How is she?" Cameron whispered when they drew apart, his gaze sweeping over his sleeping sister.

Granger motioned him out into the corridor. "She should be okay except for some minor cuts and a whole bunch of bruises. Oh, and a fractured clavicle. They're keeping her to watch for signs of concussion or internal bleeding. She'll probably be released tomorrow."

Cameron sagged in relief. "Oh. Wow. That's good news."

"Yeah. We dodged a bullet."

"You look like hell, Dad," Cameron said.

Granger almost smiled. "Been up all night."

"There's a motel down the road. You could get a room later. Get some sleep."

"I don't want to leave her alone."

Cameron gave him a gentle shoulder punch. "That's why I'm here."

"Maybe." Granger wasn't ready to agree to anything just yet. "Meanwhile, what do you think about doing a coffee run?"

"I'm on it."

Chapter Thirty-Two

In the days and weeks following Cassie's accident, Granger worked less, but he was more tired than he'd ever been. If he'd walked on eggshells with Cassie before, now he tiptoed around broken glass, afraid of doing anything that might upset her further.

When he absolutely had to be away, either his dad and stepmom stayed at the house or else Marcy came. Cassie insisted she didn't need a babysitter, but Granger cajoled her into allowing it for his own peace of mind.

Most frightening of all was the way she gave in. No glares. No sarcasm. No disrespectful one-liners. Just a meek, "Okay, Dad." The accident had taken all the snark out of her but left her with none of her former spunk and sparkle.

She kept to her room unless she needed the bathroom or something from the kitchen. But she had little interest in food, and Granger worried about that too. How could she heal if she didn't eat?

He'd had about as much well-meaning advice as he could take from his dad and Alison, the doctors, the counselor from the school, the parents of Cassie's friends and, in some cases, the friends themselves.

Leave her alone. Try to get her to talk. She'll eat when she's hungry. Let her sleep. She needs to get out more.

Granger's head spun with suggestion overload, and he started to resent it all. Cassie was his daughter. He'd deal with her as he saw fit.

Yeah, he asked himself. *How'd that work out?*

In truth, if he'd been drowning in doubt about his parenting abilities before the accident, now he found himself sinking to the bottom. And bad news just kept on coming.

Early this morning, Zak Lajeski had died without ever regaining consciousness. It wasn't an unexpected outcome. He hadn't worn a seatbelt and he'd been thrown from the vehicle. There'd been little hope of his survival. Granger dreaded telling Cassie, but he wanted her to hear it from him. He wanted to be there for her. He sent Marcy away as soon as he finished a job he couldn't put off. Now he stood outside Cassie's room, steeling himself for what he had to do.

He knocked lightly, hoping against hope she might be sleeping, and he could delay his unpleasant task longer. But she called for him to come in. She'd propped herself up against the headboard and had her laptop open, a textbook nearby.

"Hi, Dad."

"Hi, honey." Granger stepped into the room and turned her desk chair around so he could sit next to her. "What are you doing?"

"Trying to catch up on homework." She held up her right hand. "Not easy typing a 1500-word essay one-handed.

"Are you feeling better?"

"Not really. But if I get too far behind, I'll never catch up."

Granger didn't reply. What he had to say weighed too heavily on his mind.

She read the look on his face. "What happened?"

His gaze skittered away from hers. "I have some bad news."

"Is it Kye?"

"No. Not Kye." As far as Granger knew, Kye was recovering from his injuries at home, same as Cassie. "It's about Zak."

"Tell me."

There was no easy way to say it. "He died this morning."

"He died?" Tears surged into her eyes. She pushed the laptop aside and reached for a tissue from the box on her nightstand. "Are you sure?"

"I'm sure. The patient liaison from the hospital called."

"It's all my fault," Cassie burst out. Tears began to flow in earnest.

"Cassie," Granger said, horrified she thought so. "None of this is your fault."

"It's *all* my fault, Dad."

There was the drama he'd been missing from Cassie, but now he wished she'd go back to her listless doldrums.

"If I hadn't sneaked out of the house, if I hadn't lied about spending the night at Lindsey's, if I hadn't gone to the concert, if I hadn't been in that van," she sobbed, "I wouldn't have given Zak a hard time about driving drunk. He wouldn't have taken the exit. There wouldn't have been an accident."

Cassie cried until she started to hiccup, cried like she'd never stop. Granger pushed the book and laptop farther away and sat on the bed next to her and put his arm around her shoulders, careful of her sling. She didn't push him away. She just kept crying.

"Cassie," he said, smoothing a hand over her tangled hair. He tried to think of the best way to phrase what he wanted to say. "Let's think about this logically for a minute, okay?"

She huffed, like a little kid, after an outburst. But she didn't try to escape his embrace and didn't tell him to shut up.

"I'm not going to argue the points about you sneaking out and lying. You did those things."

Cassie hiccupped again and pressed the tissue to her nose. Blotted at the tears. She bowed her head and nodded. Granger's heart broke for her. It was no relief to him that he didn't have to ground her or take away her privileges. Nothing he could do would be worse than her own guilt and remorse.

"You didn't help Zak drink, though, did you? He made that decision entirely on his own."

He continued to stroke her hair, comforting himself perhaps more than her, giving him the strength somehow to get through this. "You didn't tell him to get behind the wheel, did you?"

"No," she said, her voice clogged with tears. "I tried to talk him out of it, but—"

"But he's legally an adult, and he didn't listen to you."

"I should have called you," she said dully. "That's what I should have done."

Granger was almost afraid to ask, but he wanted to hear her say it. "Why didn't you?"

Beneath his hand, Cassie's head moved back and forth. "Because even if you weren't mad at me for getting in a car with a drunk driver, I knew I'd be in big trouble for everything else."

Unfortunately, Granger couldn't argue with that. He knew he'd have been livid with her, even if she'd belatedly used the good sense he knew she had.

"Cassie, you know you can't go back and change anything you did, any choice you made. But consider if you hadn't been in the van, but everyone else was. Zak was still drunk. He could have caused an even worse accident. He could have collided with another car and hurt a lot of other people, even killed them. Kye and Patrick might have been injured worse than they are."

Cassie sighed like an exhausted toddler and leaned against him. Granger took that as encouragement to keep talking. He couldn't remember the last time he'd hugged her or touched her before the accident. Somehow, he'd got out of the habit, and she hadn't sought any affection from him. Or had she and he hadn't picked up her signals? He could berate himself later. Right now, the important thing was to lift the cloud of misplaced guilt hovering over her.

"You did some things wrong, but you did some things right, too. Kye could have been hurt much worse if he'd been sitting upright. So could you."

He gave her shoulders a squeeze. "You can't take responsibility for what others choose to do."

"I wish she'd told you." Cassie's voice held a wistful note, one filled with regret, and Granger had no idea what she was talking about.

He relaxed his hold on her and looked down, but he couldn't see her face very well. "She who?"

"Joy."

A chill ran through him. "Told me what?"

"That she saw me sneak out."

Granger changed positions so he could see Cassie's face. "When was this?" He tried to keep his tone soft and coaxing but failed miserably.

Cassie either didn't notice or didn't care. She gave a slight shrug. "I don't know. A few weeks after she moved in, I guess."

Granger thought back. Prior, possibly, to any real relationship starting between the two of them. But still. "How do you know she saw you?"

"She told me."

"What did she tell you?"

"That she saw me sneak out. She said she wouldn't tell you unless she caught me doing it again."

"Did she?"

Cassie looked at him directly, her eyes still wet, her face blotchy. "Did she catch me again?"

"No. I meant, is that really what she said? That she wasn't going to tell me unless she caught you again."

"That's what she said. She said I reminded her of her daughter. And of herself."

Granger didn't respond, too busy fighting the feelings building inside of him.

"I keep thinking if she'd told you, I don't know. Maybe you'd have done something to keep me from going to the concert. Chained me to my bed or something." Her attempt to lighten the mood fell flat. "But like you said, I can't be responsible for what other people choose to do."

"No. You can't." Somehow, the words escaped through his clenched jaw.

"Can we go to the service?" she asked, sounding like the little girl she once had been.

"Service?"

"For Zak." Cassie's eyes pleaded with him. "I feel like I should go. And I don't know if Kye..." Her voice trailed off, the rest of the sentence easily filled in. She didn't know what kind of shape Kye would be in, or if he'd be able to attend the service with her.

Granger fought with the feeling of honor that she was essentially asking if he'd go with her and his very real aversion to attending any kind of memorial service. Every one he went to sent him right back to that bewildered eight-year-old boy he'd been when his mother died.

"Sure, Cass. We can do that."

She nodded in relief.

"Do you need anything? Are you hungry?"

"No. Miss Marcy made grilled cheese earlier. I think she left a sandwich for you in the fridge."

"Great." He faked enthusiasm. "I'll rustle up something for dinner, okay? Or order pizza, maybe."

"Sure. Just cheese and peppers for me."

"Got it." He turned to go, but he turned back. He bent down and hugged his daughter. "I love you, Cassie. Maybe I didn't say it enough before, or even act like it. Maybe if I had..." His throat clogged. Why was it so difficult to tell his own daughter how much she meant to him? He couldn't even imagine, nor did he want to, how Zak's parents must be feeling.

"I know, Dad." She patted his shoulder. She sniffed. "I love you too."

When the embrace ended, they were both teary-eyed. "God, we're a pair, aren't we?"

She half-laughed through her tears and shooed him in the direction of the door. "Go. Eat your sandwich. I have to write an essay."

He left, but he'd be shocked if Cassie went back to her laptop. Not if she was anywhere near as churned up as he was.

He went to the kitchen, but food was the last thing on his mind. He braced his hands on the countertop and stared into the sink. A sparkling sink, thanks to Marcy. The dishwasher hummed, and a couple of pans were clean and drying on the drainer.

Not so long ago, he'd been on top of the world. His "art" had been well-received. A couple of pieces even sold. His business ran smoothly. He'd started a relationship with Joy that not only put a smile on his face but made him start thinking about the future. Something he'd been avoiding for a long time. He'd started to feel hope.

Of course, he hadn't known what Cassie was up to, and okay, their relationship hadn't been great. But the rest of his life? He'd been doing better than okay. Pretty well, he'd have said if asked.

But Cassie's accident shattered his sense of well-being, his trust in the future. And her revelation today? About Joy? He could hardly wrap his head around it. And when he did, he felt nothing but rage. No. More than that. Disappointment. Whatever he thought he and Joy were building was an illusion. She hadn't told him about Cassie sneaking out. What else hadn't she told him? What else *wouldn't* she tell him if they could have moved forward? Bottom line? He didn't trust her. She'd withheld critical information. And he couldn't overlook it.

Joy hadn't been in any hurry to share about her own daughter's past, either. The sense of connection he thought he felt? This idea that they were meant to be together seemed like nothing more than a pipe dream when he realized he knew very little about her. A huge gap of time and space existed between them which, up until now, he'd refused to acknowledge.

He felt sick to his stomach. Probably where all the emotions were, roiling around in there. He didn't know what to do with them all. He'd been ignoring his feelings for a long time. Now that they were confronting him, he couldn't deal. Didn't know how. Didn't want to.

Someone knocked on the back door. Why couldn't everyone just leave him alone for one minute? He hadn't had a moment of peace since the accident. He needed time to sort through things. Try to get his equilibrium back.

But instead, he yanked the door open. Joy stood there holding covered bowls and a loaf of bread on top of them. "Hi," she said. She didn't try to mask the uncertainty in her voice as she looked him over. "How's Cassie doing?"

"She's a mess. How do you think she's doing?" he snarled.

"I'm sorry. I hoped she'd be feeling better. Maybe if she gets—"

"You know what, Joy? I really don't have time for this. And frankly, you are the last person who should be offering parenting advice. You fucked up with your daughter and you sure as hell fucked up with mine. We're done here." He slammed the door in her face.

Chapter Thirty-Three

J oy stared at the door, hardly able to believe the way Granger had spoken to her. Part of her wanted to pound on the door until he opened up and told her what kind of burr was up his butt, but another part advised caution. She'd had hardly any contact with Granger since the accident. She didn't quite know where to step to keep from overstepping in their relationship. Granger had to be going through some heavy-duty shit with Cassie. Joy wanted to help any way she could, which is why she brought over some chicken Alfredo and a Caesar salad with garlic bread.

Only to have the door slammed in her face.

A third part of her thought, screw him. If he didn't want her offering, maybe someone else would. She went back to her place and called Brian. He sounded pleased with her suggestion of bringing dinner over later.

"Now what?" she asked herself after she stowed the food in the fridge. Every summer Brian hired college students to work at the gallery and design studio, so he had plenty of help. She had hours before dinnertime.

The work on the new retail space was humming along. The painters had finished yesterday, and flooring would be laid today. She could make good use of the rest of the afternoon, digitally organizing the rest of the file Brian had of crafters and artisans in the surrounding area. She could cross reference it with the vendor contact file she already had and delete any duplicates. Perhaps later she'd do more research online. If nothing else, it would take her mind off Granger's surprising behavior.

She thought fleetingly of calling her mother and asking if she knew what was up. Granger held the place of surrogate son, or at least favored nephew with her mother. Would he have confided in her?

Doubtful. Granger wasn't the confiding type, and he wouldn't choose her mother as a confidante anyway because of his relationship with her daughter.

No. She'd have to confront Granger at some point and find out what set him off. But until then, she'd do her best not to angst over it excessively. She was hurt, yes, but everyone had misunderstandings. She hoped they could have a conversation about whatever it was that caused him to react so nastily. He'd lashed out at her. Actually, he'd insulted her. That's what stung the most. He said she'd fucked up with Devonny.

"All evidence to the contrary," she muttered under her breath as she began picking through the file, laying out brochures, business cards, and scraps of paper on the table.

Devonny might have done some things that didn't make her mother proud. But she'd turned into a wonderful person, a loving mother. A smart woman and entrepreneur who'd found love not once, but twice. She owned her decisions and stood up for herself. Devonny hadn't turned out badly at all. Joy admired her daughter.

"You're the one who's misguided," she said as if Granger were standing right there.

But how did he think she had screwed up with Cassie? Joy barely knew the girl. Cassie made no secret of the fact that Joy was not her favorite person. She seemed to have some misguided sense that Joy was trying to take Granger away from her. Cassie had already done a good job of driving her father away all by herself. "I don't see how anything I did could make things worse."

She continued to sort the contents of the file into various piles, separating each item into a category: Fabrics and textures. Glass/breakables. Decorative. Sculpture. Wood. Home goods.

Her vision for the space she'd be creating continued to take shape, even though all she'd seen was the bare bones when she'd walked through it with Brian. But getting an idea of what might be offered there excited her.

"Oh!" she exclaimed as she came across information on handmade cards. They looked exquisite. "We need a rack for those," she decided. She got up to get a legal pad to make notes about displays for the additional artists whose work she wanted.

She began to sort the stacks she'd made, placing sticky notes on each and securing them with binder clips.

She also scribbled down possible names for the store. Craft Fair. Artisans. Fair Maiden.

"Hmm," she mused. "I kind of like Fair Maiden." She wondered what Brian would think of the name.

Joy clapped her hands, envisioning how the store would look on opening day. They'd have to have a grand opening celebration, she decided. With cookies and lemonade for customers to enjoy.

She opened her laptop and began to browse, not really sure what she was looking for. But the search absorbed her for the rest of the afternoon, so when Brian's text came saying he was heading home, she realized she'd hardly dwelt on the Granger issue at all.

She replied quickly, got herself together and carried the food to her car, not caring if Granger saw the dinner intended for him and Cassie headed elsewhere. Screw him, she thought, even though she didn't mean it. Sadness began to replace indignation as she drove to Brian's. She'd thought she and Granger were building something together, that their relationship was going somewhere solid. That they were connected to each other.

Idiot.

She berated herself for letting her heart get ahead of her head. For sleeping with him, dammit, which had sealed the deal with a stamp of approval on the physical attraction component.

She'd been drawn in by what? His penetrating gaze. His reluctant smile. His talent. And yes, his pain. She'd wanted to soothe every sharp edge that still hurt him.

Make him see that he was valued and wanted and that he was a freaking great guy. And what did it get her? A door slammed in her face. Rejection.

By the time she got to Brian's it all hit her. What she thought she'd found. What she may have lost. He took one look at her face, set everything she'd carried in on the kitchen counter and said, "Come here, baby."

The minute his arms went around her, she burst into tears.

"Oh, dear," he said. "Oh, baby."

When her crying jag ended, she stepped back. He handed her a paper towel, and she cleaned up her face. "I'm a great dinner companion, huh?"

"Sweetheart," he deadpanned. "You know I'm a sucker for drama." He poured them each a glass of wine and led her to the big sofa. "Spill."

She took a fortifying sip of the crisp white he'd chosen before she admitted, "It's Granger."

"I knew it." He looked grim.

After she explained what happened, which didn't take long, Brian got up to refill their glasses. "You're probably not hungry, but I'm starving, so let's make plates and you can tell me the rest of it."

"There's nothing else to tell."

"Oh, honey, there's *always* more to tell. This is just the tip of the iceberg." He set the wine back in the fridge and withdrew everything else she'd brought. "We can nuke the Alfredo, right? Stick the bread under the broiler? Yum, garlic," he enthused as he unwrapped it. He set the oven temperature and took the lid off the other bowl. "Salad. Perfect."

"Such as?" Joy asked as he filled plates with pasta.

"How was the sex?" He looked at her from beneath his brows.

"How do you know if I even slept with him?"

"Oh, honey. You wouldn't be this upset if you hadn't."

"True," she said begrudgingly. "Maybe you're in the wrong line of work. Maybe you should go into counseling instead of design."

"Ugh," he said. "All those random people with their problems? Pretending I care? I don't think so."

"You want me to shut up?"

Brian looked appalled at the idea. "No. You should tell me *everything* right from the beginning. Because I do care about my friends and *their* drama. But answer my question first."

"What question?"

"How was the sex?"

Joy stared into her glass of wine, knowing she had to be honest with herself. "Incredible."

Brian snapped his fingers and took a big slug of wine. "I knew it! It's always the quiet ones."

"The thing is—"

He held up a finger to stop her. "Let's get the food ready first. I'm a better listener on a full stomach."

By the time Joy finished telling him everything, they'd emptied the first bottle of wine and opened a second.

"Men." Brian shook his head, a bitter twist momentarily taking over his features. "You want to know what I think?"

"Of course."

"I think things were moving a little too fast for Granger and he found a reason to put the brakes on. Same thing happened to me a couple of years ago. His name was Royce. I know. It's a stupid name, but he was perfect. We were perfect. I thought so anyway. Next thing I know, he's picking a fight with me over something stupid. No matter what I said or how I tried to apologize, he wouldn't budge. He'd never admit it, but I think he got scared. He couldn't handle how intense it got between us and he bailed."

"He wasn't ready for the relationship to move forward is what you're saying."

"He wasn't ready for a relationship period. And if that's Granger's problem, you know what I say?" Brian asked as he picked up his plate and brought it to the sink. "Screw him." He gestured so wildly with the hand holding his glass, liquid sloshed over the top. "He doesn't deserve you."

Hadn't Granger said exactly those words to her not so long ago? Hadn't he told her in one of their very first conversations that he still had issues about his divorce?

"Yeah, well, the problem is, I think I might be in love with him."

Chapter Thirty-Four

G ranger spent the rest of the afternoon in his office catching up on paperwork and looking at the backlog list of project requests, but he didn't return calls to schedule any. Weariness overtook him to the point he sacked out on the couch with the TV on ESPN. He wasn't even watching it. He closed his eyes and replayed his encounter with Joy earlier. He'd shocked himself with the depth of his anger and judging by the look on her face before he'd slammed the door, he'd shocked Joy as well.

He wasn't sure where he wanted to go from here. He tried to envision apologizing to Joy and couldn't. He felt the way he felt about what she'd done. He couldn't take it back and pretend any different.

His thoughts churned the way his stomach had earlier, and finally he dropped off into a temporary, uneasy sleep. He woke groggy and disoriented, his brain wrapped in fog. This, he recalled, was why he never napped.

At 6:30, Granger tapped on Cassie's door and stuck his head in. He'd hardly heard a peep out of her all afternoon except for a single trip to refill her water cup.

She followed him to the kitchen. "Smells good," she said, indicating the food he'd set on the table. She got a can of soda from the fridge and plates from the cabinet while Granger opened the boxes of pizza, garlic knots, and brownie bites. "Wow, Dad. You went a little crazy."

That comment covered a lot of territory, but Granger chose to believe she was merely referring to the amount of food he'd ordered. Usually, he begrudgingly sprung for one large pizza and nothing else, appalled at the prices for what was essentially one meal and not a very nutritious one at that.

"I guess I was hoping to tempt your appetite. You haven't been eating much."

"I know." Again, Cassie's lack of fight surprised and worried Granger. Her attitude seemed to have done a complete one-eighty.

He thought about having a beer with his meal and couldn't think of a good reason not to, so he grabbed one and sat.

He reached for the pizza but froze when Cassie said, "Can we pray first?"

They used to say grace before meals all the time. But somehow when Adele left and with Cam already gone to college, he and Cassie had gotten out of the habit. Maybe because Granger got tired of hearing Cassie's put-upon sigh of annoyance when he tried to continue the tradition.

I gave up. The realization smacked him in the face. *I gave up on her.* That was the truth of it. He'd stopped fighting to have a relationship with his daughter because he'd deemed it too difficult. She'd turned into too much of a challenge. He'd essentially abandoned her. They'd abandoned each other in the wake of Adele's desertion, when they should have stuck together and been there for each other. At the very least, he should have been there for Cassie. He vowed right then and there to do better by her in the future.

"Sure," he said. He folded his hands and bowed his head, expecting her to recite the same prayer they'd always said before meals.

"God," she began, her voice filled with a reverence Granger'd never heard from her before. "Thank you for this food. Bless everyone in this house and all our family and friends. Especially bless Zak's family and watch over his soul. Amen."

"Amen." Granger echoed, hesitating before he straightened. Cassie took a slice of pizza and a garlic knot, so he did the same.

They ate in silence for a few minutes, before Cassie said, "You know, Dad, it's not her fault."

"What's not whose fault?"

"Me sneaking out. The accident. It's not Joy's fault."

Granger regarded her.

"I overheard you. When she stopped by earlier."

Granger turned his bottle of beer around in circles, not sure what to say. Not sure this was any of Cassie's business.

"I wasn't eavesdropping. I was on my way back from the bathroom. I heard what you said to her."

He wasn't sure he could explain the source of his rage. He wasn't even sure he knew where it all came from, only that it had exploded in that moment with Joy as the intended target.

"I'd rather not talk about it," Granger said.

Cassie's expression softened but she didn't back down. "I think that's been part of our problem. Ever since Mom left, we'd rather not talk about anything. So, we don't."

Granger looked down the road at his future. He saw a lot of uncomfortable conversations there. He'd have to man up and have them, he supposed, or keep living this half-life with the broken relationships he'd had before.

"Okay," he managed. "Let's talk."

That got a glimmer of a smile out of Cassie. "I don't like it either, you know. I'm so tired of crying."

Granger half-laughed. "Me too."

"But us shutting down," Cassie said carefully, "after Mom left, and *never* talking about her leaving, made it so we never talked about *anything*."

"And we got farther and farther apart." Granger saw that now. Maybe he always had, but it had been one of the things he didn't want to acknowledge because he didn't know how to fix it. That's what he did. He fixed things. Things. Not people. He couldn't fix his relationship with Adele. Or with Cassie. Or even the one he had with himself. Instead, he'd shut down. He'd driven Cassie away when she might have needed him the most. And he'd only opened back up after Joy moved in.

Started to open up, anyway. Before he slammed the door in her face.

"Wow," he said in regretful awe during his moment of clarity, his gaze falling squarely on his daughter as if seeing her, really seeing her for the first time in a long time. "I really screwed up, didn't I?"

"Everybody screws up."

If she meant to comfort him, it didn't work. "I wasn't there for you."

She didn't deny it or try to make him feel better about his shortcomings. "You're here for me now. And I want to be here for you."

Her unspoken *we're all we've got* hung in the air between them.

Cassie pulled apart a garlic knot before she said, "I thought you liked her." She ate a small bite. "Joy," she added when he didn't respond.

"I do." Granger thought he might need a second beer to get through this.

"Until today." Cassie gave him a look of consternation. "Now I feel like I ruined that, too." She looked away. "I screw everything up."

"Cassie!" Granger moved to the chair next to her and squeezed her wrist. "That is not true. Please don't think that."

"I'm the one who Joy saw sneaking out. You're mad at her because she didn't tell you. But you should be mad at me."

"Can I be mad at both of you?"

Cassie choked out a laugh. "Stop it. It's not funny."

"I guess not."

"You were starting to get happy again. Because of her."

Granger couldn't deny that. "I didn't think you liked her."

"Honestly, Dad, I don't really know her. I think I just couldn't stand to see anyone else be happy when I wasn't."

"How old are you again?" Granger teased.

Cassie's eyes showed a glint of their old sparkle. "Almost sixteen."

"You seem a lot smarter about things than the average sixteen-year-old."

The wistfulness returned. "I've grown up a lot in the last week or so."

"I'm sorry you had to."

Cassie covered the hand resting on her wrist. "All I'm saying is, it isn't her fault."

"And I shouldn't have let her have it the way I did."

"How did she mess up with her daughter?"

"It's not important."

"Was it worse than what I did?"

Cassie wasn't going to leave it alone. Granger thought for a moment before he answered. "Let's just say no parent would be proud of what she did."

"So, you think Joy's a bad parent because of whatever her daughter did?"

"Cassie, it's complicated."

"Not really," she insisted. "If she's a bad parent because of what her daughter did, then doesn't that make you a bad parent because of what I did?"

Granger looked at her in consternation wishing he could find fault in her logic.

Before he could come up with an answer she went on. "Dad, you're not a bad parent. Just because a kid does something stupid, doesn't make it the parents' fault."

Weariness washed over Granger once again. His tired brain couldn't pursue this conversation any further. At least not tonight.

To make it stop he said, "You could be right. Now I have one more question."

"What?"

He glanced at the box on the table. "How many of those brownie bites do you think we can eat?"

Cassie glanced at the brownies and back to him. "Dad, are you deflecting?"

Chapter Thirty-Five

J oy awoke the next morning to discover her hurt feelings had disappeared. Or maybe they were still there, but they were buried under a thick layer of resentment. She also had a slight headache, probably caused by too much wine, too many tears, and an excessive amount of carbs.

She yanked her door open and stared at Granger's house. She'd like to catch him if he headed out early and give him a piece of her mind, or at least try to figure out what was going on with him. She kept one ear open as she brewed coffee and got dressed for the day. She wanted to get started on contacting the creatives and finish setting up the database. If Brian had time, she wanted to review her plans with him and stop over at the new location and see how the rest of the renovations were progressing.

The sweet sense of excitement about starting this endeavor warred with the ball of resentment burning inside her.

Granger had been out of line, pure and simple. He'd acted like a child throwing a tantrum instead of an adult capable of a reasonable conversation about something that had upset him.

"And I deserve better," she reminded her reflection as she finished with her makeup.

She peeked out the door before she poured a cup of coffee to see Granger crossing the yard to his truck, his stride fast and determined. Maybe he was trying to escape before she caught him.

She let the screen slam behind her and pounded down the steps before he could get his truck door open. "I want to talk to you," she said.

When he looked at her, she remembered how intrigued she'd been those first couple of times she'd met him. Like those times, he didn't say anything. Arms crossed, feet planted, he watched and waited. He didn't look surprised at all by her approach or demeanor.

"What's going on?" she asked.

"What do you mean?"

She growled in frustration. "Don't act like you don't know. Yesterday. You slammed the door in my face after saying some truly nasty things to me."

He looked chagrined, but not at her. "Yeah, that was inexcusable."

"Damn right it was."

"I shouldn't have said what I said."

"No. You shouldn't have."

"Saying you caught me at a bad time sounds lame, I know, but Cassie had just told me you caught her sneaking out and—"

"*That's* what this is about?"

"You never told me." Granger took on a sullen tone, like somehow *he* was the wronged party.

"Told you what?" Joy was beside herself. "For the record, given the fact that you were obviously having a difficult time with her, I thought you knew. But in any case, she's *your* daughter, and I didn't consider it my responsibility to tell you what she was up to. And at the time, I barely knew you. I didn't think you'd appreciate me sticking my nose in."

"You could have told me after we got to know each other better."

Joy stared at him, dumbfounded. He wasn't going to apologize. This conversation was going nowhere. Her hope to resolve what was between them dissolved and left her deflated and defeated. "You know what, Granger? You want to blame someone for what happened to Cassie, find somebody else. You were right yesterday when you said we're done here. Congratulations. Your ploy to get out of this relationship worked."

She turned her back on him and went up to her apartment, knowing he watched her climb the stairs and close the door. She locked it, leaned against it, and burst into tears. She slid to the floor with bent knees, crossed her arms on top of them and sobbed like a broken-hearted child.

Granger got in the truck and stared at the steps to Joy's apartment before he started the engine. He should go up there and apologize. Really apologize. Some part of him knew that's all she wanted. But he stubbornly refused to admit he'd been wrong.

She hasn't apologized for not telling me what she knew, either he reminded himself as he put the truck in gear and backed out. If she had, it would have made it easier for him to offer his own apology. Maybe.

He still didn't understand why he didn't want to back down. Was he looking for a scapegoat to explain what had happened to Cassie? He could have lost her for good. That thought had stayed with him ever since the accident and he couldn't shake it. To admit that he and he alone was solely responsible for that possibility? He couldn't. There had to be other factors at work.

He could admit to a lot of things he'd done wrong with her. But Joy had critical information, and she should have shared it with him. *She should have.*

But was he willing to lose her because she didn't? Was he subconsciously looking for a way to sabotage the relationship as she'd implied? He didn't have an answer at the moment. He was too raw inside, too unsettled. Too much had come at him too quickly. The only bright spot on his otherwise bleak horizon was his improved relationship with Cassie.

Sheesh. Was he capable of only one decent relationship with a woman at a time? A better question was, did he really want a life, a future, without Joy in it?

Eventually, Joy cried herself out and picked herself up off the floor. She stared at her reflection in the bathroom mirror. Being a wreck over a man was new to her, and she didn't like it one bit. She pressed a cold washcloth over her eyes and face until some of the blotchiness abated.

"Get it together," she scolded herself. Losing Granger wasn't the end of the world. A world she now didn't feel ready to face today.

She texted Brian to tell him she'd be at home this morning, contacting some of the people from the file he'd given her and maybe she'd stop by later in the afternoon to check on the progress of the new store.

The flexibility of the schedule was one of the reasons she'd been so excited to start her own business. Even after they opened, she wouldn't have to be at the store full-time. If she set it up correctly, it should be easy for capable part-timers to handle things without her.

The door to Art's church office was ajar. Granger tapped on the jamb and stuck his head in. "Art? Got a minute?"

Art looked up from the papers covering his desk. "Granger. Come in. I need a break from drawing up next year's budget before the elders meeting next week. How are you? How's Cassie?"

Granger closed the door and took one of the no-nonsense chairs facing the desk. "That's actually what I wanted to talk to you about."

"Oh? But I thought she was doing well. Healing. Isn't she back in school?"

"Yes. She is healing. Physically, anyway. And she did go back to school."

"But...?"

Granger rubbed the back of his neck. "I don't know, Art. It's like all the fight went out of her after the accident."

Art gave him a gentle smile. "Isn't that, on some level at least, what you wanted?"

Granger looked chagrined. "I didn't want everything to be a fight with her. But now? It's like her spark is gone. I'm worried about her."

"Tell me more about what's concerning you."

"Before, no matter what I said or did, it was always met with defiance and sarcasm. She'd be downright disrespectful at times and didn't seem fazed by my attempts at discipline. She'd find a way around it or she'd cut me off even further. She had as little to do with me as possible."

"And now?"

"It's almost like she's a zombie. Not that she's zoned out, but she goes along with everything, never makes an objection, never makes a fuss. She comes home after school. Does her homework. I hardly ever hear her talking on the phone and she doesn't seem to text much, either. She leaves her bedroom door open in the afternoons, Art. She hasn't done that since she was twelve. I'm worried about her."

Art relaxed back in his chair. "Not to discount your concern, but I'm intrigued by the fact that she leaves her door open. Perhaps it's an invitation."

Granger cocked his head. "Sorry?"

"To you. She was closed off before, not just physically behind a closed door, but emotionally. Trauma can have some surprising effects. One of which is it breaks down walls. Especially in a life-or-death situation such as Cassie's accident. Makes us re-evaluate our behavior, our relationships. Everything."

"I hadn't thought of it like that."

"Cassie may be sending you signals she's not even consciously aware of. By not defying you or arguing with you, by leaving the door open, she wants you to see her as approachable. She may not know how to make the first move to repair your relationship. It's possible she's waiting for you to do that."

"Got any words of wisdom?"

Art chuckled. "You'll figure it out, with God's help. Sometimes all we can do is love them through the difficult times and hope we come out triumphant on the other side."

"Thanks for taking the time, Art. I'll see if I can talk to her."

"Any time. You know that. I have confidence in Cassie. And in you. She'll be okay. Just give it some time."

"I will. See you later."

Take that, Dr. Phil. You got nothing on me.

Art's satisfied grin faded. Advising others on how to deal with their children came so easily, but when it came to his own daughter, he had failed miserably. Spectacularly. He hadn't loved her through anything. Not the good times or the bad. He'd turned his back on her and now he was paying the price.

He'd been wrong. Christ Almighty, he'd been wrong.

Why had it taken him so long to acknowledge the error of his ways, even when the truth had been staring him in the face all these years? He'd been too full of pride and ego and arrogance. Had he done his best with Joy? Not even close. Worse, he hadn't even tried.

In a way, he'd lost Marcy when Joy left. Instead of recapturing what had once been, he'd created a divide between them. No matter how hard he tried over the years to bridge the gap or pretend it wasn't there, Marcy drew farther and farther away from him.

Rather than be an instrument of peace, he'd sewn discontent and heartache through his misguided self-righteousness.

Sadness at his own inadequacies swamped him and he did what he always did when life got the better of him. He prayed. For forgiveness. For change. For a way back.

Momentarily overwhelmed by the amends he knew he needed to make, Art at least knew where to start and who would help him. He picked up the phone and called Ty.

Chapter Thirty-Six

G ranger thought about what Art said as he drove home. He made a pact with himself that if Cassie's door was open, he'd walk through. Be the parent. He prayed for the strength, the wisdom, the words. God knew words were not his strong suit.

Cassie looked up from the book she was reading when he tapped on her open door. "Got a minute?"

She set the book aside and scooted over on the bed. "Sure."

Granger sat on the end of the bed, bringing one leg up so he could face her. "How are things going?"

"Like school, you mean?"

"Sure. Let's start there."

"Okay. It was kind of weird the first few days. Everyone wanted to ask me about what happened. I know a lot of the kids were talking about me. Kye too. But then Robbie Hawkins and Seth Greeley got arrested for stealing Robbie's grandma's car. The police chased them down. They were both drunk and Seth threw up all over one of the cops."

"Gross." Granger couldn't help the grin tugging at the corners of his mouth.

Cassie almost smiled too. "Took everybody's minds off the accident, anyway."

Granger's humor faded. "I've been worried about you."

"I've been worried about you, too."

"You don't need to worry about me."

"It's Joy, isn't it? Did you apologize to her? For what you said?"

"No. Not yet."

"Why not?"

"It's complicated." *And none of your business.*

"Not unless you're making it complicated. You tend to do that. Maybe it's because you're an engineer."

He wasn't following her logic, but he said, "Cassie, I'm here to talk about you."

"Okay, but after that we'll talk about you." He thought he saw a spark in Cassie's eye. The first he'd seen in a while. She was defying him, but it was a friendly kind of defiance. He'd take it.

"You've been real quiet lately," he said. "And," he searched for the right word and came up with, "agreeable."

Cassie giggled but not for long. "I've had a lot to think about. One of the grief counselors suggested journaling might help me sort out my feelings. So, I've been trying that."

Granger hadn't known she'd been journaling. "Is it helping?"

"I don't know. I think so. It's like everything I thought was so important before doesn't seem as important now."

"I was afraid you'd lost your spark."

Again came that quick giggle. "You're funny, Dad."

Relief threatened to overwhelm Granger, but he made himself look his daughter in the eye. "I love you, Cassie. You might get sick of hearing that because I'm going to be telling you every day that I love you. There's nothing I wouldn't do for you. I don't want things to go back to how they were. I want us to talk to each other, okay?"

"Okay. Now tell me why you haven't apologized to Joy."

Granger looked at her in consternation, afraid she wouldn't leave it alone until he gave her some kind of answer. "The short version is I'm not ready to apologize."

Cassie tilted her head. "But don't you want to get back together with her?"

"I don't know, Cassie. I haven't sorted it all out yet. I'm not sure I can trust her."

"Does this have something to do with Mom?"

His discomfort talking about feelings made Granger squirm. In a moment of quiet revelation, he acknowledged Adele's efforts to get him to open up made him feel the exact same way he did now.

"You were happy when you were with Joy," Cassie went on. "That's all I'm saying. So, don't let it go too long. Remember what you said before about Zak? What if he kept driving? He might have hurt a lot more people. What if you don't get a chance to tell Joy you're sorry?"

Granger decided it was beyond time to change the subject. He wiggled her ankle. "Are you sick of grilled cheese yet?" It was one of the few things he had mastered in the culinary arena.

"Make chicken noodle soup, too, okay?"

For just a moment, his little girl was back. It made Granger smile.

"You got it."

Chapter Thirty-Seven

Each and every morning and several times throughout the day, Joy gave thanks that Brian had agreed to partner with her on a business that required focused attention. Pulling together the new retail space, visiting local artisans and crafters, acquiring product, deciding on price and placement kept her from thinking too much about, well, everything else.

Her parents. Granger. Cassie. The impending arrival of Devonny, Luke, and Lucy. The family reunion her mother insisted on going full steam ahead with in spite of the situation with her husband.

At two o'clock, when Joy took a fifteen-minute break for a snack, she couldn't keep her thoughts at bay any longer. How, she wondered, had she created this path of destruction simply by trying to reconcile with her family?

Her parents weren't speaking to each other. Granger treated her as if she were a leper. Cassie? Well, she didn't know how Cassie was faring because she couldn't get close enough to Granger to ask, and if she tried to approach Cassie directly, she might get a door slammed in her face.

At least her daughter still spoke to her. And Brian. God bless Brian whose attitude about all of it seemed to be "Fuck 'em." He was of the assured opinion that none of them deserved to have Joy in their lives, nor did they have any idea how to treat her properly. He further insisted that they all owed Joy a huge heartfelt apology for their behavior toward her.

Joy smiled at the thought, because Brian had uttered that sentiment with a glass of wine in his hand the other night, standing and sloshing the vino over the rim of his glass as he gestured wildly in agitation on her behalf.

Joy opened the foil packet of trail mix and twisted the top off a bottle of mineral water. She took a seat in a lovely cane-backed rocking chair she'd acquired on one of her buying jaunts. The recently retired woodshop teacher had been more than happy to participate in the consignment plan she'd offered him, and they'd had a delightful conversation about the state of public-school education.

Joy rocked, nibbled, and drank her water, letting her gaze wander around the not quite finished space, seeing in her mind's eye her and Brian's vision come to life.

They'd agreed on a warm and welcoming palette of beiges and tans and grays for the décor. Natural wood shelving with live edges for some of the smaller pieces, pottery, glass, and the like. Broad ladders to display quilts, rugs and woven goods. Antique mirrors and old-time fixtures encased the section for the handmade soaps, candles and toiletries. Placed throughout would be pieces like the rocker, tables and other handcrafted furniture. She'd set the tables using woven table runners and placemats, hand-painted napkins and the delicate work of glass artists.

Joy finished the trail mix and drained the water just as the ancient door with its wavy panes of glass opened. They weren't officially doing business, but Joy wasn't going to turn any visitors or curiosity seekers away.

She stood to discard the trash and froze when she saw her father coming toward her. He stopped a few feet away and fixed her with a look she couldn't readily decipher. It wasn't his cold, stern, disapproving expression. But it wasn't exactly friendly either. If she had to guess, she'd say his expression spoke of uncertainty, as though unsure of his welcome. But unsure wasn't a word she'd ever have used to describe her father.

"Hello, Joy."

His greeting couldn't be called friendly, but at least it was neutral. Civil. "Dad."

She moved behind the counter to throw the snack leftovers away.

"How are you?" he asked.

Her father treating her as a—what? Casual acquaintance he'd met on the street? Decidedly weird. Even so, it was better than she'd been treated as his daughter. "I'm well, thank you for asking," she lied. "How are you?" She could play this game with him. For a few minutes anyway.

"I'm..." He seemed to reach for words, blinking at her as if hoping she could interpret his non-verbal communication. But she didn't know what he expected her to say or how she could help.

"...lost," he finally said, his gaze holding hers.

Again, Joy had the sense that she and her father were more alike than either wanted to admit. "Welcome to the club," she said. She tried to smile, but it wouldn't quite come. Something seemed to shift between them.

"You?" he asked. "But you always seem so sure of yourself."

Joy laughed without humor. "So do you, Dad. You always have. Especially when it came to right and wrong."

Art's gaze dropped, and he shook his head slowly. "I'm not so sure I should have been sure of anything." His head came up. "Could we talk? Not now, I know you're working. But later. Would you have dinner with me? Or—or coffee or something?"

Joy thought quickly. She didn't think it'd be a good idea to meet with her father in a public place where anything could happen. The last thing she wanted to do was create more chaos and scandal. She needed to be in a safe space. Her space. "Why don't you come to my place? We could have dinner," she said. "Around six-thirty."

Art appeared to debate her offer as if there might be a trap he couldn't see hidden in the invitation. "All right." He dipped his chin in acknowledgment, turned, and left.

Joy watched him retreat until the door closed behind him. Had that just happened? Had her dad, her strong, stoic, always right father, just approached her of his own free will, spoken to her without disapproval in his tone, and admitted to being lost?

The phrase *when hell freezes over* flitted across Joy's thoughts. How strange would it be having him in her little apartment? Sitting across the table from him? Sharing a meal. A conversation.

It would be a novelty. Possibly unsettling. But she found herself looking forward to it. What if she and her father cleared the air between them once and for all? Decided to either part company forever or settle their differences. What if, she couldn't help thinking, she could finally have a relationship with her father?

Chapter Thirty-Eight

By the time Joy left work, it was nearly six. Both the deliveries scheduled for the afternoon arrived late, and there'd been the inevitable discussions with the vendors about placement and pricing. Cutting those conversations short wouldn't be in the store's best interest. Acquiring future merchandise meant maintaining pleasant working relationships with the artisans.

She'd left it too late to run to the supermarket and realized she didn't feel like preparing anything anyway. She hadn't had Chinese since she'd gone that time with Granger and decided on takeout. A vague recollection of an outing to the Cincinnati Zoo had been teasing around the edges of her mind all afternoon. She hadn't been more than seven or eight at the time, and it was one of the few fairly harmonious family memories she had.

There'd been a discussion about where to go to dinner before driving home. Her father, as she recalled, wanted to try a Chinese place he'd read about in the Sunday paper, but her mother wasn't keen.

"I want Chinese, too," Joy had piped up from the back even though they hadn't asked her.

"You don't even know what it is," her mother pointed out.

"How will I ever know if I don't try it?"

She saw her parents exchange a look, and to the Chinese restaurant they went. Her mother had ordered the simplest thing on the menu, chicken fried rice, and ate little of it.

Her father if she recalled correctly, got chicken chow mein, and cleaned his plate.

Joy couldn't recall what she had. Shrimp lo mein, perhaps, her mother thinking something resembling spaghetti might not be too objectionable to her young palate.

Joy ordered the same two meals and added a six-pack of Kirin. She recalled her father enjoying the occasional beer but didn't know if he still did. When she arrived home, she found her father chatting with Granger in the driveway. She parked and approached with the takeout bags.

"Joy," her father said. "You're here."

She glanced at Granger. "Hello," she said, somehow managing to keep her tone neutral.

He nodded. Evidently, he didn't want to waste one of his few words on her. She turned back to her father. "Want to come up?" She didn't wait for an answer but started for the stairs. Art said goodbye to Granger and followed her.

"Let me take that," he said, as she juggled the bags while fumbling with her keys.

She handed the bags to him and unlocked the door. "You can put those on the counter." She pulled out the six-pack. She'd have to move. That was all there was to it. She hadn't seen Granger in days, and now, just that brief interaction had rattled her and driven her to drink. She used a can opener to pop the top and took a long drink while her father looked on.

"Sorry. Would you like a beer? I brought Chinese. I thought I remembered..." she trailed off. She hadn't had a meal with her father since her return. She honestly had no idea what his preferences were.

"Chinese?" He seemed surprised but not displeased. "That's a treat. Your mother doesn't care for it, you know. And yes, a beer would be fine." She handed him one of the bottles and stowed the others in the fridge. She set out plates and began unpacking the food.

"I got chicken chow mein," she said. "And shrimp lo mein. I thought I remembered..." Again, she trailed off, feeling foolish.

"Cincinnati. The zoo. You must have been, what? Seven? Eight?"

She glanced up in surprise. "You remember?"

"Of course, I do. I think that was the last time I had Chinese food."

Were his eyes twinkling? He looked amused. Friendly, even.

She fixed plates for both of them and brought them to the table. Once they were seated, Joy picked up her fork, realizing how hungry she was after only having a snack earlier. But Art folded his hands and bowed his head. She set her fork down and followed suit, respecting his tradition of a prayer before meals, something she should have taught Devonny. But her rejection of her parents' ways had been complete.

Ironic how Devonny began attending church once she moved to Iowa. She'd embraced, if not religion, at least a sense of spirituality. There were things about Devonny's life Joy envied. How she'd become part of the community, the way she'd built a new life for herself. Joy thought she might be able to do the same. But now it seemed less and less likely. She couldn't even decide if she wanted to stay in Liberty.

The prayer concluded and they both began to eat. "Thank you for agreeing to meet me," Art said after a few bites.

Joy made eye contact with him, finding his expression not nearly as forbidding as it had been before today. "You said you wanted to talk." Whatever he wanted to say, she told herself she was ready for it. A lie. She drank more of her beer while she waited.

"I wanted to ask you..." He took a breath, as if to fortify himself before he continued. "If you would talk to your mother for me."

Her father wanted her to run interference for him. He wasn't here to clear the air between *them*. It was about her mother. He had some nerve. Nothing had changed.

"Why should I?" she asked, not trying to hide her bitterness. "You made your bed. Now you can lay in it. Isn't that your life philosophy?"

He could no longer hold her gaze. He looked away. She saw his Adam's apple move as he swallowed hard. "I should never have said that to you," he admitted, his voice hoarse with emotion. "Should never have hung up on you."

Joy waited. He looked her in the eye again. "Instead of trusting in the Lord, I let fear get the better of me."

"What were you afraid of?"

His shoulders lifted slightly, then dropped. "Everything, as it turns out. It was easier to push you away than face my own inadequacies as a father and husband. As a man."

"You need to explain that." Joy edged her plate aside, her appetite gone. She might need another beer, though.

Art cleared his throat. "I was never much of a father to you. You'd almost cost me my wife, and I never forgave you for that." He put up a hand as if to squelch Joy's objection. "I know. It wasn't your fault. You were completely innocent. But the thought of losing Marcy..." He made a helpless gesture with the same hand. "It was more than I could bear. It didn't matter how wrong or irrational my thinking was. I blamed you."

Joy could see how that might make a certain amount of sense, given the situation. She'd never doubted the depth of feeling her father had for her mother. He'd displayed a tenderness toward her he'd never shown toward Joy.

"It ate at me, but I couldn't let it go. The longer I held onto believing you were to blame, the stronger my conviction got. I'd counseled parishioners about similar situations, about death, even, but I couldn't be objective when it was my wife. My child.

"If it wasn't God's fault, then maybe it was mine. But everyone assured me I'd done everything right, going to the doctor visits, making sure Marcy got enough rest, consulting with the specialist.

"Her being so sick after you were born? I couldn't make sense of it. I needed to make sense of it. There had to be a reason."

"Me," Joy put in.

"Your mother resented me, and our marriage suffered, but I held on to the fear, the *wrongness* of how I felt because I was so afraid of losing her."

"And now you've lost her anyway."

Art nodded.

"I guess you've figured out by now that sometimes things just happen and we don't know the reason why, if there is one. The world we live in? It can be kind of random. Maybe we aren't always supposed to understand the why. Maybe we aren't even capable of that level of understanding."

"Theoretically, I knew all of that. In actual practice? I stupidly wanted answers."

"Listen, about Mom..."

"She refuses to speak to me. She won't see me or talk to me on the phone. Won't answer the door and Ginny won't let me in when I stop by."

"She's angry and she's hurt. You've lost her trust," Joy said, knowing once again she wasn't telling her father anything he didn't already know.

"Yes. But I thought if you tried..."

Now she understood her father's behavior. But Joy still needed to process how she felt. He hadn't apologized to her, although he'd admitted to knowing what he'd done was wrong. Was she looking for an apology? Or was understanding enough? Did he expect her to explain her actions? She still didn't think she owed him an apology.

"I'm not going to try to talk Mom into anything. But I will tell her that we met. That you explained yourself to me."

"I appreciate that."

"Mom's changed. She's got a mind of her own."

Art turned his beer bottle around in circles, staring at the ring of condensation on the tabletop. "I'm afraid she won't forgive me."

Joy tipped her head to one side to study him. "That depends. I haven't heard you say you're sorry or that you regret anything you did."

His chin dropped to his chest, and he looked up at her from beneath his brows. "I know. It's pretty hard to admit to being wrong for most of your life."

Joy scooted her chair back and went to the fridge to get two more beers. She didn't know if her father would drink a second, but she wanted one. "If you were wrong all this time, I was too."

He picked his head up and gave her a keen look. "How so?"

"I let all the bitterness and resentment I had for you inform every decision I made. I didn't want you to be in charge of my life, but, in a way, you still were." She shook her head, stunned at the stupidity of it, the waste of it.

Art reached across the table. Joy hesitated for just a moment before she put her hand in his. "Maybe," he said, his words choked once again. "If we say it together, it won't be so hard."

Breathless, Joy nodded. As if they knew the moment the other would speak, they said in unison, "I'm sorry."

Tears welled in Joy's eyes, the release of pain and bitterness and resentment too much for her to hold back. They rose and for the first time in longer than she could remember, her father's arms wrapped around her, and the tears continued to flow, wetting his shirt, but she couldn't let go. Every tear she'd refused to shed for all those years wanted out right now.

Minutes went by before she calmed and still, she stood in his arms. What was it about her father's embrace? The warmth and protection? Safety and security which she'd never felt from him before?

Finally, she stepped away and dabbed at her eyes with one of the takeout paper napkins. Art did the same.

"I feel like I lost about fifty pounds," he said with a chuckle.

"It's true." Lightness descended on her, allowing her to shed a weight she hadn't realized she'd been carrying around.

He put his hands on her shoulders. "Can we start over, do you think? Will you give me a chance to try to be the father I never was to you?"

Isn't that why she'd come back home?

"Yes, Dad. Let's start over."

Chapter Thirty-Nine

The next morning, Joy knocked on her Aunt Ginny's front door bright and early. Joy didn't know what Ginny's habits were, but she knew her mother would be up, probably having coffee by now.

She looked around at Ginny's neat cottage-style home, where the flower beds were a glory of color and the green grass recently trimmed. A twig wreath woven with dried flowers and slender bits of ribbon adorned the yellow front door, which accented the gray siding perfectly.

Ginny, still in her nightgown and robe, answered the door. "My goodness, Joy. You're up and about early this morning." She welcomed Joy in and embraced her in a tight squeeze. "Come on to the kitchen. We're just pouring coffee."

Marcy turned from the counter. "Joy? Is everything all right?"

"Everything's fine, Mom. I just wanted to talk to you."

Ginny took the hint. "I'm going back to bed with the crossword and my coffee. You two have a nice talk."

Marcy poured two cups and they settled themselves at the table.

"How have you been?" Joy asked.

"I'm fine." Marcy narrowed her eyes as if suspicious of the question. "Why?"

They'd avoided the subject of Art ever since the night Marcy left, but Joy braved it anyway. "How are you getting along being away from Dad?"

Marcy bristled. "I'm perfectly capable of surviving on my own, Joy."

Joy refrained from pointing out that she wasn't exactly on her own. Instead, she said, "I thought you might be missing him by now."

"I don't miss being deceived by him. Or being lied to or dictated to."

Joy said, "He came to see me yesterday."

"Did he?" Marcy kept her tone neutral.

"Yes. We had dinner together last night."

If she'd surprised her mother, Marcy didn't show it.

"He admitted the way he handled things with me was wrong." Joy waited, but still her mother said nothing. "We've agreed to start over, give each other another chance at being father and daughter."

"I'm glad."

"It's what you wanted, Mom."

"It is. It's an answer to prayer. I just didn't think..."

For the first time, emotion showed in Marcy's expression. She looked away, blinking rapidly.

Joy covered her mother's hand with her own. "Didn't think you wouldn't be part of it?"

"I never dreamed," Marcy choked out, "that he could do something so underhanded. So despicable."

"I understand why he did it," Joy said softly.

Marcy's eyes flashed at her. "It doesn't matter why he did it. He can't justify it. It's unforgiveable."

"Is it, Mom? Is anything truly unforgiveable?"

"For me this is."

"Maybe you need more time."

"I do. Twenty-five years sounds about right." Marcy sneered, something Joy hadn't thought her mother capable of.

"He asked me to come and see you. Can't you at least talk to him?"

"Yes. When hell freezes over." Joy'd never seen this side of her mother. So sure of herself. So determined and immoveable.

"I'm sorry, Mom. I feel like I caused all of this. And now I can't make it right between you."

"It isn't your fault, Joy. It's his. He's made his bed. Now he can lay in it."

"Wow, Mom. We *really* need to stop using that expression."

"I suppose." Marcy got up and went to the counter for the coffee carafe, conveniently turning her back to Joy to make her point. "I'm glad you stopped by today because I do want to discuss the reunion with you," she said before she refilled their cups and resumed her seat. "The pavilion in Shannon Woods is available that

Saturday. You remember that park in Ridgeville. They've got that bandstand that looks like a gazebo, remember?" Without waiting for a response from Joy she went on. "It's a convenient location for all of us and, I already talked to the caterers. They've worked there before so they know how to set everything up."

"Didn't we do a big family picnic there when I was little?" Joy asked.

"Yes. For Memorial Day one year, I think. Or maybe July 4ᵗʰ. I can't recall."

"I remember a big playground."

"It's still there. Plus, horseshoes and shuffleboard. They also cultivated a butterfly garden. Prettiest thing you ever saw."

"It sounds lovely, Mom. Do you need help with anything?"

"Are you kidding? Everyone's so excited to see you again and to meet Devonny and her family. Ginny's been helping me and so have Mary Lee and Ellen," she said, naming two more of her sisters.

Beneath the table Joy crossed her fingers, praying that nothing would rain on her mother's plans for the big day.

Granger hammered away at the bent piece of metal deciding it must be reinforced with steel because it refused to bend the way he wanted. He'd had an idea to do a play on a figure in the style of Rodin's *The Thinking Man,* but it wasn't coming together at all the way he'd envisioned. It looked more like a man defeated, crumpled into a sitting position, head in hands. Perhaps he should figure out how to fashion tears falling from its eyes.

He walked around the figure with a critical eye before he froze in front of it as realization dawned. *That's me.* He'd managed a partially finished self-portrait in metal that somehow perfectly portrayed his air of defeat, his feelings of frustration and sadness.

He pulled up a stool and sat to face it, studying it. He'd been tinkering for days but nothing had come together for him. Somehow, he'd lost his drive to create. Whatever had inspired him before was gone. Until this sad half-finished figure somehow sprang to life and now forced him to take a good hard look at himself.

This is what he was or at least how he felt. Incomplete. Not quite finished. Not a whole man. It didn't take a genius to figure out why. He'd been pushing love away his whole life, so afraid of losing it he was afraid to reach out and fully embrace it. He was sure now he'd driven Adele away, refused her love in small ways over the years, until she'd had enough of his subtle rejection and disappeared from his life.

And idiot that he was, he'd done the same thing with Joy. If he didn't man up and break the pattern, he'd be just like the sad metal half-man before him.

He stood abruptly. He didn't know how he was going to do it. Whatever it took, he decided. Apologize. Beg. Cajole. Make a grand gesture. Get down on his knees and beg her forgiveness if that's what he had to do. But he wasn't going to be that sad man any longer. He wasn't going to go through life without Joy.

Joy decided she loved the overhead bell that dinged every time the door to the shop opened or closed. It gave just the right amount of vintage atmosphere, while at the same time alerting her to new Fair Maiden customers.

The shop was coming together nicely, she thought, and even though it wasn't officially open yet, she'd already made a few sales. The "Opening Soon" signs didn't stop snoopy shoppers from trying the door. Joy liked to think the arrangement of items in the front window made it irresistible. She'd mixed some of the repurposed furniture with a variety of textures and colors from fabric and glass.

Front and center, she'd placed one of Granger's pieces—two children holding hands. She loved the way the abstractness of it played off the easily recognized conventional things. But mostly it seemed people who were already downtown were curious and most were polite, asking if they could come in and check out the store. Joy didn't turn anyone away. The counters and registers were already set up, and the equipment was online. Neither she nor Brian saw a reason to wait for the Labor Day weekend grand opening if customers wanted to make purchases.

Every sale, even the smallest, thrilled Joy. It reinforced her belief that she was on to something. Plus, it gave her an idea of what items generated the most interest and who she'd need to contact for more merchandise.

She turned from fussing with the kitchen corner and froze when she saw Cassie Sullivan.

Joy made herself move closer to the front of the store and took up a position behind the counter. "Can I help you?" she asked.

Cassie came closer and Joy saw no hostility in her expression. Still, her presence made Joy wary. The Sullivan sting might last only a moment, but the barb buried itself deep. Joy still heard Granger's words every time she relived that awful encounter.

"Hi." Cassie didn't seem quite so brash or sure of herself as when Joy had met her before. She glanced around the store. "Nice place."

"Thank you." Joy decided to treat her like a customer. "Is there something in particular you're looking for?"

Cassie's attention returned to her. Those clear green eyes with flecks of gold, so like her father's. Joy wondered if she'd ever get over losing him.

"Forgiveness, I guess. That's what I'm looking for."

"Unfortunately, Cassie, we don't sell that here."

"I wanted to say I'm sorry is all."

"You don't owe me an apology for anything as far as I know."

Cassie set her backpack down near one of the cane-backed rocking chairs. "I feel like I messed things up between you and my dad."

I know exactly how you feel. A humorless laugh escaped Joy. "I'm pretty sure we did that all by ourselves."

"I told him you caught me sneaking out that time. And maybe if you'd told him, I wouldn't have done it again. There wouldn't have been an accident."

Tears filled Cassie's eyes. She brushed them away, as though annoyed with the show of emotion.

"Sorry." She sniffed. "I cry a lot now. I don't know why."

"I think you probably have good reasons." This girl knocked down all Joy's defenses, much the same way her father had. Joy wanted to comfort her. Soothe away all those hurt places inside of her. "Want to sit for a minute? Those rocking chairs are the bomb."

Cassie sat and Joy came around the counter and took the one adjacent to her. "This is a great place," Cassie said, turning her head to look around again, trying to take it all in. "You don't need any help, do you?"

"Are you looking for a job?"

Cassie turned back to her. "You probably wouldn't want to hire me. Because of my dad."

A smile tugged at Joy's lips. "I'm an equal opportunity employer."

"I could work during the summer." she said. "Maybe Saturdays and a bit after school or something. School holidays."

"You've thought a lot about this."

Cassie gave a little laugh. "Not really. I just thought of it when I came in here. It'd be a cool place to work."

"I'll talk to Brian—Mr. Crowley about it. If you want to stop in again in a few days, I'll have an answer for you."

"Okay. Sure." Cassie glanced around again before she looked back at Joy. "I really am sorry. About you and my dad."

"I didn't think you wanted us to get together, anyway."

"I guess I didn't. Or I was jealous or something. But ever since the accident, things aren't the same, you know? I heard what he said to you that day. I told him it wasn't your fault, and he should apologize."

Joy didn't have a response to that revelation.

"He started getting happier because of you."

"Cassie..." Joy struggled to speak. *We're so over we need a new word for over.* The line had been playing in her head the last few days, but she couldn't remember where she'd heard it. But was it true for her and Granger? Were they over? Or could they figure out a way to fix things between them?

"The thing is," Cassie rushed on, "my dad's not good with feelings."

Joy strangled a laugh. Granger? Not good with feelings? Understatement of the year.

"I mean, like, he has them. He'd just rather not deal with them. And he'd especially rather not talk about them."

Joy bit her lip at Cassie's earnest explanation of her father. The girl had him pegged.

"Could you...?" Cassie looked around wildly as if the words were hiding behind the reclaimed wood chest of drawers or beneath one of the hand-woven throws. "Could you, like, not give up on him? Because when he figures it out, I don't want it to be too late."

"Cassie." *I've already given up on him.* Her heart rejected the thought, unconvinced that it was true. She certainly didn't need to say those words to Cassie. The girl wanted to help. There couldn't be any harm in allowing her to think she'd done so. "First of all, let's get something straight." Someone had to be the adult this time. "None of what happened between me and your dad is your fault, okay? I won't give up on him, but I don't want you to expect something that may not happen, either. I'm not going to."

Cassie breathed a sigh of relief. "Thanks. Thanks for talking to me. I know I wasn't very nice to you before." Her hand fluttered through the air. "But if you hire me, I will be. I mean, I will be anyway. But..."

"I understand." Joy stood. Cassie reached for her backpack. Joy walked her to the door and locked up. She'd had about all the visitors she could handle for one day.

Chapter Forty

That night Joy got ready for bed with a heavy heart. But when she pulled the covers up and tucked her pillow under her head, she couldn't sleep.

Coming back home had been a mistake. Even though she'd reconciled with her father, she couldn't think otherwise. From the moment she'd arrived, her parents had been at odds and now they were living apart. Because of her.

Granger's daughter had been injured. Maybe Joy should have tattled on Cassie when she caught her sneaking out. It hadn't been her place to try to befriend Cassie. If she'd gone to Granger then and told him, he'd have been keeping closer tabs on her. She'd never have been in that van when it rolled down the embankment. If Cassie had been killed, Joy would never have been able to forgive herself. Could she fault Granger for needing someone to blame?

Tears filled Joy's eyes. She'd made a grave miscalculation with Granger. It didn't matter that he was four years out from a divorce, he wasn't ready for another relationship. Joy laughed bitterly. Over twenty years after Mike's death, she wasn't sure she was ready for a relationship, either. Or she hadn't been until Granger. With him, she'd felt ready. Interested. Excited.

And pregnant. When the double lines appeared on the home test she'd taken a few days ago "just in case," her worst fears were literally brought to life. She couldn't process what they'd allowed to happen. Too many other things consumed her thoughts, and she'd done her best to push an unplanned pregnancy to the back burner.

Joy swiped at her tears and fell into an uneasy sleep, where confusing dreams swirled through her head until she woke with a start. Another gut-twisting cramp rolled through her, and she realized she was wet.

She stumbled to the toilet, bent in half as her body expelled the barely begun life. She didn't know if her sobs were due to relief or grief. She hadn't convinced herself that she wanted to try motherhood again, especially at her age and with the uncertainty of her future right now. But she'd also thought maybe she was being given a second opportunity to love and raise a child.

It was better this way, she assured herself as the cramping subsided. She got to her feet unsteadily, holding onto the vanity for support as she stared at the blood and tissue before she flushed it all away. Tears continued to leak from her eyes as she allowed herself to mourn what she'd lost.

Every bit of strength she'd built over the years dwindled away. She didn't like being vulnerable or weak. Or emotional. She told herself it didn't matter. No one else was here to see. And at that acknowledgment of her aloneness, more tears dribbled down her cheeks.

She took a quick, hot, semi-comforting shower, put on clean nightclothes and changed the sheets before she settled down with a box of tissues nearby. Which, as it turned out, she didn't need. She fell asleep, comforted by praying for blessings on the soul of her baby who would never be.

Joy woke groggy and disoriented to a persistent tapping on the door. She pulled the covers over her head. Whoever it was would go away eventually. She'd never felt less ready for a visitor.

Her senses went on high alert, however, when she heard the creak of the screen and the inner door open. She poked her head out of the covers, listening intently as someone crossed the threshold and closed the door with a soft click.

She half sat up.

"Joy?"

She fell back on her pillow. "Brian?"

A few more steps brought her friend into view. He looked huge, as if he were towering over her from the end of the bed.

"What are you doing here?"

"What's wrong?"

She knew Brian wouldn't miss a trick. It wouldn't take a genius or a best friend to tell she was nowhere near her best at the moment.

She picked at the duvet. "I had a rough night."

Brian tilted his head. "You're not hung over. Somebody beat you up?"

Joy's laugh came out harsh. "Life."

"Ouch. Not a fair fight." Brian sat at the edge of the bed. Joy scooted over to make room for him as the mattress dipped beneath his weight. He took her hand in his, rubbing his thumb over the back of it. "What happened, honey?"

The annoying tears began their aggravating trickle down her cheeks. "Miscarriage," she finally managed to say.

"Oh, sweetie." His arms came around her and he held her, stroking her hair until she sniffed and sat back, propping herself against the headboard and wiping the tears away with a tissue.

"What can I do?" Brian asked. "How about some tea?"

"I'd rather have coffee."

"On it." Brian strode into the kitchen. She heard him rummaging around. He'd have no trouble finding the coffee in a kitchen the size of hers. Then again, maybe he would.

"Why are you up?" he asked in dismay when she came around the corner. "Get back in bed."

She almost laughed at his stern tone, which reminded her a bit of her father. "I'm not sick." She patted his forearm. "I have to use the bathroom."

"Okay," he said, stepping aside. "But then you get back in bed."

"Yes, doctor." She gave him a salute before she closed the bathroom door behind her.

She stared in the mirror while she washed her hands. She looked a bit like death warmed over. Her cheeks were puffy, her hair a disaster, and eyes swollen from crying.

"No more," she muttered to herself as she combed her hair and clipped it back. She splashed cold water on her face, applied moisturizer and lip balm.

"Stay there," she told Brian, who was pouring coffee into mugs. "I'm going to get dressed."

She did so quickly and took the mug of coffee over to the table. Brian frowned but followed her.

"How did you get in, anyway? Did I forget to lock the door?"

"No, but it's a flimsy lock. I used the old credit card trick, just like on TV."

"Sounds like I need to step up the security arrangements." Joy took a careful sip of the coffee.

"Talk to your jerk of a landlord about it."

Joy noticed the set of Brian's jaw. Granger had just shot to the top of his shit list. "He didn't know. Doesn't know."

"No," she said.

Brian clenched his mug. "Clueless bastard."

Joy squeezed his wrist. "Please don't let what's between me and him color your judgment when it comes to his work. One has nothing to do with the other."

"Clueless talented bastard."

"Why are you here checking up on me on a Saturday, anyway?"

"You rescheduled that meeting with Janie Klein, remember? She wanted to stop by before the craft show in Springboro."

Joy groaned, remembering. "The stained-glass artist. How did I forget?"

"Don't worry, I took care of Janie, it's all squared away. But it's not like you to miss appointments and not call. I was worried."

"What about the store? Oh, Brian, I'm so sorry. I don't even know what I did with my phone. I think I turned the volume off yesterday and forgot to turn it back on."

"Francie's covering the store. Don't worry about it." Francie was one of the interns Brian had hired for the summer.

"Thank you for that. I'm sorry to be so irresponsible."

"Don't be ridiculous. I'm just glad you're okay. You are okay, aren't you? Do you need to see a doctor or anything?"

Joy attempted a reassuring smile. "I don't think so. If I rest over the weekend, I'll probably be fine on Monday."

"You're sure."

"If I'm not, I'll let you hold my hand at the doctor's office, okay?"

"Promise?"

Joy laughed.

Brian scooted his chair back and took his mug to the sink. "I have to get going. How about if I stop by later with chicken soup?"

"You're always welcome, but it's not necessary.

Chapter Forty-One

G ranger frowned as he stared out of the kitchen window to see Brian's van parked at the edge of the road. He wondered why Brian would be visiting Joy so early on a Saturday morning. As far as he knew, Brian rarely came by Joy's place.

But as with so many things, he supposed he hadn't been paying that close attention, so maybe he didn't know anything about the frequency of their visits. They worked together, however. Surely, they saw enough of each other during the week.

He carried what was left of his coffee out to the garage workshop, switching on the lights and opening the overhead door. He set the coffee on a shelf and brought the garbage can out to the curb for pickup later. As he went back for the small can designated for Joy's use, Brian came down the steps toward him.

"Morning," Granger offered as their paths crossed.

Brian nodded but didn't return the greeting. He passed by on the way to his van.

"Everything all right?" Granger called after him. Brian lifted a hand in a dismissive wave but did not reply or turn around as he got into his vehicle and left. Granger frowned. Evidently, everything was not all right. If he wasn't mistaken, he'd just been dissed by a guy who had always been fairly friendly toward him.

The lid on the small garbage can was askew and didn't fit quite flat. He took it off and a loosely tied plastic supermarket bag spilled out. Granger bent to pick up a used-up tube of toothpaste, a cardboard toilet paper roll, and an empty shampoo bottle along with another flattened package.

He set the small carton back in the bag ready to tie the handles more securely when a word jumped out at him and gave him pause. He loosened the bag and stared at the box. *Early pregnancy test.* An instruction pamphlet and a plastic device were shoved inside. He shook the box and the tube fell out. He glanced up at Joy's apartment. Thought for a split second about the way Brian had behaved a minute ago. Didn't think twice before he took the stairs two at a time and pounded on her door.

When she didn't open it right away, he pounded again. He prepared to go for a third time when the door swung back and she stood there, looking tired and pale. He froze at her appearance, the confrontation he hadn't even planned fell by the wayside. His heart turned over as he stared at her, the love he felt for her all that mattered. Except he'd screwed up. Said things he couldn't take back. Hurt her in such an elemental way she'd never forgive him.

His ten-year-old self took over, making him nervous and uncertain and extra shy whenever he came close to his secret crush.

"Hi," he said, shocked at the stupidity of the greeting.

She didn't reply, merely waited for him to explain his presence.

"Can I come in?"

"Why?"

"I want to talk to you."

"This isn't a good time." She stepped back and started to close the door.

"Wait," he said, keeping it open. "Are you pregnant?" He said it softly, like a secret he didn't want anyone to overhear. Not that anyone would.

She blinked at him as if she didn't understand the question.

"A box fell out of the trash can," he explained.

She tried to close the door again, but he slid inside before she could. She closed it anyway and crossed her arms, refusing to look at him.

"Go away."

"Joy. Please. I need to know."

That got her attention. "Do you, Granger? Why? You've avoided me for weeks. And now you think you deserve something from me? You don't. I'll ask you again, please go."

"Joy, look." He reached out to cup her elbow and she jerked away, her eyes flashing blue fire at him. He raked the rejected hand back through his hair. "I'm sorry for all the things I said. The way I've been acting. I know I don't deserve your forgiveness." His voice refused to cooperate. He slumped against the wall and pressed the heels of his hands against his eyes as the sense of loss overwhelmed him.

This was so much worse than when he found out she'd left town all those years ago. The one girl, the woman he'd always wanted. He'd had a chance. One chance. And he'd lost it. Again, he wondered what the hell was wrong with him. Why he kept screwing up his relationships with the females in his life. So afraid of losing them that he somehow drove them away.

He heard Cassie's voice in his head. *What if something happened to Joy? Don't wait too long to apologize.*

Granger knew how bleak his life would be without her. Being with Joy, he'd begun to feel more like himself. Younger. Carefree. *Happy.* Without her? He didn't want to go back there.

He dropped his hands, not caring if she could see how wet his eyes were. He coughed and cleared his throat.

"If you are." He stopped and tried to find his voice. "I'll do whatever you need. Child support. Whatever you want." He swiped at his eyes and peered at her, trying to gauge her reaction. "I'd marry you in a heartbeat, but I guess I blew that." Not only did he need to say the words, he needed her to know.

"I'm not." She said it so softly he almost couldn't hear it. Tears welled in her eyes. "I was but..." She gave a slight shake of her head. "I'm not."

Granger didn't think about how she'd react. He wrapped his arms around her as the full meaning of her answer hit him. Had some part of him hoped they'd created a child together? Even if their relationship couldn't be repaired, that would have been something. He wouldn't have lost her completely

Joy stiffened when he hugged her, but eventually her body softened into his and she let him hold her. "I'd still marry you in a heartbeat." He repeated the words next to her ear.

He could have held her indefinitely, but too soon she squirmed away and stepped back.

He clasped her shoulders and looked into her eyes made brighter than ever with unshed tears.

"I love you. This is a terrible time to tell you, but I'm in love with you. I know I don't deserve you but if you could ever give me a second chance, I swear I'll do everything I can not to screw it up again."

When she didn't say anything, he buried his fingers in her hair and dropped a kiss on her forehead. He looked into her eyes again. "If you need anything..."

"I'm fine," she said, although it sounded like she might choke on the words.

He stepped back and went out.

Maybe he still had a chance. About a one in a million chance.

A few days later, Joy was back to feeling more like her old self, although a million thoughts jumbled through her mind and refused to settle. She and Brian had agreed to delay the official opening of Fair Maiden until after the family reunion. Joy felt as though she had too much on her plate with Devonny's arrival in a few days, her parents' situation, her feelings about Granger, nerves over starting a business. Added to that everything that came with recovering from the loss of an unplanned pregnancy.

So, when her father called and asked to meet with her again, Joy wasn't sure how to respond. She couldn't do more than she'd already done to help him reconcile with her mother. And she wasn't sure she wanted to step into the land mine of feelings there when her feelings about everything else were all over the place.

"I have an idea about the reunion I'd like to run past you," he said.

Joy hesitated. He'd been so adamantly against the reunion from the start, and Joy was still concerned about how he'd react to Devonny's presence there. And yet if he planned to attend, that meant he was making an effort, didn't it? She agreed to meet him at Fair Maiden the next morning. He promised to pick up coffee for both of them.

Joy barely had the door unlocked and the lights on before he arrived bearing a skinny latte for her and a black coffee for himself. Joy rearranged the display on one of the tables so they could sit.

Art regarded her intently for a minute. Not unkindly, but still Joy had to resist the urge to squirm. "How are you?" he asked.

"I'm fine." Her automatic response. Their relationship, such as it was, hadn't progressed to the point where she could share everything going on in her life with him. Certainly not her botched relationship with Granger.

He covered her hand with one of his. "I don't think you are. Fine, that is. I've got a lot to make up for as a father, but if there's ever anything I can do to help, I want to."

Emotion surged through Joy, and she had to look away from his gaze, from the sincerity in his voice. Her father had never shown her this gentle side of himself. If it had been there all along, she could see what had drawn her mother to him.

When she could speak again, she said, "Thanks, Dad. That's good to know."

He patted her hand and pulled a piece of paper from his shirt pocket. He smoothed out the creases before he said, "I've been thinking about this reunion."

"You're planning to attend?"

"I am. It's important to your mother. But I want to add something to it, as well. What do you think about a forgiveness ceremony?"

Joy sat back. "A forgiveness ceremony? I've never heard of such a thing."

Art gave her a small smile. "That's because I made it up. Or, the idea was put into my head, I should say. Into my heart."

From there he went on to outline his plan. Joy began to see how it could work. How beneficial it could be. Not just to her immediate family, but for all those attending. Was it true, she suddenly wondered? That old saying about hurting the ones we love. It certainly seemed so in her experience. Her parents. Devonny. Granger.

What her father proposed was something to which her mother would respond. Joy was sure of it. When he'd finished speaking, she covered his hand with hers. "I think it's a terrific idea, Dad. I'll help any way I can."

Chapter Forty-Two

J oy hadn't thought through the logistics of getting a cooler layered with ice, drinks, and food down the stairs. The cooler, which she'd borrowed from Brian, was sturdy and thick-walled. She'd made the mistake of adding cans of juice and soda and two bags of ice to the bottom. On top, she'd set plastic containers of sandwiches, pasta salad and fruit. Devonny and Luke were bringing chips, paper plates, napkins, and utensils.

Joy hefted the cooler by the handles, surprised at how heavy it was. She dragged it closer to the door, trying to decide if she should attempt to lug it down the stairs on her own. What choice did she have? She'd been on her own for most of her life, and today was no different. It was more the narrowness of the staircase and the awkwardness of the cooler transport that gave her pause.

She'd just go slow, she decided. What was the worst that could happen? A vision appeared of her tumbling ass over teakettle and ending in a splat at the bottom of the stairs with the cooler contents spilled around her. But Joy was stronger than she looked. She'd take her time and keep her grip and her balance.

She dragged the cooler to the landing, locked the door, and trotted down to the car where she popped the trunk and left her purse. Back at the top of the stairs, she stepped behind the cooler, grasped the handles, and hefted it up. Not so bad, she assured herself. The only problem was she couldn't see the stairs. But she'd traversed them often enough. There shouldn't be any surprises.

She took two steps before she heard Granger's voice. "Can I help you with that?"

Before she knew it, he was halfway up the steps.

"I'm fine. I don't need help."

"I'm here," he said, when he reached her. "I'm here, Joy."

Joy looked into his eyes and knew on some level he was asking for more than just to help with the cooler. She didn't want to soften her stance with him, even in light of his declaration a few days ago. Once he gave her the apology she wanted, forgiveness should logically follow. But she couldn't seem to get there, even though her heart yearned for him.

Her arm muscles began to scream in protest.

Granger fixed her with a look. He wasn't going to move. He gave her no choice when he took hold of the cooler, pivoted, and started back down the steps. He muttered something under his breath, but she couldn't hear it. She suspected it might have been a comment about her stubbornness.

Joy followed him to the car and after he deposited the cooler in the trunk, she picked up her purse and keys and slammed the lid, more irritated than she should be. He retreated to the garage door, feet planted, arms crossed.

Joy pretended to ignore him as she started the car and backed out. But her insides were shaking, her hands not quite steady. She turned at the corner and as soon as she knew she was out of sight of the house, she stopped long enough to get hold of herself.

Why did Granger still have this effect on her? *Because you're still in love with him.* True. But she didn't want to be. She wanted to get over him and move on. Move out. But she hadn't taken much time to look for another place to live. She'd been focused on the Fair Maiden, family issues, the reunion. And the truth was, her little apartment was almost perfect for her needs. But what had once been an upside to living there, being so close to Granger, had turned into a downside.

He'd been both unnecessarily cruel and unusually loving toward her. She didn't know which side to believe. She'd heard the opposite of love wasn't hate but indifference. What she felt wasn't indifference, but a mix of anger, disappointment, frustration mixed in with the love. If she didn't care, she wouldn't be so upset by the mere sight of the man. But she wasn't sure she could believe his words. She wasn't sure what to believe about him. She needed something more.

I'd marry you in a heartbeat. Granger's words lodged themselves deep inside her and somehow gave her hope that they could get past this wedge they'd created and still be together.

But she refused to let thoughts of Granger ruin her day.

On the drive to pick up her mother-in-law, Joy couldn't help thinking what Mike might have thought about the upcoming reunion. Of course, if he hadn't died, perhaps the estrangement from their families wouldn't have been. She had no one to blame but herself. Trying to pick up the pieces now was all she could do.

Dot must have been on the lookout for Joy's car because no sooner had she parked next to the trailer than Dot came out holding a baking pan. She locked the door and came down the steps. She didn't look much different from the other time Joy had seen her, but today she wore faded red cropped pants and a matching striped top. Her sandals had seen better days and the fake leather purse had long ago lost its sheen.

In that moment, Joy hated herself. Beyond setting up the annuity for her mother-in-law, she'd never bothered to contact her. Never tried to have a relationship with her. Not that she would have if she wasn't going to have one with her own family. But would it have been so hard to check on Dot periodically? To see how she was doing? The truth was, she'd written Dot off a long time ago. She'd been relegated to the past, to this town, to everything Joy'd wanted so desperately to escape.

But with Dot's only son dead she had no family. Joy had left Dot alone. No call at Christmas, not even a birthday card.

Another twinge of regret worked its way through Joy. She'd hadn't been back to visit Dot and had only called her a few times to discuss the plan for today. Joy decided to make more of an effort with her starting right now.

Dot opened the door and got in, greeting her in a panting breath, before setting the pan in her lap, the purse at her feet, and buckling the seatbelt. Joy smiled at her. "It's good to see you."

"I made carrot cake. Cream cheese frosting. I hope it doesn't melt in the heat."

"I've got a cooler filled with ice in the trunk. We'll set it in there until we're ready for it."

"Oh. That should be fine, then."

"I'm sorry," Joy said aloud, startling herself.

"Sorry?" Dot looked at her. "They're not coming, are they? They don't want to meet me." She stared at the cake pan in her lap, head bowed. "Can't say I blame them."

"What? No. Devonny and Luke are meeting us at the park. That's not what I meant."

"Oh," Dot said, her relief evident. She plucked at a stray thread on her slacks. "What did you mean, then? What are you sorry about?"

"I was thinking that after Mike died, you maybe didn't have any other family. And I ignored you for all these years. I never sent you a birthday card or a Christmas present."

Dot started to laugh, which turned into a fit of coughing. She covered her mouth with one hand and flapped the other back and forth until the spasms in her chest eased.

"If you'd a sent me a present back then, I probably would have hocked it for drug money. Don't feel bad about what's in the past. You're here now, treating me like a real person. Taking me to meet my family. That's enough for me."

Joy slid a look her way. "But if I wanted to make up for lost time, say, if it would make me feel better, would you let me buy you some presents and not get weird about it and tell me I shouldn't have?"

Dot considered it for a moment. "As long as you don't go overboard. It's not like I sent you any cards or anything, either. Not even a thank you. I could have, too, now that I think about it. I had that attorney's address. He could have forwarded mail to you."

"Well, but I never expected anything."

Dot glanced over at her with a small smile. "Neither did I. So, we're even."

Joy hadn't sent her own mother cards or presents, either. That first Mother's Day she'd thought about it. Especially since she had become a mother herself by then. But she'd reminded herself her mother had taken her father's side against her. After that, she still thought about her parents at holidays, but it got easier to justify ignoring them.

"Dot?" Joy said as they pulled into the park entrance. "If you ever need anything, please let me know, okay? I wasn't there for you before. But I want to be now." She parked and turned the engine off to look at Dot. "You understand?"

Dot's eyes watered and she looked away for a second. "Sure, honey. If that's what you want."

Joy patted her hand. "Bring your cake. Let's have a picnic."

Never had Joy been prouder of her daughter. Devonny's genuine interest in her paternal grandmother warmed Joy's heart. During lunch, she encouraged Dot to talk about herself and her life. Little Lucy also seemed fascinated by the woman, going to her willingly, exploring her face and hair with her tiny hands.

Dot seemed delighted with her newfound family, and Joy found herself liking the person her mother-in-law was more and more. There was an appealing sense of peace and lack of artifice about Dot. She knew who she was and although she didn't think highly of herself, she didn't shy away from the bald truth of her life, either.

When she needed a nicotine fix, she stepped away from the table, pacing back and forth in the grass nearby. Everyone oohed and ahhed over the carrot cake. Even though Lucy wasn't on solid food yet, Devonny offered her tiny tastes of the frosting. She made everyone laugh at her demands for more.

As they finished dessert, Devonny set a small box in front of Dot. "This is a little something for you," she said.

Dot glanced at her with uncertain eyes before she undid the wrapping and opened the box. She lifted a silver locket suspended from a slender chain. Her fingers trembled as she opened it. "Oh!" Dot teared up. "I've never had anything so nice." She offered a shaky smile.

"It's something for you to remember us by," Devonny said. "That's all."

Dot laughed. "As if I could ever forget, now that I've met you."

She passed the locket to Joy. Inside were tiny photos. One of Devonny and one of Lucy. The engraving on the back said, "Family."

After they packed everything up, they took photos. Devonny promised to send prints to Dot.

All in all, the day had been a grand success and Joy could only hope the upcoming reunion with her extended family would be as well. She drove home with a sense of accomplishment after dropping Dot off. If she achieved nothing else by returning to Liberty, she'd at least allowed Devonny to connect with her extended family. Lucy would grow up knowing she had kin, blood relations. Somehow, that seemed important now in a way it hadn't been when Joy took off at eighteen. Maybe, being surrounded by family her whole life, she'd taken it for granted. Maybe she'd never even thought about how important it was.

But she couldn't help feeling a bit sad about depriving Dot, who had no one except the granddaughter Joy had foolishly withheld from her all these years.

As much as she tried not to look back at the past, sometimes it proved impossible. She knew she couldn't go back and change anything, but still she felt this need to review it, examine it, learn from it. There had to be some value in the past, otherwise what was the point of remembering it?

"Think you can trust her?" Brian asked that evening after she told him about Cassie's visit.

They were at the wine bar down the street from the gallery. Joy still couldn't get over the transformation of Liberty's downtown, but she'd underestimated the drive of the folks who lived here. They'd applied for grants from the state and federal coffers, found which buildings qualified for historic preservation status, and made the most of it.

The wine bar had once been a general store dating from the early 1800s and sported the original brick to prove it. A couple who'd been a few years behind Joy and Brian in school owned and ran it. They offered top quality wines, daily specials, and tasty appetizers. At the moment, Joy and Brian were slowly working their way through a margherita flatbread pizza along with glasses of Sauvignon Blanc.

Joy thought before she answered. "I don't have a reason not to."

"She sounded like she was quite the bee-otch when you first met her."

"True." Joy took a sip of wine. "But she seemed, I don't know, softer, somehow. Genuine in a way she wasn't before."

"So, the Miss Nasty act was an act?"

"Probably." Joy thought some more. "She's been through a lot, even before the accident. I mean, it can't be easy having your mother abandon you, but gosh, she was what? Eleven? Twelve? Old enough to have a relationship with the woman. And she left without a backward glance. What kind of person does that?"

"A cold one." Brian took another slice of the flatbread. "Your boy Granger must have married an ice queen."

Joy wondered if that was true. He hadn't said much about his ex-wife. She couldn't help herself from recalling the way he made love. His depth. His intensity. How could that combination fail to thaw even the coldest female?

A yawning sympathy for him opened inside her. He hadn't had it easy, either. Realistically, she knew no one did, but he and his daughter tugged at her heartstrings. They had from the first.

"I'd like to give her a chance. If it doesn't work out, it doesn't work out."

"Okay," Brian agreed easily, evidently done with playing devil's advocate. "How goes it with the parental units?"

"It doesn't," Joy said, not even trying to hide the glumness the subject made her feel. "But while we're discussing potential part-time employees, what do you think about offering my mother a job?"

"Your mother?"

"She's never worked a real job, but she could learn our system. It would give her something to do besides sit at my aunt's house or volunteer at the church. I think earning her own money would be a good thing for her."

"Could be a good thing for us, too. She knows practically everyone in town. Just being who she is would bring in a lot of traffic."

Joy grinned, delighted with the idea of offering her mother a job. Another idea struck. "What about Dot?"

"Dot?"

"My mother-in-law."

Brian frowned. "From the way you've described her, I'm not sure she's exactly what we're looking for."

"Maybe not as a clerk, but she could work in the warehouse," Joy mused, referring to the back third of the store they'd allocated for shipping and receiving stock. "Inventory. Set-up. Cleaning."

"Are we planning to hire all of your relatives and acquaintances? You want to offer Aunt Ginny a job, too?"

Joy lifted her glass. "I might."

"You hire, you fire if it doesn't work out. No drama, okay?"

"Oh, come on. You enjoy drama. Admit it."

"Only in love, sweetheart. Not in business."

Chapter Forty-Three

Art's Bible was open in his lap. He'd planned to make notes about a few of the verses he wanted to include at the forgiveness ceremony. What he did instead was study Marcy's desk. The African violet she kept near the window looked droopy and sad. When Marcy was here, it looked green and healthy and probably bloomed non-stop, although Art never noticed how often it flowered.

In her absence, however, he noticed everything. How quiet the house could be. The empty kitchen, her pride and joy, lost its luster. A layer of dust coated every piece of furniture. Art knew he should clean up, but he couldn't muster the enthusiasm. Even the refrigerator had changed its hum, as if mourning its nearly empty state.

Art wrestled with the question of how he could make things right again, trying his damnedest to consider others instead of himself and his own comfort and convenience.

Squaring things with Joy hadn't brought Marcy back. Her heels were dug in. He wasn't sure if she would ever come back, or if she'd even forgive him. He sighed and turned back to the Bible, turning the thin pages, praying for inspiration to find the words that would reach her heart.

The doorbell rang and Art's heart lifted. Maybe it was Marcy. Silly. Of course, it wasn't. Marcy had a key. He set the Bible aside and peeked out the front door. He saw a young woman he didn't recognize, but who looked familiar.

He opened the door and peered at her. "Yes?"

"Arthur Harmon?"

"Yes?"

"I'm Devonny Bradshaw. Your granddaughter. I'd like to speak with you."

Now he knew why she looked familiar. She had her mother's blue eyes, and he could see bits of Joy in her facial features. Some of her father there too. The jawline, Art thought, the picture of Mike Laurence dim in his memory. *Should have tried harder with that one,* he reprimanded himself. A lost kid, looking for something to believe in. The sort of kid he was supposed to help, not spurn.

Still, even though the afternoon was overcast, Devonny seemed to radiate light. He found himself immediately drawn to her.

Art pushed the screen back and said, "Come in." He indicated the living room. "Have a seat."

Devonny chose a corner of the sofa. Art took his usual recliner. "I didn't expect to see you until the reunion," he said.

"I thought we should meet ahead of time." Her clear, direct gaze pinned him in his seat. "Get a few things squared away."

"All right." He hoped the uncertainty he felt didn't come through in his voice. But he was afraid it did. The Reverend Arthur Harmon, always so sure he was right. Quoting Scripture backward and forward, offering a solution for life's dilemmas while mucking up his own life, his marriage, his family, and driving away the people he loved.

What a hypocrite he'd been. Joy forgave him. Someday Marcy might. But he wondered if he'd ever be able to forgive himself.

"I understand you kept tabs on my mother and me. That you know I acted in adult films, and you have a problem with it."

He remembered how self-righteous he'd been up until a couple of weeks ago. It had cost him precious time with his daughter and driven his wife away. Deprived him of a relationship with his granddaughter. And *her* daughter. He had a great-grandchild he'd never met and if he didn't handle this meeting right, might never get to know.

"I did. But I've since realized it's not my place to sit in judgment on other people."

"Oh." Devonny seemed surprised by his answer. A little deflated, as well. "I had a whole speech prepared. I guess I don't need it now."

Her disappointment made Art smile. "You can still use it if you want. I probably deserve whatever condemnation you planned to heap on my head."

"No. I try to avoid judgment, too. I just wanted to say I had my reasons for doing those films. They're something I did, not who I am."

"And who are you?" Art asked. "I'd really like to know."

Devonny gave him a look but instead of answering said, "You're not what I expected."

"Not an ogre spitting out fire and preaching hell and damnation?"

"You're, I don't know, softer than I thought you'd be. More receptive."

Art chuckled. "It's a recent transformation. I'm trying to become a better version of myself than I was for most of my life. I have your mother to thank for that. You as well, come to think of it."

Devonny tilted her head in question but said nothing.

"If your mother hadn't come back here..."

Art paused as another lightning bolt of clarity hit him. "Sorry," he said as he tried to grasp his train of thought. "Her being here started a chain reaction, I guess you could say. She blew up my life the same way she did after she was born." He shook his head, unable to make sense of it all or adequately put it into words. "That explosion, *my* explosion, was at least in part because of you. What you'd done. Who I thought you must be."

He shook his head again. "The blast knocked me on my rear. It woke me up and forced things out into the open. Things I'd kept hidden. If it wasn't for you, for her, this reunion..."

Art drifted off. Would he have continued living in the false world he'd built for himself forever? The blow-up sent him reeling, and the aftermath caused him pain like nothing had before. But, in a way, he also felt more alive. Maybe it was simply that he was *feeling* after such a long time of going through the motions and keeping up the pretense.

"But my grandmother left you."

"I'm praying that's temporary."

"You don't blame us? My mom and me?"

"I blame myself." He had to own his behavior, his choices, his deception. No one made him be the way he'd chosen to be. In fact, several people and God Himself had tried to talk him out of it. He'd been so blind and stubborn.

"This is not the conversation I expected to have with you," Devonny said.

Something about her, this granddaughter of his, made him want to smile. "Is that a good thing or a bad thing?"

"It's better than I thought it would be."

"Well, in that case," Art said, getting to his feet. "Can I offer you something to drink? I have root beer and ginger ale. And Mallomars. Your grandmother usually won't buy them. She's got this crazy idea that sugar is bad.

Unless, of course, it's in something she baked. But I had to go to the store or starve and she wasn't there to tell me what was good for me."

Devonny followed him to the kitchen.

"I got salami, too," he told her, as if imparting the greatest conspiracy of the century. "And a box of fried chicken."

Chapter Forty-Four

Art stepped to the top of the bandstand and picked up the microphone. No awkward screech of static sounded when he turned it on and spoke, just the soothing baritone that made him such a success from the pulpit. A voice you automatically listened to. "Can I have everyone's attention please?"

Just like that, the assembled relatives stopped what they were doing and quieted. Taking it as their cue, Devonny and Joy each picked up a bucket holding long-stemmed roses and began threading through the crowd, handing one to everyone there. Art could see some people were confused, so he spoke above the whispered questions and thank yous.

"I'm somewhat of an unscheduled speaker today, but as we're all together here, there are a few things I want to say while I have the opportunity and the audience." He paused and cleared his throat. He looked at Marcy to find her studying him with a stern expression, arms crossed defensively. He had a plan. With Joy's help, he'd committed to this course of action, and he'd see it through with God's grace.

"I think almost all of you know of my estrangement from my daughter, Joy. There aren't very many secrets within families, are there? It's taken me too many years and Joy's return to make me clearly see the part I played in our separation.

"Ephesians 4:31 says, 'Let all bitterness and wrath and anger and clamor and slander be put away from you, along with all malice.' But I confess to you all here today that I didn't put away any of those things. I held onto my bitterness and my anger and carried both as a shield against the truth about myself I was unwilling to accept. I blamed my daughter for things that weren't her fault. I was never the father to her that I should have been. Never the father she deserved."

He allowed his gaze to wander over the members of his and Marcy's extended families who were hanging on his every word. Even giving his best Sunday sermon, he didn't receive the rapt attention displayed now.

"I drove my daughter away. My pride, my ego, my lack of forgiveness kept her away all this time."

He scanned the crowd again, people he'd known all his life, the ones he'd grown up with, the ones who'd raised him. "I've spent a lot of time in self-reflection these past few months since Joy returned. A lot of time spent with my spiritual director. I didn't like what I saw. Luke 6:37 became my constant companion. 'Do not judge, and you will not be judged. Do not condemn, and you will not be condemned. Forgive, and you will be forgiven.'

"God continues to forgive us, even when we don't deserve it. But people? People often have a harder time with forgiveness than God does."

He saw that all everyone had received a rose. As planned, she took up her position near him.

Art softened his tone. "I know we all struggle with each other from time to time. Wives with husbands. Children with parents. Brothers with sisters. We're family and we love each other, but still we struggle. Joy and I"—he held out his hand to her and circled his arm around her shoulders— "came up with this idea when we forgave each other after all these years. That's what your roses are for.

"Let's bow our heads and meditate for a moment. Think about who you may have wronged in the past and who you need to ask for forgiveness. What we're suggesting you do today is take petals from your roses and offer them to each of those individuals as you ask for their forgiveness. Accept the petals as you offer forgiveness in return. Some of us might need to offer the entire rose to one individual, our need is so great. You might want to hold onto a few petals, as well, because sometimes we have the hardest time forgiving ourselves.

"Holding grudges holds us back from love. I've learned this the hard way. Maybe you have too." He paused, encouraged by the bowed heads. "Lack of forgiveness separates us from those we love most." He paused again and softened his voice further. "Today let's do our best to forgive and pray for one another going forward, that we might all be healed."

Art turned off the mic and offered his rose to Joy. "Thank you for forgiving me."

She accepted it with a smile and gave him hers. "Thank you for forgiving me."

They stepped to where Devonny stood next to Luke, who held Lucy. Joy went first. "Devonny, I said some terrible things to you in the past. I know we've reconciled, but I'm sorry and I ask for your forgiveness."

Devonny hugged Joy. "There's nothing to forgive, okay, Mom? We're good."

Joy nodded against her daughter's shoulder, closing her eyes against the wave of emotion and the sudden spurt of tears. "I love you."

"I love you too."

After a minute, they let go. "Take this," Joy insisted, offering the entire rose to Devonny. "Now it's official," she said when Devonny accepted it.

"Un unh," Devonny said. "You take mine. *Now* it's official."

Joy stepped aside so Art could say his piece to his granddaughter and went to her mother, who remained seated and alone while it seemed everyone else interacted with those around them. Her rose lay limply in her lap. Joy knelt in front of her mother and offered the rose to her. Marcy looked at her in surprise and started to say something.

"I'm sorry, Mom. For all the pain I caused you. For leaving and staying away. For the rift I caused between you and Dad. For everything. I'd like your forgiveness."

Marcy cupped her chin and looked into her eyes. "You have it. You've always had it." She took the rose from Joy and gave her the one in her lap. "Can you forgive me for not trying harder to find you? For letting things go on as long as they did when I knew it was wrong? When I was too afraid to change what was?"

"You have my forgiveness," Joy said. "I love you, Mom."

"And I love you." Marcy smiled through a sheen of tears before she looked up to see Art waiting his turn.

Joy got to her feet and moved away. Whatever happened next, she'd done what she could to bring them together today. If nothing changed, she'd have to accept it. She needed a few minutes to compose herself, to face the rest of the afternoon.

She started off toward the corner of the park designated as a butterfly garden. Exploring the paths and the benches under the pergolas would be the perfect respite. She found a tissue in her pocket and dabbed at her eyes and nose. Her emotions were running high after greeting so many of her extended family members earlier and spending time with Devonny, Luke, and Lucy the past couple of days, along with the picnic with Dot yesterday. Seeing Dot's pleasure in meeting everyone, her delight with Lucy, had touched them all.

The garden paths were deserted. The benches unoccupied. She dropped onto one gratefully, listening to the buzz of bees and watching butterflies flit by. She closed her eyes, savoring the warmth of the sun, the slight breeze, the ultimate peace she'd found with her decision to return to Liberty. Only one thing could make it better. She needed the forgiveness of one other person. She didn't know how or when, but she wanted, more than anything, to make things right with Granger.

Her solitary peace didn't last long. A shadow fell across her, and she opened her eyes to see Granger holding a rose. She didn't know Granger was at the reunion and wondered who had invited him.

"Art suggested we stop by today," he told her, as if he'd read her mind. He looked down at the rose for a moment. "I gave one to Cassie, but this one's for you." He knelt next to her. "I know it's not enough. I know I don't deserve it." He gazed up at her with those compelling eyes of his and she couldn't look away.

"Joy, I'm sorrier than I can say for what I said to you that day. For the way I've behaved. I could give you twelve reasons why I lost it with you, but none of them excuse what I did or what I said." He waited, but she couldn't think of a response. She hadn't expected him to be here. Hadn't expected him to approach her again, after she'd ignored his first apology.

"I'm sorry too," she said, not sure if he heard her.

"I talked to Art. Got his blessing, actually." He gave her a lopsided smile. "He told me about the forgiveness ceremony."

She reached for his hand wanting to trust the spurt of hope his words encouraged.

"The thing is," he went on doggedly. "I love you. If you can forgive me, I'd like to spend the rest of my life making it up to you." He paused. "If you stay."

Joy stared at the rose that represented so much. Things she never thought she'd have. A man like Granger. A partner in life. One with faults as big as her own, but who wasn't afraid to admit it. She, more than anyone, knew the power of forgiveness. Of the weight it lifted. The freedom it offered. Only a fool would turn it down. And Joy was done being a fool.

"I like your hair," he said.

"Oh." Joy had arrived at a salon yesterday without an appointment, knowing the time for change had come. She fingered the shorter strands the stylist had created before she held the rose her mother had given her out to him.

"Granger Sullivan." She cupped his jaw, noticing he'd finally had his too-long hair trimmed as well, but there was still enough to tickle her fingertips. "Not only am I here to stay. I accept your rose."

"Really?"

"Really."

In seconds they were on their feet, their arms wrapped around each other, the roses dangling from their hands.

The three Rs, Joy thought. Reconciliation. Redemption. Reconnection. She'd achieved everything she'd hoped to by returning home. When Granger kissed her, she decided to add another R to the list. Because even though she hadn't been looking for it, romance made having all the others even sweeter.

Dear Readers

Dear Readers,

I hope you enjoyed Joy's journey. I have plans for a fourth book in the Red Bud series entitled If You Touch, featuring a mixed-race male friend of Devonny's, Dex, who also relocates to Red Bud and leaves the porn industry behind. His love interest in *If You Touch* will be Melody, (from If You Knew) who runs the daycare center.

If you enjoyed If You Stay, I hope you will leave a brief review on the site where you purchased it, and/or on Goodreads. Reviews are so helpful to authors, especially indie authors. I also hope you will tell others about the book.

I love hearing from readers. You can contact me, follow my blog, and sign up for my monthly newsletter at www.barbarameyers.com.

All the best,
Barbara Meyers

About Author

Barbara Meyers writes contemporary romance and women's fiction, comic fantasy, song lyrics and Dr. Seuss-like poetry (for adults). Her novels are a mix of comedy, suspense and spice and often feature a displaced child.

Originally from Southwest Missouri, she currently resides in Central Florida.

Also By

Look for these titles by Barbara Meyers
Books Now Available:
Misconceive
Scattered Moments
Not Quite Heaven
Cleo's Web
White Roses in Winter
Training Tommy
A Family for St. Nick (Christmas Novella)

Red Bud, Iowa Series (Connected, Stand Alone)
If You Knew (Book One)
If You Dare (Book Two)

Phantom (Romantic Suspense, Manuscripts Under the Bed)
The Color of Nothing (Young Adult, Manuscripts Under the Bed)

The Braddocks Series (Connected, Stand Alone)
A Month From Miami (Book One)
A Forever Kind of Guy (Book Two)
The First Time Again (Coming Soon)
What A Rich Woman Wants (Book Four)

Coming Soon: The Red Bud Series
If You Touch

Barbara Meyers writing as AJ Tillock:
The Grinding Reality Series:
The Forbidden Bean (Book One)
Cool Beans (Book Two)

Acknowledgments

As always, I thank God for every bit of writing talent and ability He gave me, and for the daily inspiration and assistance He sends me.

To Bill for everything he has done for me for the past 40+ years.

To my wonderful beta readers: Ellen Holder and Margaret Ellison.

To Cathy, Sandy, Kerry, and Danielle. They know why.

To my editor, Noah Chinn.

To my cover artist, Steven Novak, Novak Illustration.

To my Facebook, Twitter, Instagram, TikTok, and newsletter followers for their support and feedback on everything from research to covers.

To Lakeland Writers, Novelists, Inc., and Florida Writers Association friends for their assistance and support.

CPSIA information can be obtained
at www.ICGtesting.com
Printed in the USA
BVHW061202020522
635882BV00004B/134